"ALL THE TEY MAGIC . . . ! SUPERB!"

—*San Francisco Chronicle*

"The unalloyed pleasure of watching a really cultivated mind in action! Buy and cherish!"

—*Boston Sunday Globe*

"Steadily absorbing . . . ! Rich . . . ! Lively!"

—*New York Herald Tribune*

"Movie stars, astrology, Balkan politics, crackpot religion, a marvelous 17-year-old girl and a magnificent corpse . . . richly rewarding . . . a joy absolute!"

—*The New York Times*

Books by Josephine Tey

Brat Farrar
The Daughter of Time
The Man in the Queue
A Shilling for Candles
The Singing Sands

Published by POCKET BOOKS

Josephine Tey

A SHILLING
FOR CANDLES

PUBLISHED BY POCKET BOOKS NEW YORK

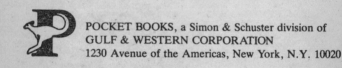

POCKET BOOKS, a Simon & Schuster division of
GULF & WESTERN CORPORATION
1230 Avenue of the Americas, New York, N.Y. 10020

Originally published in England in 1936.
First published in the United States of America in 1954 by
Macmillan Publishing Co., Inc.

ISBN: 0-671-80974-1

First Pocket Books printing December, 1980

10 9 8 7 6 5 4 3 2

POCKET and colophon are trademarks of Simon & Schuster

Printed in the U.S.A.

1

IT WAS A LITTLE AFTER SEVEN ON A SUMMER MORNING, and William Potticary was taking his accustomed way over the short down grass of the cliff-top. Beyond his elbow, two hundred feet below, lay the Channel, very still and shining, like a milky opal. All around him hung the bright air, empty as yet of larks. In all the sunlit world no sound except for the screaming of some sea-gulls on the distant beach; no human activity except for the small lonely figure of Potticary himself, square and dark and uncompromising. A million dewdrops sparkling on the virgin grass suggested a world new—come from its Creator's hand. Not to Potticary, of course. What the dew suggested to Potticary was that the ground fog of the early hours had not begun to disperse until well after sunrise. His subconscious noted the fact and tucked it away, while his conscious mind debated whether, having raised an appetite for breakfast, he should turn at the Gap and go back to the Coastguard Station, or whether, in view of the fineness of the morning, he should walk into

Westover for the morning paper, and so hear about the latest murder two hours earlier than he would otherwise. Of course, what with wireless, the edge was off the morning paper, as you might say. But it was an objective. War or peace, a man had to have an objective. You couldn't go into Westover just to look at the front. And going back to breakfast with the paper under your arm made you feel fine, somehow. Yes, perhaps he would walk into the town.

The pace of his black, square-toed boots quickened slightly, their shining surface winking in the sunlight. Proper service, these boots were. One might have thought that Potticary, having spent his best years in brushing his boots to order, would have asserted his individuality, or expressed his personality, or otherwise shaken the dust of a meaningless discipline off his feet by leaving the dust on his boots. But no, Potticary, poor fool, brushed his boots for love of it. He probably had a slave mentality, but had never read enough for it to worry him. As for expressing one's personality, if you described the symptoms to him he would, of course, recognize them. But not by name. In the Service they call that "contrariness."

A sea-gull flashed suddenly above the cliff-top, and dropped screaming from sight to join its wheeling comrades below. A dreadful row these gulls were making. Potticary moved over to the cliff edge to see what jetsam the tide, now beginning to ebb, had left for them to quarrel over.

The white line of the gently creaming surf was broken by a patch of verdigris green. A bit of cloth. Baize, or something. Funny it should stay so bright a color after being in the water so—

Potticary's blue eyes widened suddenly, his body becoming strangely still. Then the square black boots began to run. *Thud, thud, thud,* on the thick turf, like a heart beating. The Gap was two hundred yards away, but Potticary's time would not have disgraced a track performer. He clattered down the rough steps hewn in the chalk of the gap, gasping; indignation welling through his excitement. That was what came of going into cold water before breakfast! Lunacy, so help him. Spoiling other people's breakfasts, too. Schaefer's best, except where ribs broken. Not likely to be ribs broken. Perhaps only a faint after all. Assure the patient in a loud voice that he is safe. Her arms and legs were as brown as the sand. That was why he had thought the green thing a piece of cloth. Lunacy, so help him. Who wanted cold water in the dawn unless they had to swim for it? He'd had to swim for it in his time. In that Red Sea port. Taking in a landing party to help the Arabs. Though why anyone wanted to help the lousy bastards— That was the time to swim. When you had to. Orange juice and thin toast, too. No stamina. Lunacy, so help him.

It was difficult going on the beach. The large white pebbles slid maliciously under his feet, and the rare patches of sand, being about tide level, were soft and yielding. But presently he was within the cloud of gulls, enveloped by their beating wings and their wild crying.

There was no need for Schaefer's, nor for any other method. He saw that at a glance. The girl was past all help. And Potticary, who had picked bodies unemotionally from the Red Sea surf, was strangely moved. It was all wrong that someone so young should be lying there when all the world was waking up to a brilliant day; when so much of life lay in front of her. A pretty girl, too, she must have been. Her hair had a dyed look, but the rest of her was all right.

A wave washed over her feet and sucked itself away, derisively, through the scarlet-tipped toes. Potticary, although the tide in another minute would be yards away, pulled the inanimate heap a little higher up the beach, beyond reach of the sea's impudence.

Then his mind turned to telephones. He looked around for some garment which the girl might have left behind when she went in to swim. But there seemed to be nothing. Perhaps she had left whatever she was wearing below high-water level and the tide had taken it. Or perhaps it wasn't here that she had gone into water. Anyhow, there was nothing now with which to cover her body, and Potticary turned away and began his hurried plodding along the beach again, and so back to the Coastguard Station and the nearest telephone.

"Body on the beach," he said to Bill Gunter as he took the receiver from the hook and called the police.

Bill clicked his tongue against his front teeth, and jerked his head back. A gesture which expressed with eloquence and economy the tiresomeness of circumstances, the unreasonableness of human beings who get themselves drowned, and his own satisfaction in expecting the worst of life and being right. "If they want to commit suicide," he said in his subterranean voice, "why do they have to pick on us? Isn't there the whole of the south coast?"

"Not a suicide," Potticary gasped in the intervals of hulloing.

Bill took no notice of him. "Just because the fare to the south coast is more than to here! You'd think when a fellow was tired of life he'd stop being mean about the fare and bump himself off in style. But no! They take the cheapest ticket they can get and strew themselves over our doorstep!"

"Beachy Head get a lot," gasped the fair-minded Potticary. "Not a suicide, anyhow."

"Course it's a suicide. What do we have cliffs for? Bulwark of England? No. Just as a convenience to suicides. That makes four this year. And there'll be more when they get their income tax demands."

He paused, his ear caught by what Potticary was saying.

"—a girl. Well, a woman. In a bright green bathing-dress." (Potticary belonged to a generation which did not know swim-suits.) "Just south of the Gap. 'Bout a hundred yards. No, no one there. I had to come away to telephone. But I'm going back right away. Yes, I'll meet you there. Oh, hullo, Sergeant, is that you? Yes, not the best beginning of a day, but we're getting used to it. Oh, no, just a bathing fatality. Ambulance? Oh, yes, you can bring it practically to the Gap. The track goes off the main Westover road just past the third milestone, and finishes in those trees just inland from the Gap. All right, I'll be seeing you."

"How can you tell it's just a bathing fatality," Bill said.

"She had a bathing-dress on, didn't you hear?"

"Nothing to hinder her putting on a bathing-dress to throw herself into the water. Make it look like accident."

"You can't throw yourself into the water this time of year. You land on the beach. And there isn't any doubt what you've done."

"Might have walked into the water till she drowned," said Bill, who was a last-ditcher by nature.

"Ye'? Might have died of an overdose of bull's-eyes," said Potticary, who approved of last-ditchery in Arabia but found it boring to live with.

2

THEY STOOD AROUND THE BODY IN A SOLEMN LITTLE group: Potticary, Bill, the sergeant, a constable, and the two ambulance men. The younger ambulance man was worried about his Stomach, and the possibility of its disgracing him, but the others had nothing but business in their minds.

"Know her?" the sergeant asked.

"No," said Potticary. "Never seen her before."

None of them had seen her before.

"Can't be from Westover. No one would come out from town with a perfectly good beach at their doors. Must have come from inland somewhere."

"Maybe she went into the water at Westover and was washed up here," the constable suggested.

"Not time for that," Potticary objected. "She hadn't been that long in the water. Must have been drowned hereabouts."

"Then how did she get here?" the sergeant asked.

"By car, of course," Bill said.

"And where is the car now?"

"Where everyone leaves their car: where the track ends at the trees."

"Yes?" said the sergeant. "Well, there's no car there."

The ambulance men agreed with him. They had come up that way with the police—the ambulance was waiting there now—but there was no sign of any other car.

"That's funny," Potticary said. "There's nowhere near enough to be inside walking distance. Not at this time in the morning."

"Shouldn't think she'd walk anyhow," the older ambulance man observed. "Expensive," he added, as they seemed to question him.

They considered the body for a moment in silence. Yes, the ambulance man was right; it was a body expensively cared for.

"And where are her clothes, anyhow?" The sergeant was worried.

Potticary explained his theory about the clothes; that she had left them below high-water mark and that they were now somewhere at sea.

"Yes, that's possible," said the sergeant. "But how did she get here?"

"Funny she should be bathing alone, isn't it?" ventured the young ambulance man, trying out his stomach.

"Nothing's funny, nowadays," Bill rumbled. "It's a wonder she wasn't playing jumping off the cliff with a glider. Swimming on an empty stomach, all alone, is just too ordinary. The young fools make me tired."

"Is that a bracelet around her ankle, or what?" the constable asked.

Yes, it was a bracelet. A chain of platinum links. Curious links, they were. Each one shaped like a C.

"Well," the sergeant straightened himself, "I suppose there's nothing to be done but to remove the body to the mortuary, and then find out who she is. Judging by appearances that shouldn't be difficult. Nothing 'lost, stolen or strayed' about that one."

"No," agreed the ambulance man. "The butler is probably telephoning the station now in great agitation."

"Yes." The sergeant was thoughtful. "I still wonder how she came here, and what—"

His eyes had lifted to the cliff face, and he paused.

"So! We have company!" he said.

They turned to see a man's figure on the cliff-top at the Gap. He was standing in an attitude of intense eagerness, watching them. As they turned towards him he did a swift right-about and disappeared.

"A bit early for strollers," the sergeant said. "And what's he running away for? We'd better have a talk with him."

But before he and the constable had moved more than a pace or two it became evident that the man, far from running away, had been merely making for the entrance to the Gap. His thin dark figure shot now from the mouth of the Gap and came towards them at a shambling run, slipping and stumbling, and giving the little group watching his advent an impression of craziness. They could hear the breath panting through his open mouth as he drew near, although the distance from the Gap was not long and he was young.

He stumbled into their compact circle without looking at them, pushing aside the two policemen who had unconsciously interposed their bulk between him and the body.

"Oh, yes, it is! Oh, it is, it is!" he cried, and without warning sat down and burst into loud tears.

Six flabbergasted men watched him in silence for a moment. Then the sergeant patted him kindly on the back and said, idiotically, "It's all right, son!"

But the young man only rocked himself to and fro and wept the more.

"Come on, come on," rallied the constable, coaxing.

(Really, a dreadful exhibition on a nice bright morning.) "That won't do anyone any good, you know. Best pull yourself together—sir," he added, noting the quality of the handkerchief which the young man had produced.

"A relation of yours?" the sergeant inquired, his voice suitably modulated from its former businesslike pitch.

The young man shook his head.

"Oh, just a friend?"

"She was so good to me, so good!"

"Well, at least you'll be able to help us. We were beginning to wonder about her. You can tell us who she is."

"She's my—hostess."

"Yes, but I meant, what is her name?"

"I don't know."

"You—don't—know! Look here, sir, pull yourself together. You're the only one that can help us. You must know the name of the lady you were staying with."

"No, no; I don't."

"What did you call her, then?"

"Chris."

"Chris, what?"

"Just Chris."

"And what did she call you?"

"Robin."

"Is that your name?"

"Yes, my name's Robert Stannaway. No, Tisdall. It used to be Stannaway," he added, catching the sergeant's eye and feeling apparently that explanation was needed.

What the sergeant's eye said was, "God give me patience!" What his tongue said was, "It all sounds a bit strange to me, Mr.—er—"

"Tisdall."

"Tisdall. Can you tell me how the lady got here this morning?"

"Oh, yes. By car."

"By car, eh? Know what became of the car?"

"Yes. I stole it."

"You what?"

"I stole it. I've just brought it back. It was a swinish thing to do. I felt a cad so I came back. When I found she wasn't anywhere on the road, I thought I'd find her stamping about here. Then I saw you all standing around something—oh, dear, oh dear!" He began to rock himself again.

"Where were you staying with this lady?" asked the sergeant, in exceedingly businesslike tones. "In Westover?"

"Oh, no. She has—had, I mean—oh dear!—a cottage. Briars, it's called. Just outside Medley."

"'Bout a mile and a half inland," supplemented Potticary, as the sergeant, who was not a native, looked a question.

"Were you alone, or is there a staff there?"

"There's just a woman from the village—Mrs. Pitts—who comes in and cooks."

"I see."

There was a slight pause.

"All right, boys." The sergeant nodded to the ambulance men, and they bent to their work with the stretcher. The young man drew in his breath sharply and once more covered his face with his hands.

"To the mortuary, Sergeant?"

"Yes."

The man's hands came away from his face abruptly.

"Oh, no! Surely not! She had a home. Don't they take people home?"

"We can't take the body of an unknown woman to an uninhabited bungalow."

"It isn't a bungalow," the man automatically corrected. "No. No, I suppose not. But it seems dreadful—the mortuary. Oh, God in heaven above!" he burst out, "why did this have to happen!"

"Davis," the sergeant said to the constable, "you go

back with the others and report. I'm going over
to—what is it?—Briars? with Mr. Tisdall."

The two ambulance men crunched their heavy way
over the pebbles, followed by Potticary and Bill. The
noise of their progress had become distant before the
sergeant spoke again.

"I suppose it didn't occur to you to go swimming
with your hostess?"

A spasm of something like embarrassment ran across
Tisdall's face. He hesitated.

"No. I—not much in my line, I'm afraid: swimming
before breakfast. I—I've always been a rabbit at games
and things like that."

The sergeant nodded, noncommittal. "When did she
leave for a swim?"

"I don't know. She told me last night that she was
going to the Gap for a swim if she woke early. I woke
early myself, but she was gone."

"I see. Well, Mr. Tisdall, if you've recovered I think
we'll be getting along."

"Yes. Yes, certainly. I'm all right." He got to his feet
and together and in silence they traversed the beach,
climbed the steps at the Gap, and came on the car
where Tisdall said he had left it: in the shade of the
trees where the track ended. It was a beautiful car, if a
little too opulent. A cream-colored two-seater with a
space between the seats and the hood for parcels, or, at
a pinch, for an extra passenger. From this space, the
sergeant, exploring, produced a woman's coat and a
pair of the sheepskin boots popular with women at
winter race-meetings.

"That's what she wore to go down to the beach. Just
the coat and boots over her bathing things. There's a
towel, too."

There was. The sergeant produced it: a brilliant
object in green and orange.

"Funny she didn't take it to the beach with her," he
said.

"She liked to dry herself in the sun usually."

"You seem to know a lot about the habits of a lady whose name you didn't know." The sergeant inserted himself into the second seat. "How long have you been living with her?"

"Staying with her," amended Tisdall, his voice for the first time showing an edge. "Get this straight, Sergeant, and it may save you a lot of bother: Chris was my hostess. Not anything else. We stayed in her cottage unchaperoned, but a regiment of servants couldn't have made our relations more correct. Does that strike you as so very peculiar?"

"Very," said the sergeant frankly. "What are these doing here?"

He was peering into a paper bag which held two rather jaded buns.

"Oh, I took these along for her to eat. They were all I could find. We always had a bun when we came out of the water when we were kids. I thought maybe she'd be glad of something."

The car was slipping down the steep track to the main Westover-Stonegate road. They crossed the high-road and entered a deep lane on the other side. A signpost said "Medley 1, Liddlestone 3."

"So you had no intention of stealing the car when you set off to follow her to the beach?"

"Certainly not!" Tisdall said, as indignantly as if it made a difference. "It didn't even cross my mind till I came up the hill and saw the car waiting there. Even now I can't believe I really did it. I've been a fool, but I've never done anything like that before."

"Was she in the sea then?"

"I don't know. I didn't go to look. If I had seen her even in the distance I couldn't have done it. I just slung the buns in and beat it. When I came to I was halfway to Canterbury. I just turned her around without stopping, and came straight back."

The sergeant made no comment.

"You still haven't told me how long you've been staying at the cottage?"

"Since Saturday midnight."

It was now Thursday.

"And you still ask me to believe that you don't know your hostess's last name?"

"No. It's a bit queer, I know. I thought so, myself, at first. I had a conventional upbringing. But she made it seem natural. After the first day we simply accepted each other. It was as if I had known her for years." As the sergeant said nothing, but sat radiating doubt as a stove radiates heat, he added with a hint of temper, "Why shouldn't I tell you her name if I knew it!"

"How should I know?" said the sergeant, unhelpfully. He considered out of the corner of his eye the young man's pale, if composed, face. He seemed to have recovered remarkably quickly from his exhibition of nerves and grief. Light-weights, these moderns. No real emotion about anything. Just hysteria. What they called love was just a barn-yard exercise; they thought anything else "sentimental." No discipline. No putting up with things. Every time something got difficult, they ran away. Not slapped enough in their youth. All this modern idea about giving children their own way. Look what it led to. Howling on the beach one minute and as cool as a cucumber the next.

And then the sergeant noticed the trembling of the too fine hands on the wheel. No, whatever else Robert Tisdall was he wasn't cool.

"This is the place?" the sergeant asked, as they slowed down by a hedged garden.

"This is the place."

It was a half-timbered cottage of about five rooms; shut in from the road by a seven-foot hedge of briar and honeysuckle, and dripping with roses. A godsend for Americans, week-enders, and photographers. The little windows yawned in the quiet, and the bright blue door stood hospitably open, disclosing in the shadow the gleam of a brass warming pan on the wall. The cottage had been "discovered."

As they walked up the brick path, a thin small

woman appeared on the doorstep, brilliant in a white apron; her scanty hair drawn to a knob at the back of her head, and a round bird's-nest affair of black satin set insecurely at the very top of her arched, shining poll.

Tisdall lagged as he caught sight of her, so that the sergeant's large official elevation should announce trouble to her with the clarity of a sandwich board.

But Mrs. Pitts was a policeman's widow, and no apprehension showed on her tight little face. Buttons coming up the path meant for her a meal in demand; her mind acted accordingly.

"I've been making some griddle cakes for breakfast. It's going to be hot later on. Best to let the stove out. Tell Miss Robinson when she comes in, will you, sir?" Then, realizing that buttons were a badge of office, "Don't tell me you've been driving without a license, sir!"

"Miss—Robinson, is it? Has met with an accident," the sergeant said.

"The car! Oh, dear! She was always that reckless with it. Is she bad?"

"It wasn't the car. An accident in the water."

"Oh," she said slowly. *"That* bad!"

"How do you mean: that bad?"

"Accidents in the water only mean one thing."

"Yes," agreed the sergeant.

"Well, well," she said, sadly contemplative. Then, her manner changing abruptly, "And where were *you?"* she snapped, eyeing the drooping Tisdall as she eyed Saturday-night fish on a Westover fishmonger's slab. Her superficial deference to "gentry" had vanished in the presence of catastrophe. Tisdall appeared as the "bundle of uselessness" she had privately considered him.

The sergeant was interested but snubbing. "The gentleman wasn't there."

"He ought to have been there. He left just after her."

"How do you know that?"

"I saw him. I live in the cottage down the road."

"Do you know Miss Robinson's other address? I take it for granted this isn't her permanent home."

"No, of course it isn't. She only has this place for a month. It belongs to Owen Hughes." She paused, impressively, to let the importance of the name sink in. "But he's doing a film in Hollywood. About a Spanish count, it was to be, so he told me. He said he's done Italian counts and French counts and he thought it would be a new experience for him to be a Spanish count. Very nice, Mr. Hughes is. Not a bit spoiled in spite of all the fuss they make of him. You wouldn't believe it, but a girl came to me once and offered me five pounds if I'd give her the sheets he had slept in. What I gave her was a piece of my mind. But she wasn't a bit ashamed. Offered me twenty-five shillings for a pillow-slip. I don't know what the world is coming to, that I don't, what with—"

"What other address had Miss Robinson?"

"I don't know any of her addresses but this one."

"Didn't she write and tell you that she was coming?"

"Write! No! She sent telegrams. I suppose she could write, but I'll take my alfred davy she never did. About six telegrams a day used to go to the post office in Liddlestone. My Albert used to take them, mostly; between school. Some of them used three or four forms, they were that long."

"Do you know any of the people she had down here, then?"

"She didn't have any folks here. 'Cept Mr. Stanna-way, that is."

"No one!"

"Not a one. Once—it was when I was showing her the trick of flushing the W.C.; you have to pull hard and then let go smart-like—once she said: 'Do you ever, Mrs. Pitts,' she said, 'get sick of the sight of people's faces?' I said I got a bit tired of some. She said: 'Not some, Mrs. Pitts. All of them. Just sick of people.'

I said when I felt like that I took a dose of caster oil. She laughed and said it wasn't a bad idea. Only everyone should have one and what a good new world it would be in two days. 'Mussolini never thought of that one,' she said."

"Was it London she came from?"

"Yes. She went up just once or twice in the three weeks she's been here. Last time was last week-end, when she brought Mr. Stannaway back." Again her glance dismissed Tisdall as something less than human. "Doesn't *he* know her address?" she asked.

"No one does," the sergeant said. "I'll look through her papers and see what I can find."

Mrs. Pitts led the way into the living-room; cool, low-beamed, and smelling of sweetpeas.

"What have you done with her—with the body, I mean?" she asked.

"At the mortuary."

This seemed to bring home tragedy for the first time.

"Oh, deary me." She moved the end of her apron over a polished table, slowly. "And me making griddle cakes."

This was not a lament for wasted griddle cakes, but her salute to the strangeness of life.

"I expect you'll need breakfast," she said to Tisdall, softened by her unconscious recognition of the fact that the best are but puppets.

But Tisdall wanted no breakfast. He shook his head and turned away to the window, while the sergeant searched in the desk.

"I wouldn't mind one of those griddle cakes," the sergeant said, turning over papers.

"You won't get better in Kent, though it's me that's saying it. And perhaps Mr. Stannaway will swallow some tea."

She went away to the kitchen.

"So you didn't know her name was Robinson?" said the sergeant, glancing up.

"Mrs. Pitts always addressed her as 'miss.' And anyhow, did she look as if her name was Robinson?"

The sergeant, too, did not believe for a moment that her name was Robinson, so he let the subject drop.

Presently Tisdall said: "If you don't need me, I think I'll go into the garden. It—it's stuffy in here."

"All right. You won't forget I need the car to get back to Westover."

"I've told you. It was a sudden impulse. Anyhow, I couldn't very well steal it now and hope to get away with it."

Not so dumb, decided the sergeant. Quite a bit of temper, too. Not just a nonentity, by any means.

The desk was littered with magazines, newspapers, half finished cartons of cigarettes, bits of a jigsaw puzzle, a nail file and polish, patterns of silk, and a dozen more odds and ends; everything, in fact, except note paper. The only documents were bills from the local tradesmen, most of them receipted. If the woman had been untidy and unmethodical, she had at least had a streak of caution. The receipts might be crumpled and difficult to find if wanted, but they had never been thrown away.

The sergeant, soothed by the quiet of the early morning, the cheerful sounds of Mrs. Pitts making tea in the kitchen, and the prospect of griddle cakes to come, began as he worked at the desk to indulge in his one vice. He whistled. Very low and round and sweet, the sergeant's whistling was, but, still—whistling. "Sing to me sometimes" he warbled, not forgetting the grace notes, and his subconscious derived great satisfaction from the performance. His wife had once shown him a bit in the *Mail* that said that whistling was the sign of an empty mind. But it hadn't cured him.

And then, abruptly, the even tenor of the moment was shattered. Without warning there came a mock tattoo on the half open sitting-room door—*tum-te-ta-tum-tumta-TA!* A man's voice said, "So this is where

you're hiding out!" The door was flung wide with a
flourish and in the opening stood a short dark stranger.

"*We-e-ell,*" he said, making several syllables of it. He
stood staring at the sergeant, amused and smiling
broadly. "I thought you were Chris! What is the Force
doing here? Been a burglary?"

"No, no burglary." The sergeant was trying to
collect his thoughts.

"Don't tell me Chris has been throwing a wild party!
I thought she gave that up years ago. They don't go
with all those high-brow rôles."

"No, as a matter of fact, there's—"

"Where is she, anyway?" He raised his voice in a
cheerful shout directed at the upper story. "Yo-hoo!
Chris. Come on down, you old so-and-so! Hiding out
on me!" To the sergeant: "Gave us all the slip for
nearly three weeks now. Too much Kleig, I guess.
Gives them all the jitters sooner or later. But then, the
last one was such a success they naturally want to cash
in on it." He hummed a bar of "Sing to me sometimes," with mock solemnity. "That's why I thought
you were Chris; you were whistling her song. Whistling
darned good, too."

"Her—her song?" Presently, the sergeant hoped, a
gleam of light would be vouchsafed him.

"Yes, her song. Who else's? You didn't think it was
mine, my dear good chap, did you? Not on your life. I
wrote the thing, sure. But that doesn't count. It's her
song. And perhaps she didn't put it across! Eh? Wasn't
that a performance?"

"I couldn't really say." If the man would stop
talking, he might sort things out.

"Perhaps you haven't seen *Bars of Iron* yet?"

"No, I can't say I have."

"That's the worst of wireless and gramophone rec-
ords and what not: they take all the pep out of a film.
Probably by the time you hear Chris sing that song
you'll be so sick of the sound of it that you'll retch at the
ad lib. It's not fair to a film. All right for songwriters

and that sort of cattle, but rough on a film, very rough. There ought to be some sort of agreement. Hey, Chris! Isn't she here, after all my trouble in catching up on her?" His face drooped like a disappointed baby's. "Having her walk in and find me isn't half such a good one as walking in on her. Do you think—"

"Just a minute, Mr.—er—I don't know your name."

"I'm Jay Harmer. Jason on the birth certificate. I wrote 'If it can't be in June.' You probably whistle that as—"

"Mr. Harmer. Do I understand that the lady who is—was—staying here is a film actress?"

"Is she a film actress!" Slow amazement deprived Mr. Harmer for once of speech. Then it began to dawn on him that he must have made a mistake. "Say, Chris *is* staying here, isn't she?"

"The lady's name is Chris, yes. But—well, perhaps you'll be able to help us. There's been some trouble— very unfortunate—and apparently she said her name was Robinson."

The man laughed in rich amusement. "Robinson! That's a good one. I always said she had no imagination. Couldn't write a gag. Did you believe she was a Robinson?"

"Well, no; it seemed unlikely."

"What did I tell you! Well, just to pay her out for treating me like bits on the cutting-room floor, I'm going to split on her. She'll probably put me in the ice-box for twenty-four hours, but it'll be worth it. I'm no gentleman, anyhow, so I won't damage myself in the telling. The lady's name, Sergeant, is Christine Clay."

"Christine Clay!" said the sergeant. His jaw slackened and dropped, quite beyond his control.

"Christine Clay!" breathed Mrs. Pitts, standing in the doorway, a forgotten tray of griddle cakes in her hands.

3

"CHRISTINE CLAY! CHRISTINE CLAY!" YELLED THE MID-day posters.

"Christine Clay!" screamed the headlines.

"Christine Clay!" chattered the wireless.

"Christine Clay!" said neighbor to neighbor.

All over the world people paused to speak the words. Christine Clay was drowned! And in all civilization only one person said, "Who is Christine Clay?"—a bright young man at a Bloomsbury party. And he was merely being "bright."

All over the world things happened because one woman had lost her life. In California a man tele-phoned a summons to a girl in Greenwich Village. A Texas airplane pilot did an extra night flight carrying Clay films for rush showing. A New York firm cancelled an order. An Italian nobleman went bankrupt: he had hoped to sell her his yacht. A man in Philadelphia ate his first square meal in months, thanks to an "I knew her when" story. A woman in Le Touquet sang because now her chance had come. And in an English cathedral town a man thanked God on his knees.

The Press, becalmed in the doldrums of the silly season, leaped to movement at so unhoped-for a wind. The *Clarion* recalled Bart Bartholomew, their "descriptive" man, from a beauty contest in Brighton (much to Bart's thankfulness—he came back loudly wondering how butchers ate meat), and "Jammy" Hopkins, their "crime and passion" star, from a very dull and low-class poker killing in Bradford. (So far had the *Clarion* sunk.) News photographers deserted motor race tracks, reviews, society weddings, cricket, and the man who was going to Mars in a balloon, and swarmed like beetles over the cottage in Kent, the maisonette in South Street, and the furnished manor in Hampshire. That, having rented so charming a country retreat as this last, Christine Clay had yet run away to an unknown and inconvenient cottage without the knowledge of her friends made a very pleasant appendage to the main sensation of her death. Photographs of the manor (garden front, because of the yews) appeared labelled, "The place Christine Clay owned" (she had only rented it for the season, but there was no emotion in renting a place); and next these impressive pictures were placed photographs of the rose-embowered home of the people, with the caption, "The place she preferred."

Her press agent shed tears over that. Something like that *would* break when it was too late.

It might have been observed by any student of nature not too actively engaged in the consequences of it that Christine Clay's death, while it gave rise to pity, dismay, horror, regret, and half a dozen other emotions in varying degrees, yet seemed to move no one to grief. The only outburst of real feeling had been that hysterical crisis of Robert Tisdall's over her body. And who should say how much of that was self-pity? Christine was too international a figure to belong to

anything so small as a "set." But among her immediate
acquaintances dismay was the most marked reaction of
the dreadful news. And not always that. Coyne, who
was due to direct her third and final picture in England,
might be at the point of despair, but Lejeune (late
Tomkins), who had been engaged to play opposite her,
was greatly relieved; a picture with Clay might be a
feather in your cap but it was a jinx in your box-office.
The Duchess of Trent, who had arranged a Clay
luncheon which was to rehabilitate her as a hostess in
the eyes of London, might be gnashing her teeth, but
Lydia Keats was openly jubilant. She had prophesied
the death, and even for a successful society seer that
was a good guess. "Darling, how wonderful of you!"
fluttered her friends. "Darling how wonderful of you!"
On and on. Until Lydia so lost her head with delight
that she spent all her days going from one gathering to
another so that she might make that delicious entrance
all over again, hear them say: "Here's Lydia! Darling
how—" and bask in the radiance of their wonder. No,
as far as anyone could see, no hearts were breaking
because Christine Clay was no more. The world dusted
off its blacks and hoped for invitations to the funeral.

4

BUT FIRST THERE WAS THE INQUEST. AND IT WAS AT THE inquest that the first faint stirring of a much greater sensation began to appear. It was Jammy Hopkins who noted the quiver on the smooth surface. He had earned his nickname because of his glad cry of "Jam! Jam!" when a good story broke, and his philosophical reflection when times were thin that "all was jam that came to the rollers." Hopkins had an excellent nose for jam, and so it was that he stopped suddenly in the middle of analyzing for Bartholomew's benefit the various sensation seekers crowding the little Kentish village hall. Stopped dead and stared. Because, between the fly-away hats of two bright sensationalists, he could see a man's calm face which was much more sensational than anything in that building.

"Seen something?" Bart asked.

"Have I seen something!" Hopkins slid from the end of the form, just as the coroner sat down and tapped for silence. "Keep my place," he whispered, and disap-

27

peared out of the building. He entered it again at the back door, expertly pushed his way to the place he wanted, and sat down. The man turned his head to view this gate-crasher.

"Morning, Inspector," said Hopkins.

The Inspector looked his disgust.

"I wouldn't do it if I didn't need the money," Hopkins said, *vox humana*.

The coroner tapped again for silence, but the Inspector's face relaxed.

Presently, under cover of the bustle of Potticary's arrival to give evidence, Hopkins said, "What is Scotland Yard doing here, Inspector?"

"Looking on."

"I see. Just studying inquests as an institution. Crime slack these days?" As the Inspector showed no sign of being drawn: "Oh, have a heart, Inspector. What's in the wind? Is there something phony about the death? Suspicions, eh? If you don't want to talk for publication I'm the original locked casket."

"You're the original camel-fly."

"Oh, well, look at the hides I have to get through!" This produced a grin and nothing else. "Look here. Just tell me one thing, Inspector. Is this inquest going to be adjourned?"

"I shouldn't be surprised."

"Thank you. That tells me everything," Hopkins said, half sarcastic, half serious, as he made his way out again. He prised Mrs. Pitts' Albert away from the wall where he clung limpet-like by the window, persuaded him that two shillings was better than a partial view of dull proceedings, and sent him to Liddlestone with a telegram which set the *Clarion* office buzzing. Then he went back to Bart.

"Something wrong," he said out of the corner of his mouth in answer to Bart's eyebrows. "The Yard's here. That's Grant, behind the scarlet hat. Inquest going to be adjourned. Spot the murderer!"

"Not here," Bart said, having considered the gathering.

"No," agreed Jammy. "Who's the chap in the flannel bags?"

"Boy friend."

"Thought the boy friend was Jay Harmer."

"Was. This one newer."

" 'Love nest killing'?"

"Wouldn't mind betting."

"Supposed to be cold, I thought?"

"Yes. So they say. Fooled them, seemingly. Good enough reason for murder, I should think."

The evidence was of the most formal kind—the finding and identification of the body—and as soon as that had been offered the coroner brought the proceedings to an end, and fixed no date for resumption.

Hopkins had decided that, the Clay death being apparently no accident, and Scotland Yard not being able so far to make any arrest, the person to cultivate was undoubtedly the man in the flannel bags. Tisdall, his name was. Bart said that every newspaper man in England had tried to interview him the previous day (Hopkins being then enroute from the poker murder) but that he had been exceptionally tough. Called them ghouls, and vultures, and rats, and other things less easy of specification, and had altogether seemed unaware of the standing of the Press. No one was rude to the Press any more—not with impunity, that was.

But Hopkins had great faith in his power to seduce the human mind.

"Your name Tisdall, by any chance?" he asked casually, "finding" himself alongside the young man in the crowded procession to the door.

The man's face hardened into instant enmity.

"Yes, it is," he said aggressively.

"Not old Tom Tisdall's nephew?"

The face cleared swiftly.

"Yes. Did you know Uncle Tom?"

"A little," admitted Hopkins, no whit dismayed to find that there really was a Tom Tisdall.

"You seem to know about my giving up the Stannaway?"

"Yes, someone told me," Hopkins said, wondering if the Stannaway was a house, or what? "What are you doing now?"

By the time they had reached the door, Hopkins had established himself. "Can I give you a lift somewhere? Come and have lunch with me?"

A pip! In half an hour he'd have a front-page story. And this was the baby they said was difficult! No, there was no doubt of it: he, James Brooke Hopkins, was the greatest newspaper man in the business.

"Sorry, Mr. Hopkins," said Grant's pleasant voice at his shoulder. "I don't want to spoil your party, but Mr. Tisdall has an appointment with me." And, since Tisdall betrayed his astonishment and Hopkins his instant putting two and two together, he added, "We're hoping he can help us."

"I don't understand," Tisdall was beginning. And Hopkins, seeing that Tisdall was unaware of Grant's identity, rushed in with glad maliciousness.

"That is Scotland Yard," he said. "Inspector Grant. Never had an unsolved crime to his name."

"I hope you write my obituary," Grant said.

"I hope I do!" the journalist said, with fervor.

And then they noticed Tisdall. His face was like parchment, dry and old and expressionless. Only the pulse beating hard at his temple suggested a living being. Journalist and detective stood looking in mutual astonishment at so unexpected a result of Hopkins' announcement. And then, seeing the man's knees beginning to sag, Grant took him hastily by the arm.

"Here! Come and sit down. My car is just here."

He edged the apparently blind Tisdall through the dawdling, chattering crowd, and pushed him into the rear seat of a dark touring car.

"Westover," he said to the chauffeur, and got in beside Tisdall.

As they went at snail's pace towards the high-road, Grant saw Hopkins still standing where they had left him. That Jammy Hopkins should stay without moving for more than three consecutive minutes argued that he was being given furiously to think. From now on—the Inspector sighed—the camel-fly would be a blood-hound.

And the Inspector, too, had food for his wits. He had been called in the previous night by a worried County Constabulary who had no desire to make themselves ridiculous by making mountains out of molehills, but who found themselves unable to explain away satisfactorily one very small, very puzzling obstacle to their path. They had all viewed the obstacle, from the Chief Constable down to the sergeant who had taken charge on the beach, had been rude about each other's theories, and had in the end agreed on only one thing: that they wanted to push the responsibility on to someone else's shoulders. It was all very well to hang on to your own crime, and the kudos of a solution, when there *was* a crime. But to decide in cold blood to announce a crime, on the doubtful evidence of that common little object on the table; to risk, not the disgrace of failure, but the much worse slings of ridicule, was something they could not find it in their hearts to do. And so Grant had cancelled his seat at the Criterion and had journeyed down to Westover. He had inspected the stumbling block, listened with patience to their theories and with respect to the police surgeon's story, and had gone to bed in the small hours with a great desire to interview Robert Tisdall. And now here was Tisdall, beside him, still speechless and half fainting because he had been confronted without warning by Scotland Yard. Yes, there was a case; no doubt of it. Well, there couldn't be any questioning with Cork in the driving seat, so until they got back to

Westover Tisdall might be left to recover. Grant took a flask from the car pocket and offered it to him. Tisdall took it shakily but made good use of it. Presently he apologized for his weakness.

"I don't know what went wrong. This affair has been an awful shock to me. I haven't been sleeping. Keep going over things in my mind. Or rather, my mind keeps doing it; I can't stop it. And then, at the inquest it seemed—I say, is something not right? I mean, was it not a simple drowning? Why did they postpone the end of the inquest?"

"There are one or two things that the police find puzzling."

"As what, for instance?"

"I think we won't discuss it until we get to Westover."

"Is anything I say to be used in evidence against me?" The smile was wry but the intention was good.

"You took the words out of my mouth," the Inspector said lightly, and silence fell between them.

By the time they reached the Chief Constable's room in the County Police offices, Tisdall was looking normal if a little worn. In fact, so normal did he look that when Grant said, "This is Mr. Tisdall," the Chief Constable, who was a genial soul except when someone jumped in his pocket out hunting, almost shook hands with him, but recollected himself before any harm was done.

"Howdyudo. Harrump!" He cleared his throat to give himself time. Couldn't do that, of course. My goodness, no. Fellow suspected of murder. Didn't look it, no, upon his soul he didn't. But there was no telling these days. The most charming people were—well, things he hadn't known till lately existed. Very sad. But couldn't shake hands, of course. No, definitely not. "Harrump! Fine morning! Bad for racing, of course. Going very hard. But good for the holiday makers. Mustn't be selfish in our pleasures. You a racing man? Going to Goodwood? Oh, well, perhaps—No. Well, I expect you and—and our friend here—" somehow one didn't want to rub in the fact of Grant's inspectorship.

Nice-looking chap. Well brought up, and all that—
"would like to talk in peace. I'm going to lunch. The
Ship," he added, for Grant's benefit, in case the
Inspector wanted him. "Not that the food's very good
there, but it's a self-respecting house. Not like these
Marine things. Like to get steak and potatoes without
going through sun lounges for them." And the Chief
Constable took himself out.

"A Freedy Lloyd part," Tisdall said.

Grant looked up appreciatively from pulling forward
a chair.

"You're a theater fan."

"I was a fan of most things."

Grant's mind focused on the peculiarity of the
phrase. "Why 'was'?" he asked.

"Because I'm broke. You need money to be a fan."

"You won't forget that formula about 'anything you
say,' will you?"

"No. Thanks. But it doesn't make any difference. I
can only tell you the truth. If you draw wrong
deductions from it then that's your fault, not mine."

"So it's I who am on trial. A nice point. I appreciate
it. Well, try me out. I want to know how you were
living in the same house with a woman whose name you
didn't know? You did tell the County Police that, didn't
you?"

"Yes. I expect it sounds incredible. Silly, too. But it's
quite simple. You see, I was standing on the pavement
opposite the Gaiety one night, very late, wondering
what to do. I had fivepence in my pocket, and that was
fivepence too much, because I had aimed at having
nothing at all. And I was wondering whether to have a
last go at spending the fivepence (there isn't much one
can do with fivepence) or to cheat, and forget about the
odd pennies. So—"

"Just a moment. You might explain to a dullard just
why these five pennies should have been important."

"They were the end of a fortune, you see. Thirty
thousand. I inherited it from my uncle. My mother's

brother. My real name is Stannaway, but Uncle Tom
asked that I should take his name with the money. I
didn't mind. The Tisdalls were a much better lot than
the Stannaways, anyhow. Stamina and ballast and all
that. If I'd been a Tisdall I wouldn't be broke now, but
I'm nearly all Stannaway. I've been the perfect fool, the
complete Awful Warning. I was in an architect's office
when I inherited the money, living in rooms and just
making do; and it went to my head to have what
seemed more than I could ever spend. I gave up my job
and went to see all the places I'd wanted to see and
never hoped to. New York and Hollywood and Buda-
pest and Rome and Capri and God knows where else. I
came back to London with about two thousand,
meaning to bank it and get a job. It would have been
easy enough two years before—I mean, to bank the
money. I hadn't anyone to help spend it then. But in
those two years I had gathered a lot of friends all over
the world, and there were never less than a dozen of
them in London at the same time. So I woke up one
morning to find that I was down to my last hundred. It
was a bit of a shock. Like cold water. I sat down and
thought for the first time for two years. I had the choice
of two things: sponging—you can live in luxury anywhere in the world's capitals for six months if you're a
good sponger: I know; I supported dozens of that
sort—and disappearing. Disappearing seemed easier. I
could drop out quite easily. People would just say,
'Where's Bobby Tisdall these days?' and they'd just
take it for granted that I was in some of the other
corners of the world where their sort went, and that
they'd run into me one of these days. I was supposed to
be suffocatingly rich, you see, and it was easier to drop
out and leave them thinking of me like that than to stay
and be laughed at when the truth began to dawn on
them. I paid my bills, and that left me with fifty-seven
pounds. I thought I'd have one last gamble then, and
see if I could pick up enough to start me off on the new

level. So I had thirty pounds—fifteen each way; that's the bit of Tisdall in me—on Red Rowan in the Eclipse. He finished fifth. Twenty-odd pounds isn't enough to start anything except a barrow. There was nothing for it but tramping. I wasn't much put out at the thought of tramping—it would be a change—but you can't tramp with twenty-seven pounds in the bank, so I decided to blue it all in one grand last night. I promised myself that I'd finish up without a penny in my pocket. Then I'd pawn my evening things for some suitable clothes and hit the road. What I hadn't reckoned with was that you can't pawn things in the west-end on a Saturday midnight. And you can't take to the road in evening things without being conspicuous. So I was standing there, as I said, feeling resentful about these five pennies and wondering what I was to do about my clothes and a place to sleep. I was standing by the traffic lights at the Aldwych, just before you turn around into Lancaster Place, when a car was pulled up by the red lights. Chris was in it, alone—"

"Chris?"

"I didn't know her name, then. She looked at me for a little. The street was very quiet. Just us two. And we were so close that it seemed natural when she smiled and said, 'Take you anywhere, mister?' I said: 'Yes. Land's End.' She said: 'A bit off my route. Chatham, Faversham, Canterbury, and points east?' Well, it was one solution. I couldn't go on standing there, and I couldn't think of a water-tight tale that would get me a bed in a friend's house. Besides, I felt far away from all that crowd already. So I got in without thinking much about it. She was charming to me. I didn't tell her all I'm telling you, but she soon found out I was broke to the wide. I began to explain, but she said: 'All right, I don't want to know. Let's accept each other on face value. You're Robin and I'm Chris.' I'd told her my name was Robert Stannaway, and without knowing it she used my family pet name. The crowd called me

Bobby. It was sort of comforting to hear someone call me Robin again."

"Why did you say your name was Stannaway?"

"I don't know. A sort of desire to get away from the fortune side of things. I hadn't been much ornament to the name, anyhow. And in my mind I always thought of myself as Stannaway."

"All right. Go on."

"There isn't much more to tell. She offered me hospitality. Told me she was alone, but that—well, that I'd be just a guest. I said wasn't she taking a chance. She said, 'Yes, but I've taken them all my life and it's worked out pretty well, so far.' It seemed an awkward arrangement to me, but it turned out just the opposite. She was right about it. It made things very easy, just accepting each other. In a way (it was queer, but it was like that) it was as if we had known each other for years. If we had had to start at scratch and work up, it would have taken us weeks to get to the same stage. We liked each other a lot. I don't mean sentimentally, although she was stunning to look at; I mean I thought her grand. I had no clothes for the next morning, but I spent that day in a bathing suit and a dressing-gown that someone had left. And on Monday Mrs. Pitts came in to my room and said, 'Your suit-case, sir,' and dumped a case I'd never seen before in the middle of the floor. It had a complete new outfit in it—tweed coat and flannels, socks, shirt, everything. From a place in Canterbury. The suit-case was old, and had a label with my name on it. She had even remembered my name. Well, I can't describe to you what I felt about these things. You see, it was the first time for years that anyone had *given* me anything. With the crowd it was take, take, all the time. 'Bobby'll pay.' 'Bobby'll lend his car.' They never thought of *me* at all. I don't think they ever stopped to look at me. Anyhow, those clothes sort of broke me up. I'd have died for her. She laughed when she saw me in them—they were reach-me-downs, of course, but they fitted quite well—and said: 'Not exactly Bruton Street, but they'll do. Don't say I can't size a man up.' So we settled down to having a good time together, just lazing around, reading, talking, swimming, cooking when Mrs. Pitts wasn't there. I put out of my head what was going to happen after. She said that in about ten days she'd have to leave the cottage. I tried to go after the first day, out of politeness, but she wouldn't let me. And after that I didn't try. That's how I came to be staying there, and that's how I didn't know her name." He drew in his breath in a sharp sigh as he sat back. "Now I know how these psychoanalysts make money. It's a long time since I enjoyed anything like telling you all about myself."

Grant smiled involuntarily. There was an engaging childlikeness about the boy.

Then he shook himself mentally, like a dog coming out of water.

Charm. The most insidious weapon in all the human armory. And here it was, being exploited under his nose. He considered the good-natured feckless face dispassionately. He had known at least one murderer who had had that type of good looks; blue-eyed, amiable, harmless; and he had buried his dismembered fiancée in an ash-pit. Tisdall's eyes were of that particular warm opaque blue which Grant had noted so often in men to whom the society of women was a necessity of existence. Mother's darlings had those eyes; so sometimes, had womanizers.

Well, presently he would check up on Tisdall. Meanwhile—

"Do you ask me to believe that in your four days together you had no suspicion at all of Miss Clay's identity?" he asked, marking time until he could bring Tisdall unsuspecting to the crucial matter.

"I suspected that she was an actress. Partly from things she said, but mostly because there were such a lot of stage and film magazines in the house. I asked her about it once, but she said: 'No names, no pack drill. It's a good motto, Robin. Don't forget.'"

"I see. Did the outfit Miss Clay bought for you include an overcoat?"

"No. A mackintosh. I had a coat."

"You were wearing a coat over your evening things?"

'Yes. It had been drizzling when we set out for dinner—the crowd and I, I mean."

"And you still have that coat?"

"No. It was stolen from the car one day when we were over at Dymchurch." His eyes grew alarmed suddenly. "Why? What has the coat got to do with it?"

"Was it dark- or light-colored?"

"Dark, of course. A sort of gray-black. Why?"

"Did you report its loss?"

"No, neither of us wanted attention called to us. What has it—"

"Just tell me about Thursday morning, will you?" The face opposite him was steadily losing its ingenuousness and becoming wary and inimical again. "I understand that you didn't go with Miss Clay to swim. Is that right?"

"Yes. But I awoke almost as soon as she had gone—"

"How do you know when she went if you were asleep?"

"Because it was still only six. She couldn't have been gone long. And Mrs. Pitts said afterwards that I had followed down the road on her heels."

"I see. And in the hour and a half—roughly—between your getting up and the finding of Miss Clay's body you walked to the Gap, stole the car, drove it in the direction of Canterbury, regretted what you had done, came back, and found that Miss Clay had been drowned. Is that a complete record of your actions?"

"Yes, I think so."

"If you felt so grateful to Miss Clay, it was surely an extraordinary thing to do."

"Extraordinary isn't the word at all. Even yet I can't believe I did it."

"You are quite sure that you didn't enter the water that morning?"

"Of course I'm sure. Why?"

"When was your last swim? Previous to Thursday morning, I mean?"

"Noon on Wednesday."

"And yet your swimming suit was soaking wet on Thursday morning."

"How do you know that! Yes, it was. But not with salt water. It had been spread to dry on the roof below my window, and when I was dressing on Thursday morning I noticed that the birds in the tree—an apple tree hangs over that gable—had made too free with it. So I washed it in the water I had been washing in."

"You didn't put it out to dry again, though, apparently?"

"After what happened the last time? No! I put it on the towel rail. For God's sake, Inspector, tell me what all this has to do with Chris's death? Can't you see that questions you can't see the reason of are torture? I've had about all I can stand. The inquest this morning was the last straw. Everyone describing how they found her. Talking about 'the body,' when all the time it was Chris. Chris! And now all this mystery and suspicion. If there was anything not straightforward about her drowning, what has my coat got to do with it anyway?"

"Because this was found entangled in her hair."

Grant opened a cardboard box on the table and exhibited a black button of the kind used for men's coats. It had been torn from its proper place, the worn threads of its attachment still forming a ragged "neck." And around the neck, close to the button, was twined a thin strand of bright hair.

Tisdall was on his feet, both hands on the table edge, staring down at the object.

"You think someone *drowned* her? I mean—like

that! But that isn't mine. There are thousands of buttons like that. What makes you think it is mine?"

"I don't think anything, Mr. Tisdall. I am only eliminating possibilities. All I wanted you to do was to account for any garment owned by you which had buttons like that. You say you had one but that it was stolen."

Tisdall stared at the Inspector, his mouth opening and shutting helplessly.

The door breezed open, after the sketchiest of knocks, and in the middle of the floor stood a small, skinny child of sixteen in shabby tweeds, her dark head hatless and very untidy.

"Oh, sorry," she said. "I thought my father was here. Sorry."

Tisdall slumped to the floor with a crash.

Grant, who was sitting on the other side of the large table sprang to action, but the skinny child, with no sign of haste or dismay, was there first.

"Dear me!" she said, getting the slumped body under the shoulders from behind and turning it over.

Grant took a cushion from a chair.

"I shouldn't do that," she said. "You let their heads stay back unless it's apoplexy. And he's a bit young for that, isn't he?"

She was loosening collar and tie and shirt-band with the expert detachment of a cook paring pastry from a pie edge. Grant noticed that her sunburnt wrists were covered with small scars and scratches of varying age, and that they stuck too far out of her out-grown sleeves.

"You'll find brandy in the cupboard, I think. Father isn't allowed it, but he has no self-control."

Grant found the brandy and came back to find her slapping Tisdall's unconscious face with a light insistent *tapotement*.

"You seem to be good at this sort of thing," Grant said.

"Oh, I ran the Guides at school." She had a voice at

once precise and friendly. "A *ve*-ry silly institution. But it varied the routine. That is the main thing, to vary the routine."

"Did you learn this from the Guides?" he asked, nodding at her occupation.

"Oh, no. They burn paper and smell salts and things. I learned this in Bradford Pete's dressing-room."

"Where?"

"You know. The welter-weight. I used to have great faith in Pete, but I think he's lost his speed lately. Don't you? At least, I *hope* it's his speed. He's coming to nicely." This last referred to Tisdall. "I think he'd swallow the brandy now."

While Grant was administering the brandy, she said: "Have you been giving him the third degree, or something? You're police aren't you?"

"My dear young lady—I don't know your name?"

"Erica. I'm Erica Burgoyne."

"My dear Miss Burgoyne, as the Chief Constable's daughter you must be aware that the only people in Britain who are subjected to the third degree are the police."

"Well, what did he faint for? Is he guilty?"

"I don't know," Grant said, before he thought.

"I shouldn't think so." She was considering the now spluttering Tisdall. "He doesn't look capable of much." This with the same grave detachment as she used to everything she did.

"Don't let looks influence your judgment, Miss Burgoyne."

"I don't. Not the way you mean. Anyhow, he isn't at all my type. But it's quite right to judge on looks if you know enough. You wouldn't buy a washy chestnut narrow across the eyes, would you?"

This, thought Grant, is quite the most amazing conversation.

She was standing up now, her hands pushed into her jacket pockets so much the much-tried garment sagged to two bulging points. The tweed she wore was rubbed at the cuffs and covered all over with "pulled" ends of thread where briars had caught. Her skirt was too short and one stocking was violently twisted on its stick of leg. Only her shoes—scarred like her hands, but thick, well-shaped and expensive—betrayed the fact that she was not a charity child.

And then Grant's eyes went back to her face. Except her face. The calm sureness of that sallow little triangular visage was not bred in any charity school.

"There!" she said encouragingly, as Grant helped Tisdall to his feet and guided him into a chair. "You'll be all right. Have a little more of Father's brandy. It's a much better end for it than Father's arteries. I'm going now. Where is Father, do you know?" This to Grant.

"He has gone to lunch at The Ship."

"Thank you." Turning to the still dazed Tisdall, she said, "That shirt collar of yours is far too tight." As Grant moved to open the door for her, she said, "You haven't told me *your* name?"

"Grant. At your service." He gave her a little bow.

"I don't need anything just now, but I might some day." She considered him. Grant found himself hoping with a fervor which surprised him that he was not being placed in the same category as "washy chestnuts." "You're much more my type. I like people broad across the cheekbones. Goodbye, Mr. Grant."

"Who was that?" Tisdall asked, in the indifferent tones of the newly conscious.

"Colonel Burgoyne's daughter."

"She was right about my shirt."

"One of the reach-me-downs?"

"Yes. Am I being arrested?"

"Oh, no. Nothing like that."

"It mightn't be a bad idea."

"Oh? Why?"

"It would settle my immediate future. I left the cottage this morning and now I'm on the road."

"You mean you're serious about tramping."

"As soon as I have got suitable clothes."

"I'd rather you stayed where I could get information from you if I wanted."

"I see the point. But how?"

"What about that architect's office? Why not try for a job?"

"I'm never going back to an office. Not an architect's anyhow. I was shoved there only because I could draw."

"Do I understand that you consider yourself permanently incapacitated from earning your bread?"

"Phew! That's nasty. No, of course not. I'll have to work. But what kind of job am I fit for?"

"Two years of hitting the high spots must have educated you to something. Even if it is only driving a car."

There came a tentative tap at the door, and the sergeant put his head in.

"I'm very sorry indeed to disturb you, Inspector, but I'd like something from the Chief's files. It's rather urgent."

Permission given, he came in.

"This coast's lively in the season, sir," he said, as he ran through the files. "Positively continental. Here's the chef at the Marine—it's just outside the town, so it's our affair—the chef at the Marine's stabbed a waiter because he had dandruff, it seems. The waiter, I mean, sir. Chef on the way to prison and waiter on the way to hospital. They think maybe his lung's touched. Well, thank you, sir. Sorry to disturb you."

Grant eyed Tisdall, who was achieving the knot in his tie with a melancholy abstraction. Tisdall caught the look, appeared puzzled by it, and then, comprehension dawning, leaped into action.

"I say, Sergeant, have they a fellow to take the waiter's place, do you know?"

"That they haven't. Mr. Toselli—he's the manager—he's tearing his hair."

"Have you finished with me?" he asked Grant.

"For today," Grant said. "Good luck."

5

"No. No arrest," said Grant to Superintendent
Barker over the telephone in the early evening. "But I
don't think there's any doubt about its being murder.
The surgeon's sure of it. The button in her hair might
be an accident—although if you saw it you'd be
convinced it wasn't—but her fingernails were broken
with clawing at something. What was under the nails
has gone to the analyst, but there wasn't much after an
hour's immersion in salt water . . . 'M? . . . Well, indi-
cations point one way certainly, but they cancel each
other out, somehow. Going to be difficult, I think. I'm
leaving Williams here on routine inquiry, and coming
back to town tonight. I want to see her lawyer—
Erskine. He arrived just in time for the inquest, and
afterward I had Tisdall on my hands so I missed him.
Would you find out for me when I can talk to him
tonight. They've fixed the funeral for Monday. Golders
Green. Yes, cremation. I'd like to be there, I think. I'd
like to look over the intimates. Yes, I may look in for a
drink, but it depends how late I am. Thanks."

44

Grant hung up and went to join Williams for a high tea, it being too early for dinner and Williams having a passion for bacon and eggs garnished with large pieces of fried bread.

"Tomorrow being Sunday may hold up the button enquiries," Grant said as they sat down. "Well, what did Mrs. Pitts say?"

"She says she couldn't say whether he was wearing a coat or not. All she saw was the top of his head over her hedge as he went past. But whether he wore it or not doesn't much matter, because she says the coat habitually lay in the back of the car along with that coat that Miss Clay wore. She doesn't remember when she saw Tisdall's dark coat last. He wore it a fair amount, it seems. Mornings and evenings. He was a 'chilly mortal,' she said. Owing to his having come back from foreign parts, she thought. She hasn't much of an opinion of him."

"You mean she thinks he's a wrong 'un?"

"No. Just no account. You know, sir, has it occurred to you that it was a clever man who did this job?"

"Why?"

"Well, but for that button coming off no one would ever have suspected anything. She'd have been found drowned after going to bathe in the early morning—all quite natural. No footsteps, no weapon, no signs of violence. Very neat."

"Yes. It's neat."

"You don't sound very enthusiastic about it."

"It's the coat. If you were going to drown a woman in the sea, would you wear an overcoat to do it?"

"I don't know. 'Pends how I meant to drown her."

"How *would* you drown her?"

"Go swimming with her and keep her head under."

"You'd have scratches that way, ten to one. Evidence."

"Not me. I'd catch her by the heels in shallow water and upend her. Just stand there and hold her till she drowned."

"Williams! What resource. And what ferocity."

"Well, how would you do it, sir?"

"I hadn't thought of aquatic methods. I mightn't be able to swim, or I mightn't like early-morning dips, or I might want to make a quick get-away from a stretch of water containing a body. No, I think I'd stand on a rock in deep water, wait till she came to talk to me, grip her head and keep it under. The only part of me that she could scratch that way would be my hands. And I'd wear leather gloves. It takes only a few seconds before she is unconscious."

"Very nice, sir. But you couldn't use that method anywhere within miles of the Gap."

"Why not?"

"There aren't any rocks."

"No. Good man. But there are the equivalent. There are stone groynes."

"Yes. Yes, so there are! Think that was how it was done, sir?"

"Who knows? It's a theory. But the coat still worries me."

"I don't see why it need, sir. It was a misty morning, a bit chilly at six. Anyone might have worn a coat."

"Y-es," Grant said doubtfully, and let the matter drop, this being one of those unreasonable things which occasionally worried his otherwise logical mind (and had more than once been the means of bringing success to his efforts when his logic failed).

He gave Williams instructions for his further enquiries, when he himself should be in town. "I've just had another few minutes with Tisdall," he finished. "He has got himself a waiter's job at the Marine. I don't think he'll bolt, but you'd better plant a man. Sanger will do. That's Tisdall's car route on Thursday morning, according to himself." He handed a paper to the sergeant. "Check up on it. It was very early but someone may remember him. Did he wear a coat or not? That's the main thing. I think, myself, there's no doubt of his taking the car as he said. Though not for the reason he gave."

"I thought it a silly reason myself, when I read that statement. I just thought: 'Well, he might have made up a better one!' What's you're theory, sir?"

"I think that when he had drowned her his one idea was to get away. With a car he could be at the other end of England, or out of the country, before they found her body! He drove away. And then something made him realize what a fool he was. Perhaps he missed the button from his cuff. Anyhow, he realized that he had only to stay where he was and look innocent. He got rid of the tell-tale coat—even if he hadn't missed the button the sleeve almost up to the elbow must have been soaking with salt water—came back to replace the car, found that the body had been discovered thanks to an incoming tide, and put on a very good act on the beach. It wouldn't have been difficult. The very thought of how nearly he had made a fool of himself would have been enough to make him burst into tears."

"So you think he did it?"

"I don't know. There seems to be a lack of motive. He was penniless and she was a liberal woman. That was every reason for keeping her alive. He was greatly interested in her, certainly. He says he wasn't in love with her, but we have only his word for it. I think he's telling the truth when he says there was nothing between them. He *may* have suffered from frustration, but if that were so he would be much more likely to beat her up. It was a queerly cold-blooded murder, Williams."

"It was certainly that, sir. Turns my stomach." Williams laid a large forkful of best Wiltshire lovingly on a pink tongue.

Grant smiled at him: the smile that made Grant's subordinates "work their fingers to the bone for him." He and Williams had worked together often, and always in amity and mutual admiration. Perhaps, in a large measure because Williams, bless him, coveted no one's shoes. He was much more the contented husband of a pretty and devoted wife than the ambitious detective-sergeant.

"I wish I hadn't missed her lawyer after the inquest. There's a lot I want to ask him, and heaven knows where he'll be for the weekend. I've asked the Yard for her dossier, but her lawyer would be much more helpful. Must find out whom her death benefits. It was a misfortune for Tisdall, but it must have been lucky for a lot of people. Being an American, I suppose her will's in the States somewhere. The Yard will know by the time I get up."

"Christine Clay was no American, sir!" Williams said in a well-I-*am*-surprised-at-you voice.

"No? What then?"

"Born in Nottingham."

"But everyone refers to her as an American."

"Can't help that. She was born in Nottingham and went to school there. They do say she worked in a lace factory, but no one knows the truth of that."

"I forgot you were a film fan, Williams. Tell me more."

"Well, of course, what I know is just by reading *Screenland* and *Photoplay* and magazines like that. A lot of what they write is hooey, but on the other hand they'll never stop at truth as long as it makes a good story. She wasn't fond of being interviewed. And she used to tell a different story each time. When someone pointed out that that wasn't what she had said last time, she said: 'But that's so dull! I've thought of a much better one.' No one ever knew where they were with her. Temperament, they called it, of course."

"And don't you call it that?" asked Grant, always sensitive to an inflection.

"Well, I don't know. It always seemed to me more like—well, like protection, if you know what I mean. People can only get at you if they know what you're like—what matters to you. If you keep them guessing, they're the victims, not you."

"A girl who'd pushed her way from a lace factory in Nottingham to the top of the film world couldn't be very vulnerable."

"It's *because* she was from a lace factory that she was what-d'you-call-it. Every six months she was in a different social sphere, she went up at such a rate. That takes a lot of living up to—like a diver coming up from a long way below. You're continually adjusting yourself to the pressure. No, I think she needed a shell to get into, and keeping people guessing was her shell."

"So you were a Clay fan, Williams."

"Sure I was," said Williams in the appropriate idiom. His pink cheeks grew a shade pinker. He slapped marmalade with venom onto his slab of toast. "And before this affair's finished I'm going to put bracelets on the chap that did it. It's a comforting thought."

"Got any theories yourself?"

"Well, sir, if you don't mind my saying so, you've passed over the person with the obvious motive."

"Who?"

"Jason Harmer. What was he doing snooping around at half past eight of a morning?"

"He'd come over from Sandwich. Spent the night at the pub there."

"So he said. Did the County people verify that?"

Grant consulted his notes.

"Perhaps they haven't. The statement was volunteered before they found the button, and so they weren't suspicious. And since then everyone has concentrated on Tisdall."

"Plenty of motive, Harmer has. Clay walks out on him, and he runs her to earth in a country cottage, alone with a man."

"Yes, very plausible. Well, you can add Harmer to your list of chores. Find out about his wardrobe. There's an S.O.S out for a discarded coat. I hope it

brings in something. A coat's a much easier clue than a
button. Tisdall, by the way, says he sold his wardrobe
complete (except for his evening things) to a man
called—appropriately enough—Togger, but doesn't
know where his place of business is. Is that the chap
who used to be in Craven Road?"

"Yes, sir."

"Where is he now?"

"Westbourne Grove. The far end."

"Thanks. I don't doubt Tisdall's statement. But
there's just a chance there's the duplicate of that button
on another coat. It might lead us to something." He got
to his feet. "Well, on with the job of making bricks
without straw! And talking of that Israelitish occupation, here's a grand sample of it to flavor your third
cup." He pulled from his pocket the afternoon edition
of the *Sentinel,* the *Clarion's* evening representative,
and laid it, with its staring headlines, "Was Clay's
Death an Accident?" upward, by William's plate.

"Jammy Hopkins!" Williams said, with feeling, and
flung sugar violently into his black tea.

6

Marta Hallard, as befitted a leading lady who alternated between the St. James's and the Haymarket, lived in the kind of apartment block which has deep carpet on the stairs and a cloistered hush in the corridors. Grant, climbing the stairs with weary feet, appreciated the carpet even while his other self wondered about the vacuum cleaning. The dim pink square of the lift had fled upward as he came through the revolving door, and rather than wait for its return he was walking the two flights. The commissionaire had said that Marta was at home: had arrived about eleven from the theater with several people. Grant regretted the people, but was determined that this day was not going to end without his obtaining some light on Christine Clay and her entourage. Barker had failed to find the lawyer, Erskine, for him; his man said he was suffering from the shock of the last three days and had gone into the country over Sunday; address unknown. ("Ever heard of a lawyer suffering from shock?"

Barker had said.) So the matter which most interested Grant—the contents of Christine Clay's will—must wait until Monday. At the Yard he had read through the dossier—still, of course, incomplete—which they had gathered together in the last twelve hours. In all the five sheets of it Grant found only two things remarkable.

Her real name, it appeared, was Christina Gotobed.

And she had had no lovers.

No public ones, that is. Even in those crucial years when the little Broadway hoofer was blossoming into the song-and-dance star, she seemed to have had no patron. Nor yet when, tiring of song-and-dance pictures, her ambition had reached out to drama; her rocket had shot to the stars under its own power, it would seem. This could only mean one of two things: that she had remained virgin until her marriage at twenty-six (a state of affairs which Grant, who had a larger experience of life than of psychology textbooks, found quite possible) or that her favor was given only when her heart (or her fancy, according to whether you are sentimentalist or cynic) was touched. Four years ago Lord Edward Champneis (pronounced Chins), old Bude's fifth son, had met her in Hollywood, and in a month they were married. She was at that time shooting her first straight film, and it was generally agreed that she had "done well for herself" in her marriage. Two years later Lord Edward was "Christine Clay's husband."

He took it gracefully, it was reported; and the marriage had lasted. It had become a casual affair of mutual friendliness; partly owing to the demands of time and space that her profession made on Christine, and partly to the fact that Edward Champneis's main interest in life (after Christine) was to invade the uncomfortable interiors of ill-governed and inaccessible countries and then to write books about it. During the book-writing solstice he and Christine lived more or less under one roof, and were apparently very happy.

The fact that Edward, although a fifth son, had nevertheless a large fortune of his own, inherited from his mother's brother (Bremer, the leather king), had done much to save the marriage from its most obvious dangers. And Edward's delighted pride in his wife did the rest.

Now, where in that life, as shown in the dossier, did a murder fit in? Grant asked himself, toiling up the padded stairs. Harmer? He had been her constant companion for the three months she had been in England. True, they had work in common (producers still liked to insert a song somewhere in the plot of Christine's films: the public felt cheated if they did not hear her sing), but the world which amuses itself had no doubt of their relations, whatever their colleagues thought. Or Tisdall? An ill-balanced boy, picked up in a moment of waywardness or generosity, at a time when he was reckless and without direction.

Well, he himself would find out more about Tisdall. Meanwhile he would find out about the Harmers of her life.

As he came to the top of the second flight, he heard the gentle sound of the lift closing, and he turned the corner to find Jammy Hopkins just taking his thumb from the bell-push.

"Well, well," said Jammy, "it's a party!"

"I hope you have an invitation."

"I hope you have a warrant. People shriek for their lawyer nowadays at the very sight of a policeman on the mat. Look, Inspector," he said hurriedly in a different voice, "let's not spoil each other's game. We both thought of Marta. Let's pool results. No need for crowding."

From which Grant deduced that Hopkins was doubtful of his reception. He followed Grant into the little hall without giving his name, and Grant, while appreciating the ingenuity, rebelled at providing a cloak for the press.

"This gentlemen is, I believe, from the *Clarion*," he

said to the servant who had turned away to announce them.

"Oh!" she said, turning back and eyeing Hopkins without favor. "Miss Hallard is always very tired at night, and she has some friends with her at the moment—"

But luck saved Hopkins from any necessity for coercion. The double doors to the living-room stood open, and from the room beyond came welcome in high excited tones.

"Mr. Hopkins! How charming! Now *you* can tell us what all these midday editions were talking about. I didn't know you knew Mr. Hopkins, Marta darling!"

"Who'd have thought I'd ever be glad to hear that voice!" Jammy murmured to Grant as he moved forward to greet the speaker, and Grant turned to meet Marta Hallard, who had come from the room into the hall.

"Alan Grant!" she said, smiling at him. "Is this business or pleasure?"

"Both. Do me a favor. Don't tell these people who I am. Just talk as you were talking before I came. And if you can get rid of them fairly soon, I'd like to talk to you alone for a little."

"I'd do a lot more than that for you. Every time I tie these around my neck," she indicated a rope of pearls, "I remember you."

This was not because Grant had given her the pearls but because he had once recovered them for her.

"Come and meet the others. Who is your friend?"

"Not a friend. Hopkins of the *Clarion*."

"Oh. Now I understand Lydia's welcome. And they say professional people are publicity hounds!" She led Grant in, introducing people as they came. The first was Clement Clements, the society photographer, radiant in purple "tails" and a soft shirt of a pale butter color. He had never heard of an Alan Grant, and made it perfectly clear. The second was a Captain Somebody, a nondescript and humble follower of

Marta's, who clung to his glass of whisky and soda as being the only familiar object in an unknown terrain. The third was Judy Sellers, a sulky fair girl who played "dumb" blondes from year's end to year's end, and whose life was one long fight between her greed and her weight. And the fourth was that intimate of the stars, Miss Lydia Keats, who was now talking all over Jammy Hopkins and enjoying herself immensely.

"*Mr.* Grant?" Jammy said, nastily, as Grant was introduced.

"*Isn't* it 'Mr.'?" Lydia asked, her ears pricked, her eyes snapping with curiosity.

"No, it isn't!"

But Hopkins met Grant's eye and lacked the courage of his desire. It would be folly to make an enemy of a C.I.D. Inspector.

"He has one of those Greek titles, you know, but he's ashamed to own it. Got it for rescuing a Greek royalist's shirt from a Greek laundry."

"Don't pay any attention to him, Mr. Grant. He loves to hear himself talk. I know, you see. He has interviewed me so often. But he never listens to a word I say. Not his fault, of course. Aries people are often talkative. I knew the first time he crossed my threshold that he was April born. Now you, Mr. Grant, are a Leo person. Am I right? No, you don't need to tell me. I know. Even if I couldn't feel it—here—" she thumped her skinny chest, "you have all the stigmata."

"I hope they're not very deadly?" Grant asked, wondering how soon he could disengage himself from this harpy.

"Deadly! My dear Mr. Grant! Don't you know anything of astrology? To be born in Leo is to be a king. They are the favorites of the stars. Born to success, predestined to glory. They are the great ones of the world."

"And when does one have to be born to qualify for a Leo benefit?"

"Between the middle of July and the middle of

August. I should say that you were born in the first
weeks of August." Grant hoped he didn't look as
surprised as he felt. He had certainly been born on the
4th of August.

"Lydia's uncanny," Marta broke in, handing Grant a
drink. "She did poor Christine Clay's horoscope about
a year ago, you know, and foretold her death."

"And wasn't that a break!" drawled the Judy girl,
poking among the sandwiches.

Lydia's thin face was convulsed with fury, and Marta
hastened to pour oil. "You know that's not fair, Judy! It
isn't the first time Lydia has been right. She warned
Tony Pickin about an accident before he was smashed
up. If he'd listened to her and taken a little more care,
he'd have two legs today. And she told me about not
accepting the Clynes' offer, and she—"

"Don't bother to defend me, Marta darling. The
credit is not mine, in any case. I only read what is there.
The stars don't lie. But one does not expect a Pisces
person to have either the vision or the faith!"

"Seconds out of the ring," murmured Jammy, and hit
the rim of his glass with his fingernail so that it made a
light "ping."

But there was to be no fight. Clements provided a
distraction.

"What I want to know," he drawled, "is not what
Lydia found in the stars but what the police found at
Westover."

"What I want to know is who did her in?" Judy said,
taking a large bite of sandwich.

"Judy!" Marta protested.

"Oh, bunk!" said Judy. "You know we're all thinking the same thing. Going around the possibilities.
Personally I plump for Jason. Has anyone any advance
on Jason?"

"Why Jason?" Clements asked.

"He's one of these smoldering types, all passion and
hot baths."

"Smolder! Jason!" Marta protested. "What non-sense! He simmers. Like a merry kettle." Grant glanced at her. So she was sticking up for Jason? How much did she like him? "Jason's much too volatile to smolder."

"Anyhow," Clements said, "men who take hot baths don't commit murder. It's the cold-plungers who see red. They are possessed by a desire to get back on life for the suffering they have endured."

"I thought masochists were rarely sadists," Grant said.

"Whether or not, you can put Jason out of it," insisted Marta. "He wouldn't hurt a fly."

"Oh, wouldn't he," Judy said, and they all paused to look at her.

"What exactly does that mean?" Clements asked.

"Never mind. My bet's on Jason."

"And what was the motive?"

"She was running out, I suspect."

Marta interrupted sharply. "You know that's non-sense, Judy. You know quite well that there was nothing between them."

"I know nothing of the sort. He was never out of her sight."

"A bitch thinks all the world a bitch," murmured Jammy into Grant's ear.

"I suspect"—it was Lydia's turn to break into a growing squabble—"that Mr. Hopkins knows much more about it than we do. He's been down at Westover today for his paper."

Jammy was instantly the center of attraction. What did he think? What had the police got? Who did they think had done it? Were all these hints in the evening papers about her living with someone true?

Jammy enjoyed himself. He was suggestive about murderers, illuminating on murder, discursive about human nature, and libelously rude about the police and their methods, all with a pleased eye on the helpless Grant.

"They'll arrest the boy she was living with," he

finished. "Take it from me. Tisdall's his name. Good-looking boy. He'll create a sensation in the dock."

"Tisdall?" they said, puzzled. "Never heard of him."

All but Judy Sellers.

Her mouth opened in dismay, stayed that way helplessly for a moment, and then shut tightly; and a blind came down over her face. Grant watched the display in surprised interest.

"I think it's utterly ridiculous," Marta was saying, scornfully. "Can you imagine Christine Clay in a furtive business like that! It's not in the part at all. I'd as soon—as soon—I'd as soon believe that Edward could commit a murder!"

There was a little laugh at that.

"And why not?" asked Judy Sellers. "He comes back to England to find his adored wife being unfaithful, and is overcome with passion."

"At six of a morning on a cold beach. Can't you see Edward!"

"Champneis didn't arrive in England till Thursday," offered Hopkins, "so that lets him out."

"I do think this is the most heartless and reprehensible conversation," Marta said. "Let's talk of something else."

"Yes, do," said Judy. "It's a profitless subject. Especially since *you*, of course, murdered her yourself."

"I!" Marta stood motionless in an aura of bewildered silence. Then the moment broke.

"Of course!" Clement said. "You wanted the part she was due to play in the new film! We'd forgotten that!"

"Well, if we're looking for motives, Clement, my sweet, you were raving mad with fury because she refused to be photographed by you. If I remember rightly, she said your works were like spilt gravy."

"Clement wouldn't drown her. He'd poison her," Judy said. "With a box of chocolates, Borgia-wise. No, come to think of it, Lejeune did it, in case he'd have to act with her. He's the virile type. His father was a butcher, and he probably inherited a callous mentality! Or how about Coyne? He would have killed her on the *Iron Bars* set, if no one had been looking." She apparently had forgotten about Jason.

"Will you all kindly stop this silly chatter!" Marta said, with angry emphasis. "I know that after three days a shock wears off. But Christine was a friend of ours, and it's disgusting to make a game of the death of a person we all liked."

"Hooey!" said Judy, rudely. She had consumed her fifth drink. "Not one of us cared a brass farthing for her. Most of us are tickled to death she's out of the way."

7

In the bright cool of Monday morning Grant drove himself down Wigmore Street. It was still early and the street was quiet; Wigmore Street's clients do not stay in town for weekends. The flower shops were making up Saturday's roses into Victorian posies where their errant petals could be gently corseted. The antique shops were moving that doubtful rug to the other side of the window out of the too questioning gaze of the morning sun. The little cafés were eating their own stale buns for their morning coffee and being pained and haughty with inconsiderates who asked for fresh scones. And the dress shops took Saturday's bargains out of the cupboard and restored the original prices.

Grant, who was en route to see Tisdall's tailor, was a little disgruntled at the perversity of things. If Tisdall's coat had been made by a London tailor it would have been a simple matter to have the button identified by them as one used by them for coats, and for Tisdall's coat in particular. That wouldn't clinch the matter but it would bring the clinching appreciably nearer. But Tisdall's coat had been made, of all places, in Los Angeles. "The coat I had," he explained, "was too heavy for that climate, so I got a new one."

Reasonable, but trying. If the coat had been made by a London firm of standing, one could walk into their shop at any time in the next fifty years and be told without fuss and with benevolent politeness (provided they knew who you were) what kind of buttons had been used. But who was to say whether a Los Angeles firm would know what buttons they put on a coat six months ago! Besides, the button in question was wanted here. It could not very well be sent to Los Angeles. The best one could do was to ask them to supply a sample of the buttons used. *If* they remembered!

Grant's main hope was that the coat itself would turn up. An abandoned coat which could be identified as Tisdall's, with one button missing, would be the perfect solution. Tisdall was wearing the coat when he drove away the car. That was Sergeant William's contribution to the cause of justice and due promotion. He had found a farmer who had seen the car at the Wedmarsh cross-roads a little after six on Thursday morning. About twenty past, he reckoned, but he hadn't a watch. Didn't need one. Tell the time any time of day, sun or no sun. He was driving sheep, and the car slowed down because of them. He was positive that the man driving was young and wore a dark coat. He didn't think he'd be able to identify the man, not on his oath, he wouldn't—but he had identified the car. It was the only car he had seen that morning.

Williams's other contribution had not been so happy. He reported that Jason Harmer had not stayed at the hotel he had given as his sleeping place at Sandwich. Had not stayed at Sandwich at all, in fact.

Grant had left his Sunday kidney and bacon untouched and had gone out without ado to interview Mr. Harmer. He found him in his pinkish flat at Devonshire

House, covered in a purple silk dressing gown, black stubble, and sheet music.

"It's not often I'm up at this hour," he offered, pushing sheets of scrawled paper off a chair to make room for Grant. "But I've been sort of upset about Chris. Very good friends, we were, Inspector. Some people found her difficult, but me, no. 'Cause why? D'you know why? 'Cause we both felt no-account and were afraid people'd find it out. Humans are awful bullies, you know. If you look and act like a million dollars they'll lick your boots. But you let them suspect that you don't think much of yourself and they're on you like ants on a dying wasp. I knew Chris was bluffing first time I set eyes on her. You can't tell me anything about bluffing. I bluffed my way into the States and I bluffed the publishers into printing my first song. They didn't find out about it till the song was a wow, and then they sort of thought it might be a good idea to forget about having one put over on them. Have a drink? Yes, it's a bit early. I don't usually myself till lunch time, but it's the next best thing to sleep. And I've got two songs to finish on contract. For—for—" his voice died away—"for Coyne's new film," he went on with a rush. "Ever tried writing a song without an idea in your head? No. No, I suppose you haven't. Well, it's just plain torture. And who's going to sing them anyhow? That Hallard dame can't sing. Did you hear Chris sing: 'Sing to me sometimes'?"

Grant had.

"Now that's what I call putting over a song. I've written better songs, I admit. But she made it sound like the best song that was ever written. What's the good of writing songs anyway, for that up-stage Hallard bird to make a mess of?"

He was moving about the room, picking up a pile of papers here only to set it down in an equally inappropriate place there. Grant watched him with interest. This was Marta's "merry kettle" and Judy's "smoldering type." To Grant he seemed neither. Just one of those rather ordinary specimens of humanity from some poor corner of Europe who believes he's being continually exploited and persecuted by his fellow men, self-pitying, ill-educated, emotional, and ruthless. Not good-looking, but attractive to women, no doubt. Grant remembered that two such widely differing types as Marta Hallard and Judy Sellers had found him remarkable; each reading her own meaning into her personality. He apparently had the ability to be all things to all men. He had been friendly to the disliked Marta, that was certain: Marta did not hotly defend indifferent worshippers at her shrine. He spent his life, that is to say, "putting on an act." He had admitted so much himself a moment ago. Was he putting on an act now? For Grant?

"I'm sorry to disturb you so early, but it was a matter of business. You know that we are investigating Miss Clay's death. And in the course of investigation it is necessary to check the movements of everyone who knew her, irrespective of persons or probabilities. Now, you told the sergeant of the County police force, when you talked to him on Thursday, that you had spent the night in a hotel at Sandwich. When this was checked in the ordinary course it was found that you hadn't stayed there."

Harmer fumbled among the music, without looking up.

"Where *did* you stay, Mr. Harmer?"

Harmer looked up with a small laugh. "You know," he said, "it's pretty funny at that! Charming gentleman calls in a perfectly friendly way about breakfast time, apologizing for disturbing you and hopes he isn't going to be a trouble to you but he's an inspector of police and would you be so very kind as to give some information because last time your information wasn't as accurate as it might have been. It's lovely, that's what it is. And you get results with it, too. Perhaps they just break down and sob, on account of all the friendliness. Pie like mother made. What I'd like to know is if that method goes in Pimlico or if you keep it for Park Lane."

"What I would like to know is where you stayed last Wednesday night, Mr. Harmer."

"The Mr., too, I guess that's Park Lane as well. In fact, if you'd been talking to the Jason of ten years back, you'd have had me to the station and scared hell out of me just like the cops of any other country. They're all the same; dough worshippers."

"I haven't your experience of the world's police forces, I'm afraid, Mr. Harmer."

Harmer grinned. "Stung you! A limey's got to be plenty stung before he's rude-polite like that. Don't get me wrong, though, Inspector. There aren't any police brands on me. As for last Wednesday night, I spent it in my car."

"You mean you didn't go to bed at all?"

"That's what I mean."

"And where was the car?"

"In a lane with hedges as high as houses each side, parked on the grass verge. An awful lot of space goes to waste in England in these verges. The ones in that lane were about forty feet wide."

"And you say you slept in the car? Have you someone who can bear witness to that?"

"No. It wasn't that kind of park. I was just sleepy and lost and couldn't be bothered going any further."

"Lost! In the east of Kent!"

"Yes, anywhere in Kent, if it comes to that. Have you ever tried to find a village in England after dark? Night in the desert is nothing to it. You see a sign at last that says 'Whatsit two and a half miles' and you think: Good old Whatsit! Nearly there! Hurrah for England and signposts! And then half a mile on you come to a place where three ways fork, and there's a nice tidy signpost on the little bit of green in the middle and every blame one of that signpost's arms has got at least three names on it, but do you think one of them mentions Whatsit? Oh, no! That would make it far too easy! So you read 'em all several times and hope someone'll come past before you have to decide, but no one comes. Last person passed there a week last Tuesday. No houses; nothing but fields, and an advertisement for a circus that was there the previous April. So you take one of the three roads, and after passing two more signposts that don't take any notice of Whatsit, you come to one that says: Whatsit, six and three-quarters. So you start off all over again, four miles to the bad, as it were, and it happens all over again. And again! And by the time Whatsit has done that on you half a dozen times, you don't care what happens as long as you can stop driving around corners and go to sleep. So I just stopped where I was and went to sleep. It was too late to drop in on Chris by that time, anyway."

"But not too late to get a bed at an inn."

"Not if you know where an inn is. 'Sides, judging by some of the inns I've seen here, I'd just as soon sleep in the car."

"You grow a heavy beard, I notice." Grant nodded at Harmer's unshaven chin.

"Yes. Have to shave twice a day, sometimes. If I'm going to be out late. Why?"

"You were shaved when you arrived at Miss Clay's cottage. How was that?"

"Carry my shaving things in the car. Have to, when you have a beard like mine."

"So you had no breakfast that morning?"

"No, I was planning to get breakfast from Chris. I don't eat breakfast anyway. Just coffee, or orange juice. Orange juice in England. My God, your coffee— What do you think they do to it? The women, I mean. It's—"

"Leaving the coffee aside for a moment, shall we come to the main point? Why did you tell the sergeant on duty that you had slept at Sandwich?"

The man's face changed subtly. Until then he had been answering at ease, automatically; the curves of his broad, normally goodnatured face slack and amiable. Now the slackness went; the face grew wary, and—was it?—antagonistic.

"Because I felt there was something wrong, and I didn't want to be mixed up in it."

"That is very extraordinary, surely? I mean, that you should be conscious of evil before anyone knew that it existed."

"That's not so funny. They told me Chris was drowned. I knew Chris could swim like an eel. I knew that I had been out all night. And the sergeant was looking at me with a Who-are-you-and-what-are-you-doing-here expression?"

"But the sergeant had no idea that the drowning was more than an accident. He had no reason to look at you in that way."

Then he decided to drop the subject of Harmer's lie to the sergeant.

"How did you know, by the way, where to find Miss Clay? I understood that she kept her retreat a secret."

"Yes, she'd run away. Gave us all the run-around, in fact, including me. She was tired and not very pleased at the way her last picture had turned out. On the floor, I mean; it isn't released yet. Coyne didn't know how to take her. A bit in awe of her, and afraid at the same time she'd put one over on him. You know. If he'd called her 'kid' and 'chocolate' the way old Joe Myers used to back in the States, she'd have laughed and worked like a black for him. But Coyne's full of his own dignity, the 'big director' stuff, and so they didn't get on too good. So she was fed-up, and tired, and everyone wanted her to go to different places for holidays, and it seemed she couldn't make up her mind, and then one day we woke up and she wasn't there. Bundle—that's her housekeeper—said she didn't know where she was, but no letters were to be forwarded and she'd turn up again in a month, so no one was to worry. Well, for about a fortnight no one heard of her, and then last Tuesday I met Marta Hallard at a sherry party at Libby Seemon's—she's going into that new play of his—and she said that on Saturday she had run into Chris buying chocolates at a place in Baker Street—Chris never could resist chocolates between pictures!—and she tried to worm out of Chris where she was hiding out. But Chris wasn't giving anything away. At least she thought she wasn't. She said: 'Perhaps I'm never coming back. You know that old Roman who grew vegetables with his own hands and was so stuck on the result that he made the arrangement permanent. Well, yesterday I helped pull the first cherries for Covent Garden market and, believe me, getting the Academy award for a picture is nothing to it!' "

Harmer laughed under his breath. "I can hear her," he said, affectionately. "Well, I went straight from Seemon's to Covent Garden and found out where those cherries came from. An orchard at a place called Bird's Green. And on Wednesday morning bright and early Jason sets off for Bird's Green. That took a bit of finding, but I got there about three o'clock. Then I had to find the orchard and the people who were working in it on Friday. I expected to find Chris straight away, but it seemed that they didn't know her. They said that when they were picking, early on Friday morning, a lady passing in a car had stopped to watch and then asked if she might help. The old boy who owned the place said they didn't need paid help, but if she liked to amuse herself good and well. 'She were a good picker,' he said. 'wouldn't mind paying her another time.' Then his grandson said he'd seen the lady—or thought he'd seen her—one day lately in the post office at Liddlestone—about six miles away. So I found Liddlestone, but the post office regular staff was 'home to her tea' and I had to wait till she came back. She said that the lady who sent 'all the telegrams'—seems they never saw so many telegrams in their lives as Chris sent—was living over at Medley. So I set out in the half-dark to find Medley, and ended by sleeping in a lane. And sleeping out or no sleeping out, that was a better piece of detective work than you're doing this morning, Inspector Grant!"

Grant grinned good-humoredly. "Yes? Well, I've nearly done." He got up to go. "I suppose you had a coat with you in the car?"

"Sure."

"What was it made of?"

"Brown tweed. Why?"

"Have you got it here?"

"Sure." He turned to a wardrobe, built in the passage where the sitting-room led into the bedroom, and pulled the sliding door open. "Have a look at my whole wardrobe. You're cleverer than I am if you can find the button."

"What button?" Grant asked, more quickly than he intended.

"It's always a button, isn't it?" Harmer said, the small pansy-brown eyes, alert under their lazy lids, smiling confidently into Grant's.

Grant found nothing of interest in the wardrobe. He had taken his leave not knowing how much to believe of Jason Harmer's story, but very sure that he had "nothing on him." The hopes of the police, so to speak, lay in Tisdall.

Now, as he pulled up by the curb in the cool bright morning, he remembered Jason's wardrobe, and smiled in his mind. Jason did not get his clothes from Stacey and Brackett. As he considered the dark, small, and shabby interior which was revealed to him as he opened the door, he could almost hear Jason laugh. The English! They'd had a business for a hundred and fifty years and this was all they could make of it. The original counters probably. Certainly the original lighting. But Grant's heart warmed. This was the England he knew and loved. Fashions might change, dynasties might fall, horses' shoes in the quiet street change to the crying of a thousand taxi-hooters, but Stacey and Brackett continued to make clothes with leisured efficiency for leisured and efficient gentlemen.

There was now neither a Stacey nor a Brackett, but Mr. Trimley—Mr. Stephen Trimley (as opposed to Mr. Robert and Mr. Thomas!)—saw Inspector Grant and was entirely at Inspector Grant's service. Yes, they had made clothes for Mr. Robert Tisdall. Yes, the clothes had included a dark coat for wear with evening things. No, that certainly was not a button from the coat in question. That was not a button they had ever put on any coat. It was not a class of button they were in the habit of using. If the Inspector would forgive Mr. Trimley (Mr. *Stephen* Trimley), the button in question was in his opinion of a very inferior make, and would not be used by any tailor of any standing. He would not be surprised, indeed, to find that the button was of foreign origin.

"American, perhaps?" suggested Grant.

Perhaps. Although to Mr. Trimley's eye it suggested the Continent. No, he certainly had no reason for such a surmise. Entirely instinctive. Probably wrong. And he hoped the Inspector would not put any weight on his opinion. He also hoped that there was no question of Mr. Tisdall being in trouble. A very charming young man, indeed. The Grammar schools—especially the older Grammar schools of the country—turned out a very fine type of boy. Better often, didn't the Inspector think so? than came from the minor public schools. There was a yeoman quality of permanence about Grammar-school families—generation after generation going to the same school—that was not matched, outside the great public schools.

There being, in Grant's opinion, no yeoman quality of permanence whatever about young Tisdall, he forbore to argue, contenting himself by assuring Mr. Trimley that as far as he knew Mr. Tisdall was in no trouble up to date.

Mr. Trimley was glad to hear that. He was getting old, and his faith in the young generation which was

growing up was too often sadly shaken. Perhaps every
generation thought that the rising one lacked due
standards of behavior and spirit, but it did seem to him
this one . . . Ah, well, he was growing old, and the
tragedy of young lives weighed more heavily on him
than it used to. This Monday morning was blackened
for him, yes, entirely blackened, by the thought that all
the brightness that was Christine Clay was at this hour
being transformed into ashes. It would be many years,
perhaps generations (Mr. Trimley's mind worked in
generations: the result of having a hundred-and-fifty-
year-old business) before her like would be seen again.
She had quality, didn't the Inspector think so? Amazing quality. It was said that she had a very humble
origin, but there must be breeding somewhere. Something like Christine Clay did not just happen in space,
as it were. Nature must plan for it. He was not what is
known, he believed, as a film fan, but there was no
picture of Miss Clay's which he had not seen since his
niece had taken him to view her first essay in a dramatic
rôle. He had on that occasion entirely forgotten that he
was in a cinema. He was dazed with delight. Surely if
this new medium could produce material of this
strength and richness one need not continue to regret
Bernhardt and Duse.

Grant went out into the street, marveling at the
all-pervading genius of Christine Clay. The mind of all
the world it seemed was in that building at Golders
Green. A strange end for the little lace-hand from
Nottingham. Strange, too, for the world's idol. "And
they put him in an oven just as if he were—" Oh, no, he
mustn't think of that. Hateful. Why should it be
hateful? He didn't know. The suburbanity of it, he
supposed. Sensible, and all that. And probably much
less harrowing for everyone. But someone whose
brilliance had flamed across the human firmament as
Clay's had should have a hundred-foot pyre. Something
spectacular. A Viking's funeral. Not ovens in the
suburb. Oh, my God, he was growing morbid, if not

sentimental. He pressed the starter, and swung into the traffic.

He had yesterday changed his mind about going to the Clay funeral. The Tisdall evidence progressing normally, he had seen no need to give himself a harrowing hour which he could avoid. But only now did he realize how very glad he was to have escaped it, and (being Grant) began instantly to wonder whether after all he should have gone. Whether his subconscious desire to get out of it had influenced his decision. He decided that it had not. There was no need for him now to study the psychology of unknown friends of Christine's. He had had a good cross-section of them at Marta's, and had learned very little, after all. The party had stubbornly refused to break up. Jammy had begun to talk again, hoping that they would dance to his piping. But Marta vetoed any more talk of Christine, and although they had come back to her several times, not even Jammy's genius for evocation could keep them on the subject. Lydia, who could never stay off her own subject for long, had read their palms, cheiromancy being a side-line of hers when horoscopes were not available (she had given a shrewd enough reading of Grant's character and had warned him about making a mistaken decision in the immediate future: "a nice safe thing to say to anyone," he had reflected) and it was not until one o'clock that the hostess had managed to shepherd them all to the door. Grant had lingered, not, curiously enough, because he had questions to ask her (the conversation had provided answers for him), but because she was anxious to question him. Was Scotland Yard called in to investigate Christine's death? What was wrong? What had they found? What did they suspect?

Grant had said that Yes, they had been called in (so much would by now be common property) but that so far there was only suspicion. She had wept a little, becomingly, with not too disastrous effect on the mascara, had treated him to a short appreciation of

Christine as artist and woman. "A grand person. It must have taken tremendous character to overcome her initial disadvantages." She enumerated the disadvantages.

And Grant had gone out into the warm night with a sigh for human nature—and a shrug for the sigh.

But there were bright spots even in human nature. Grant edged in toward the curb, and came to a halt, his brown face glad and welcoming.

"Good morning!" he called to the little gray figure.

"Oh, good morning, Mr. Grant," Erica said, crossing the pavement to him. She gave him a brief little smile, but seemed pleased to see him; so much was apparent through her schoolboy matter-of-factness. She was dressed in her "town" clothes, he noticed; but they did not seem to be an improvement on her country ones. They were neat, certainly, but they had an unused look; and the gray suit she was wearing, although undoubtedly "good," was dowdy. Her hat had been got to match, and matched also in dowdiness.

"I didn't know you ever stayed in town."

"I don't. I came up to get a bridge."

"A *bridge?*"

"But it seems you can't get them by the yard. They have to be made to measure. So I've got to come up another day. All he did today was put a lot of clay in my mouth."

"Oh, the dentist. I see. I thought only old ladies had bridges."

"Well, you see, the silly thing he put in the last time doesn't hold. I'm always picking it out of bits of toffee. I lost a lot of side teeth when Flight fell with me at a post-and-rails last winter. I had a face like a turnip. So it had to be a bridge, he says."

"A mis-nomer, Flight."

"In one way. Not in another. He was nearly at the other end of Kent before they caught him."

"Where are you going now? Can I give you a lift anywhere?"

"I suppose you wouldn't like to show me Scotland Yard?"

"I would. Very much. But in twenty minutes I have an appointment with a lawyer in the Temple."

"Oh. In that case perhaps you would drop me in Cockspur Street. I have an errand to do for Nannie."

Yes, he thought, as she inserted herself beside him, it would be a Nannie. No mother had chosen those clothes. They were ordered from the tailor just as her school clothes had been. "One gray flannel suit and hat to match." In spite of her independence and her sureness of spirit, there was something forlorn about her, he felt.

"This is nice," she said. "They're not very high, but I hate walking in them."

"What are?"

"My shoes." She held up a foot and exhibited her very modest cuban heel. "Nannie thinks they are the right thing to wear in town, but I feel dreadful in them. Teetery."

"I expect one gets used to them in time. One must conform to the tabus of the tribe."

"Why must one?"

"Because an unquiet life is a greater misery than wearing the badge of conformity."

"Oh, well. I don't come to town often. I suppose you haven't time to have an ice with me?"

"I'm afraid not. Let's postpone it until I'm back in Westover shall we?"

"Of course, you'll be back. I had forgotten that. I saw your victim yesterday," she added conversationally.

"My victim?"

"Yes, the man who fainted."

"You saw him! Where?"

"Father took me over to luncheon at the Marine."

"But I thought your father hated the Marine?"

"He does. He said he'd never seen such a set of poisonous bloaters in his life. I think 'bloaters' is a little strong. They weren't so very bad. And the melon was very good."

"Did your father tell you that Tisdall was waiting there?"

"No, the sergeant did. He doesn't look very professional. Mr. Tisdall, not the sergeant. Too friendly and interested. No professional waiter looks interested. Not really. And he forgets the spoons for the ices. But I expect you upset him pretty thoroughly the day before."

"*I* upset him!" Grant took a deep breath and expressed his hope that Erica was not going to let the plight of a good-looking young man play havoc with her heart.

"Oh no. Nothing like that. His nose is too long. Besides, I'm in love with Togare."

"Who is Togare?"

"The lion-tamer, of course." She turned to look at him doubtfully. "Do you *really* mean that you haven't heard of Togare?"

Grant was afraid that that was so.

"Don't you go to Olympia at Christmas? But you should! I'll get Mr. Mills to send you seats."

"Thank you. And how long have you been in love with this Togare?"

"Four years. I'm very faithful."

- Grant admitted that she must be.

"Drop me at the Orient office, will you?" she said, in the same tone as she had announced her faithfulness. And Grant set her down by the yellow-funneled liner.

"Going cruising?" he asked.

"Oh, no. I go round the offices collecting booklets for Nannie. She loves them. She's never been out of England because she's terrified of the sea, but she likes to sit in safety and imagine. I got her some marvelous mountain ones from the Austrian place in Regent Street in the spring. And she's very knowledgeable about the German spas. Goodbye. Thank you for the lift. How shall I know when you come to Westover? For the ice, I mean."

"I shall send you word through your father. Will that do?"

"Yes. Goodbye." And she disappeared into the office.

And Grant went on his way to meet Christine Clay's lawyer and Christine Clay's husband, feeling better.

8

IT WAS OBVIOUS AT ONCE WHY NO ONE CALLED EDWARD Champneis anything but Edward. He was a very tall, very dignified, very good-looking, and very orthodox person, with a manner of grave, if kindly, interest, and a rare but charming smile. Alongside the fretful movements of the fussy Mr. Erskine, his composure was like that of a liner suffering the administrations of a tug.

Grant had not met him before. Edward Champneis had arrived in London on Thursday afternoon, after nearly three months' absence, only to be greeted by the news of his wife's death. He had gone down immediately to Westover and identified the body, and on Friday he had interviewed the worried County Constabulary, puzzling over the button, and helped them to make up their minds that it was a case for the Yard. The thousand things waiting in town to be done as a result of his wife's death and his own long absence had sent him back to London just as Grant left it.

He looked very tired, now, but showed no emotion. Grant wondered under what circumstances this orthodox product of five hundred years of privilege and obligation would show emotion. And then, suddenly, as he drew the chair under him, it occurred to him that Edward Champneis was anything but orthodox. Had he conformed to the tribe, as his looks conformed, he would have married a second cousin, gone into the Service, looked after an estate, and read the *Morning Post*. But he had done none of those things. He had married an artist picked up at the other side of the world, he explored for fun, and he wrote books. There was something almost eerie in the thought that an exterior could be so utterly misleading.

"Lord Edward has, of course, seen the will," Erskine was saying. "He was, in fact, aware of its most important provisions some time ago, Lady Edward having acquainted him with her desires at the time the testament was made. There is, however, one surprise. But perhaps you would like to read the document for yourself."

He turned the impressive-looking sheet round on the table so that it faced Grant.

"Lady Edward had made two previous wills, both in the United States, but they were destroyed, on her instructions, by her American lawyers. She was anxious that her estate should be administered from England, for the stability of which she had a great admiration."

Christine had left nothing to her husband. "I leave no money to my husband, Edward Champneis, because he has always had, and always will have, more than he can spend, and because he has never greatly cared for money." Whatever he cared to keep of her personal possessions were to be his, however, except where legacies specifically provided otherwise. There were various bequests of money, in bulk or in annuities, to friends and dependents. To Bundle, her housekeeper and late dresser. To her Negro chauffeur. To Joe

Myers, who had directed her greatest successes. To a bellhop in Chicago "to buy that gas station with." To nearly thirty people in all, in all parts of the globe and in all spheres of existence. But there was no mention of Jason Harmer.

Grant glanced at the date. Eighteen months ago. She had at that time probably not yet met Harmer.

The legacies, however generous, left the great bulk of her very large fortune untouched. And that fortune was left, surprisingly, not to any individual, but "for the preservation of the beauty of England." There was to be a trust, in which would be embodied the power to buy any beautiful building or space threatened by extinction and to provide for its upkeep.

That was Grant's third surprise. The fourth came at the end of the list of legacies. The last legacy of all read, "To my brother Herbert, a shilling for candles."

"A brother?" Grant said, and looked up inquiring.

"Lord Edward was unaware that Lady Edward had a brother until the will was read. Lady Edward's parents died many years ago, and there had been no mention of any surviving family except for herself."

"A shilling for candles. Does it convey anything to you, sir?" He turned to Champneis, who shook his head.

"A family feud, I expect. Perhaps something that happened when they were children. These are often the things one is more unforgiving about." He glanced toward the lawyer. "The thing I remember when I meet Alicia is always that she smashed my birds'-egg collection."

"But not *necessarily* a childhood quarrel," Grant said. "She must have known him much later."

"Bundle would be the person to ask. She dressed my wife from her early days in New York. But is it important? After all, the fellow was being dismissed with a shilling."

"It's important because it is the first sign of real enmity I have discovered among Miss Clay's relationships. One never knows what it might lead us to."

"The Inspector may not think it so important when he has seen this," Erskine said. "This, which I will give you to read, is the surprise I spoke of."

So the surprise had not been one of those in the will.

Grant took the paper from the lawyer's dry, slightly trembling hand. It was a sheet of the shiny, thick, cream-colored note-paper to be obtained in village shops all over England, and on it was a letter from Christine Clay to her lawyer. The letter was headed "Briars, Medley, Kent," and contained instructions for a codicil to her will. She left her ranch in California, with all stock and implements, together with the sum of five thousand pounds, to one Robert Stannaway, late of Yeoman's Row, London.

"That," said the lawyer, "was written on Wednesday, as you see. And on Thursday morning——" He broke off, expressively.

"Is it legal?" Grant asked.

"I should not like to contest it. It is entirely handwritten and properly signed with her full name. The signature is witnessed by Margaret Pitts. The provision is perfectly clear, and the style eminently sane."

"No chance of a forgery?"

"Not the slightest. I know Lady Edward's hand very well—you will observe that it is peculiar and not easy to reproduce—and moreover I am very well acquainted with her style, which would be still more difficult to imitate."

"Well!" Grant read the letter again, hardly believing in its existence. "That alters everything. I must get back to Scotland Yard. This will probably mean an arrest before night." He stood up.

"I'll come with you," Champneis said.

"Very good, sir," Grant agreed automatically. "If I

may, I'll telephone first to make sure that the Superintendent will be there."

And as he picked up the receiver, the looker-on in him said: Harmer was right. We do treat people variously. If the husband had been an insurance agent in Brixton, we wouldn't take it for granted that he could horn in on a Yard conference!

"Is Superintendent Barker in the Yard, do you know? . . . Oh . . . At half past? That's in about twenty minutes. Well, tell him that Inspector Grant has important information and wants a conference straight away. Yes, the Commissioner, too, if he's there."

He hung up.

"Thank you for helping us so greatly," he said, taking farewell of Erskine. "And by the way, if you unearth the brother, I should be glad to know."

And he and Champneis went down the dark, narrow stairs and out into the hot sunshine.

"Do you think," Champneis asked, pausing with one hand on the door of Grant's car, "there would be time for a drink. I feel the need of some stiffening. It's been a—a trying morning."

"Yes, certainly. It won't take us longer than ten minutes along the Embankment. Where would you like to go?"

"Well, my club is in Carlton House Terrace, but I don't want to meet people I know. The Savoy isn't much better—"

"There's a nice little pub up here," Grant said, and swung the car around. "Very quiet at this time. Cool, too."

As they turned the corner Grant caught sight of the news-sellers' posters. CLAY FUNERAL: UNPRECEDENTED SCENES. TEN WOMEN FAINT. LONDON'S FAREWELL TO CLAY.And (the *Sentinel*) CLAY'S LAST AUDIENCE.

Grant's foot came down on the accelerator.

"It was unbelievably ghastly," said the man beside him, quietly.

"Yes, I can imagine."

"Those women. I think the end of our greatness as a race must be very near. We came through the war well, but perhaps the effort was too great. It left us—epileptic. Great shocks do, sometimes." He was silent for a moment, evidently seeing it all again in his mind's eye. "I've seen machine guns turned on troops in the open—in China—and rebelled against the slaughter. But I would have seen that sub-human mass of hysteria riddled this morning with more joy than I can describe to you. Not because it was—Chris, but because they made me ashamed of being human, of belonging to the same species."

"I had hoped that at that early hour there would be very little demonstration. I know the police were counting on that."

"We counted on it too. That is why we chose that hour. Now that I've seen with my own eyes, I know that nothing could have prevented it. The people are insane."

He paused, and gave an unamused laugh. "She never did like people much. It was because she found people—disappointing that she left her money as she did. Her fans this morning have vindicated her judgment."

The bar was all that Grant had promised, cool, quiet, and undemanding. No one took any notice of Champneis. Of the six men present three nodded to Grant and three looked wary. Champneis, observant even in his pain, said: "Where do *you* go when you want to be unrecognized?" and Grant smiled. "I've not found a place yet," he admitted. "I landed in Labrador from a friend's yacht once, and the man in the village store said, 'You wear your moustache shorter now, Sergeant.' After that I gave up expecting."

They talked of Labrador for a little, and then of

Galeria, where Champneis had spent the last few months.

"I used to think Asia primitive, and some of the Indian tribes of South America, but the east of Europe has them all beaten. Except for the towns, Galeria is still in the primeval dark."

"I see they've mislaid their spectacular patriot," Grant said.

"Rimnik? Yes. He'll turn up again when his party is ready. That's the way they run the benighted country."

"How many parties are there?"

"About ten, I think, not counting subdivisions. There are at least twenty races in that boiling pot of a country, all of them clamoring for self-government, and all of them medieval in their outlook. It's a fascinating place. You should go there some day. The capital is their shop-window—as nearly a replica of every other capital as they can make it. Opera, trams, electric light, imposing railway station, cinemas—but twenty miles into the country you'll find bride-barter. Girls set in rows with their dowry at their feet, waiting to go to the highest bidder. I've seen an old country woman led raving mad out of a lift in one of the town buildings. She thought she was the victim of witchcraft. They had to take her to the asylum. Graft in the town and superstition in the country—and yet a place of infinite promise."

Grant let him talk, glad that for even a few minutes he might be able to forget the horror of the morning. His own thoughts were not in Galeria but in Westover. So he had done it, that good-looking emotionalist! He had screwed a ranch and five thousand out of his hostess and then made sure that he would not have to wait for it. Grant's own inclination to like the boy died an instant death. From now on Robert Tisdall would be no more to him than the bluebottle he swatted on the windowpane, a nuisance to be exterminated as quickly and with as little fuss as possible. If, away in the depths, he was sorry that the pleasant person who was the surface Tisdall did not exist, his main and overwhelming emotion was relief that the business was going to be cleared up so easily. There was little doubt of the result of the conference. They had evidence enough. And they would have more before it came to a trial.

Barker, his Superintendent, agreed with him, and so did the Commissioner. It was a clear enough case. The man is broke, homeless, and at his wit's end. He is picked up by a rich woman at the psychological moment. Four days later a will is made in his favor. On the following morning very early, the woman goes to swim. He follows her ten minutes later. When her body is found he has disappeared. He reappears with an unbelievable tale about stealing the car and bringing it back. A black button is found twisted in the dead woman's hair. The man's dark coat is missing. He says it was stolen two days before. But a man identifies him as wearing it that morning.

Yes, it was a good enough case. The opportunity, the motive, the clue.

The only person to protest against the issue of the warrant was, strangely enough, Edward Champneis.

"It's too pat, don't you think?" he said. "I mean, would any man in his senses commit the murder the very next morning?"

"You forget, Lord Edward," Barker said, "that but for the merest chance there would be no question of murder at all."

"And moreover, time was precious to him," Grant pointed out. "There were only a few days left. The tenancy of the cottage expired at the end of the month. He knew that. She might not go bathing again. The weather might break, or she might be seized with a desire to go inland. More especially she might not go swimming in the early morning again. It was an ideal setting: a lonely beach in the very early morning, with

the mist just rising. Too perfect a chance to let go to
waste."

Yes, it was a good case. Edward Champneis went
back to the house in Regent's Park which he had
inherited with the Bremer fortune, and which between
his peregrinations he called home. And Grant went
down to Westover with a warrant in his pocket.

9

IF THERE WAS ONE THING TOSELLI HATED MORE THAN
another it was the police. All his life he had been no
poor hater, Toselli. As *commis* he had hated the maître
d'hôtel, as maître d'hôtel he had hated the management, as the management he hated many things: the
chef, wet weather, his wife, the head porter's moustache, clients who demanded to see him at breakfast
time—oh, many things! But more than all he hated the
police. They were bad for business and bad for the
digestion. It stopped his digestive juices flowing just to
see one of them walk in through the glass doors. It was
bad enough to remember his annual bill for New Year
"presents" to the local officers—thirty bottles of
Scotch, thirty of gin, two dozen champagne, and six of
liqueur brandy it had come to last year—but to suffer
the invasion of officers not so far "looked after," and
therefore callous to the brittle delicacy of hotel well-
being—well, it was more than Toselli's abundant flesh
and high-pressured blood could stand.

That is why he smiled so sweetly upon Grant—all his

life Toselli's smile had been stretched across his rage,
like a tight-rope spanning a chasm—and gave him one
of the second-best cigars. Inspector Grant wanted to
interview the new waiter, did he? But certainly! This
was the waiter's hour off—between lunch and afternoon tea—but he should be sent for immediately.

"Stop!" said Grant. "You say the man is off duty?
Do you know where he will be?"

"Very probably in his room. Waiters like to take the
weight off their feet for a little, you understand."

"I'd like to see him there."

"But certainly. Tony!" Toselli called to a page
passing the office door. "Take this gentleman up to the
room of the new waiter."

"Thank you," Grant said. "You'll be here when I
come down? I should like to talk to you."

"I shall be here." Toselli's tone expressed dramatic
resignation. His smile deepened as he flung out his
hands. "Last week it was a stabbing affair in the
kitchen, this week it is—what? Theft? Affiliation?"

"I'll tell you all about it presently, Mr. Toselli."

"I shall be here." His smile became ferocious. "But
not for long, no! I am going to buy one of those
businesses where one puts sixpence into a slot and the
meal comes out. Yes. There, but there, would be
happiness."

"Even there, there are bent coins," Grant said as he
followed Tony to the lift.

"Sanger, you come up with me," he said as they
passed through the busy hall. "You can wait for us
here, Williams. We'll bring him out this way. Much less
fuss than through the servants' side. No one will notice
anything. Car waiting?"

"Yes, sir."

Grant and Sanger went up in the lift. In those few
seconds of sudden quiet and suspended action, Grant
found time to wonder why he had not shown his
warrant and told Toselli what he had come for. That
would have been his normal course. Why was he so

anxious to have the bird in his hand? Was it just the canniness of his Scots ancestry coming out, or was there a presentiment that—That what? He didn't know. He knew only that now that he was here he could not wait. Explanations could follow. He must have the man in his hands.

The soft sound of the lift in the silence was like the sound of the curtain going up.

At the very top of the colossal building which was the Westover Marine Hotel, were the quarters of those waiters who were resident: small single rooms set in a row close together under the roof. As the page put out a bony fist to knock on a door, Grant restrained him. "All right, thank you," he said, and page and liftman disappeared into the crowded and luxurious depths, leaving the two policemen on the deserted coconut-matted landing. It was very quiet up there.

Grant knocked.

Tisdall's indifferent voice bade him come in.

The room was so small that Grant's involuntary thought was that the cell that waited would be no great change. A bed on one side, a window on the other, and in the far wall two cupboard doors. On the bed lay Tisdall in his shirt sleeves, his shoes on the floor. A book lay open, face down, on the coverlet.

He had expected to see a colleague. That was obvious. At the sight of Grant his eyes widened, and as they travelled to Sanger, standing behind Grant in the doorway, realization flooded them.

Before Grant could speak, he said, "You can't mean it!"

"Yes, I'm afraid we do," Grant said. He said his regulation piece of announcement and warning, Tisdall sitting with feet dangling on the bed's edge, not apparently listening.

When he had finished Tisdall said slowly: "I expect this is what death is like when you meet it. Sort of wildly unfair but inevitable."

"How were you so sure what we had come for?"

"It doesn't need two of you to ask about my health."
His voice rose a little. "What I want to know is why
you're doing it? What have you against me? You can't
have proved that button was mine because it wasn't.
Why don't you tell me what you have found so that I
can explain away whatever it was? If you have new
evidence you can surely ask me for an explanation. I
have a right to know, haven't I? Whether I can explain
or not?"

"There isn't anything you could explain away, Tisdall. You'd better get ready to come with us."

Tisdall got to his feet, his mind still entangled in
the unbelievableness of what was happening to him. "I
can't go in these things," he said, looking down at his
waiter's dress. "Can I change?"

"Yes, you can change, and take some things with
you." Grant's hands ran over his pockets in expert
questioning, and came away empty. "But you'll have to
do it with us here. Don't be too long about it, will you?
You can wait there, Sanger," he added, and swung the
door to, leaving Sanger outside. He himself moved
over to lean against the window-sill. It was a long way
to the ground, and Tisdall, in Grant's opinion, was the
suicide type. Not enough guts to brazen a thing out.
Not enough vanity, perhaps to like the limelight at any
price. Certainly the "everyone sorry when I'm dead"
type.

Grant watched him now with minute attention. To an
outsider he was a casual visitor, propped casually in the
window while he indulged in casual conversation. In
reality he was ready for instant emergency.

But there was no excitement. Tisdall pulled his
suit-case from under the bed, and began with automatic
method to change into his tweed and flannels. Grant
felt that if the man carried poison, it would be
somewhere in his working garments, and unconsciously
relaxed a little as the waiter's dress was cast aside.
There was going to be no trouble. The man was coming
quietly.

"I needn't have worried as to how I was going to live," Tisdall was saying. "There seems to be a moral somewhere in this very immoral proceeding. What do I do about a lawyer, by the way, when I have no money and no friends?"

"One will be provided."

"Like a table napkin. I see."

He opened the cupboard nearest to Grant, and began to take things from their hangers and fold them into his case.

"At least you can tell me what my motive was?" he said presently, as if a new thought had struck him. "You can mistake buttons; you can even wish a button on to a coat that never had it; but you can't pin a motive where there couldn't be one!"

"So you had no motive?"

"Certainly not. Quite the opposite. What happened last Thursday morning was the worst thing that has ever happened to me in my life. I should have thought that was obvious even to an outsider."

"And of course you had not the faintest idea that Miss Clay had made a codicil to her will leaving you a ranch and a large sum of money."

Tisdall had been readjusting the folds of a garment. He stopped now, his hands still holding the cloth, but motionless, and stared at Grant.

"Chris did that!" he said. "No. No, I didn't know. How wonderful of her!"

And for a moment doubt stirred in Grant. That had been beautifully done. Timing, expression, action. No professional actor could have done it better. But the doubt passed. He recrossed his legs, by way of shaking himself, recalled the charm and innocence of murderers he had known (Andrew Hamey, who specialized in marrying women and drowning them and who looked like a choir soloist, and others of even greater charm and iniquity) and then composed his mind to the peace of a detective who has got his man.

"So you've raked up the perfect motive. Poor Chris!

She thought she was doing me such a good turn. Have I any defense at all, do you know?"

"That is not for me to say."

"I have a great respect for you, Inspector Grant. I think it probable that I shall be unavailingly protesting my innocence on the scaffold."

He pushed the nearer cupboard door to, and opened the further one. The door opened away from Grant, so that the interior of the cupboard was not visible. "But you disappoint me in one way. I thought you were a better psychologist, you know. When I was telling you the story of my life on Saturday morning, I really thought you were too good a judge to think that I could have done what you suspected me of. Now I find you're just a routine policeman."

Still keeping his hand on the door-knob, he bent down to the interior of the cupboard as if to take shoes from the floor of it.

There was the rasp of a key torn from its lock, the cupboard door swung shut, and even as Grant leaped the key turned on the inside.

"Tisdall!" he shouted. "Don't be a fool! Do you hear!" His mind raced over the antidotes for the various poisons. Oh, God, what a fool he had been! "Sanger! Help me to break this open. He's locked himself in."

The two men flung their combined weight on the door. It resisted their best efforts.

"Listen to me, Tisdall," Grant said between gasps, "poison is a fool's trick. We'll get you soon enough to give you an antidote, and all that will happen is that you'll suffer hell's pain for nothing. So think better of it!"

But still the door resisted them.

"Fire axe!" Grant said. "Saw it when we came up. On wall at the end of the passage. Quick!"

Sanger fled and in eight seconds was back with the axe.

As the first blow of it fell, a half-dressed and sleepy

colleague of Tisdall's appeared from next door and announced, "You mek a noise like thet you hev the cops een!"

"Hey!" he added, seeing the axe in Sanger's grasp. "What the hell you theenk you do, eh?"

"Keep away, you fool! There's a man in that cupboard committing suicide."

"Suicide! Cupboard!" The waiter rubbed his black hair in perplexity, like a half-awakened child. "That is not a cupboard!"

"*Not a cupboard!*"

"No, that is the what you call eet—leetle back stairs. For fire, you know."

"God!" said Grant, and made for the door.

"Where does it come out—the stairway?" he called back to the waiter.

"In the passage to the front hall."

"Eight flights," Grant said to Sanger. "Lift's quicker, perhaps." He rang. "Williams will stop him if he tries to go out by the door," he said, searching for comfort.

"Williams has never seen him, sir. At least I don't think so."

Grant used words he had forgotten since he stopped campaigning in France.

"Does the man on duty at the back know him?"

"Oh, yes, sir. That's what he's there for, to stop him. But Sergeant Williams was just waiting for us."

Words failed Grant altogether.

The lift appeared.

Thirty seconds later they were in the hall.

The pleased expectancy on Williams' pink face told them the worst. Williams had certainly not intercepted anyone.

People were arriving, people were departing, people were going to tea in the restaurant, people were going to eat ices in the sun lounge, to drink in the bar, to meet other people and go to tea at Lyons—the hall of the Marine was American in the catholicity of its inhabitants. To make oneself noticeable in that assembly it

would be necessary to stand on one's hands and
proceed so.

Williams said that a young brown-haired man,
without a hat and wearing a tweed jacket and flannels
had gone out about five minutes previously. In fact, two
of them had gone out.

"Two of them! You mean together!"

No, Williams meant that two separate men answering to that description had gone out in the last five
minutes. If it came to that, here was another.

Yes, there was another. And watching him, Grant
was filled with a despair that ran up from his feet like a
wave hitting him and flooding his whole being. Yes,
indeed there would be others. In Kent alone at this
moment were ten thousand men whose description
corresponded to Tisdall's.

Grant pulled himself together and turned to the
ungrateful task of forming a police cordon.

10

THAT WAS THE BIGGEST SCOOP OF JAMMY HOPKINS'S LIFE.
The other papers that evening appeared on the street
with horrifying photographs of the mob at Golders
Green—Medusa-like heads, close-up, screaming into
the camera: dishevelled Furies with streaming locks
and open mouths clawing each other in an abandon of
hate—and thought that they were doing rather well.
Nothing, surely, was as important today as the Clay
funeral. And their photographers had done them
proud. They could afford to be pleased.

But not for nothing had Hopkins trailed Grant from
Wigmore Street, to the Orient offices, and from the
Orient offices to the Temple, and from the Temple to
the Yard. Not for nothing had he cooled his heels round
the corner while his paid henchman kept watch on the
Yard and gave him the sign when Grant left. Not for
nothing had he followed him all the way to Westover.
"CLAY MURDERED," announced the *Sentinel* posters. "CLAY MURDERED: ARREST!" And the
crowds milled around the excited newsboys. And in the

other offices there was tearing of hair, and much talk of sacking. In vain to point out to irate editors that Scotland Yard had said that when there was publishable news they should be told. What were they paid for, the editors would like to know? Sitting on their behinds waiting to be called up, and given official scraps of information? What did they think they were? Tote officials?

But Jammy was in high favor with the powers who signed his pay check. Jammy settled into residence at the Marine—much more palatially than Grant, who also had a bedroom there but was to spend most of his life in the immediate future at the police station—and gave thanks to the stars which had ordained so spectacular an end for Christine Clay.

As for Grant, he was—as he had known he would be—snowed under with information. By Tuesday noon Tisdall had been seen in almost every corner of England and Wales, and by tea-time was beginning to be seen in Scotland. He had been observed fishing from a bridge over a Yorkshire stream and had pulled his hat suspiciously over his face when the informant had approached. He had been seen walking out of a cinema in Aberystwyth. He had rented a room in Lincoln and had left without paying. (He had quite often left without paying, Grant noticed.) He had asked to be taken on a boat at Lowestoft. (He had also asked to be taken on a boat at half a dozen other places. The number of young men who could not pay their landladies and who wanted to leave the country was distressing.) He was found dead on a moor near Penrith. (That occupied Grant the best part of the afternoon.) He was found intoxicated in a London alley. He had bought a hat in Hythe, Grantham, Lewes, Tonbridge, Dorchester, Ashford, Luton, Aylesbury, Leicester, Chatham, East Grinstead, and in four London shops. He had also bought a packet of safety-pins in Swan and Edgars. He had eaten a crab sandwich at a quick lunch counter in

Argyll Street, two rolls and coffee in a Hastings bun shop, and bread and cheese in a Haywards' Heath inn. He had stolen every imaginable kind of article in every imaginable kind of place—including a decanter from a glass-and-china warehouse in Croydon. When asked what he supposed Tisdall wanted a decanter for, the informant said that it was a grand weapon.

Three telephones kept ringing like demented things, and by post, telegram, wireless, and personal appearance the information poured in. Nine-tenths of it quite useless, but all of it requiring a hearing: some of it requiring much investigation before its uselessness became apparent. Grant looked at the massed pile of reports, and his self-control deserted him for a little.

"It's a big price to pay for a moments lack of wit," he said.

"Cheer up, sir," said Williams. "It might be worse."

"Might be worse! Would you tell me what occurrence would, in your opinion, augment the horror of the situation?"

"Oh, well, so far no nut has come to confess to the crime, and waste our time that way."

But the nut arrived next morning.

Grant looked up from inspecting a dew-drenched coat which had just been brought in, to see Williams closing the door mysteriously and mysteriously advancing on him.

"What is it, Williams?" he asked, his voice sharp with anticipation.

"The nut," Williams said.

"The what?"

"The person to make a confession, sir." Williams's tone held a shade of guilt now, as if he felt that by mentioning the thing yesterday he had brought the evil to pass.

Grant groaned.

"Not a bit the usual kind, sir. Quite interesting. Very smart."

"Outside or inside?"

"Oh, her clothes, I meant, sir."

"Her! Is it a woman?"

"Yes. A lady, sir."

"Bring her in." Rage ran over him in little prickles. How dare some sensation-mad female waste his time in order to satisfy her perverted and depraved appetite.

Williams swung the door back and ushered in a bright fashionable figure.

It was Judy Sellers.

She said nothing, but came into the room with a sulky deliberation. Even in his surprise at seeing her, Grant thought how Borstal she was in spite of her soigné exterior. That air of resentment against the world in general and her own fate in particular was very familiar to him.

He pulled out a chair in silence. Grant could be very intimidating.

"All right, Sergeant," he said, "there won't be any need for you to stay." And then, to Judy as Williams went: "Don't you think this is a little unfair, Miss Sellers?"

"Unfair?"

"I am working twenty-three hours out of the twenty-four, on dreadfully important work, and you see fit to waste my time by treating us to a bogus confession."

"There's nothing bogus about it."

"It's so bogus that I have a good mind to dismiss you now, without another word."

She stayed his half-movement to the door. "You can't do that. I'll just go to another police station and confess and they'll send me on to you. I *did* it, you see!"

"Oh, no, you didn't."

"Why not?"

"For one thing, you weren't near the place."

"How do you know where I was?"

"You forget that in the course of conversation on

Saturday night it was apparent that on Wednesday night you were at Miss Keats' house in Chelsea."

"I was only there for cocktails. I left early because Lydia was going to a party up the river."

"Even so, that makes it rather unlikely that you should be on a beach near Westover shortly after dawn next morning."

"It wouldn't be at all surprising if I were in the north of England next morning. I motored down if you want to know. You can inquire at my flat. The girl I live with will tell you that I didn't come home till lunch-time on Thursday."

"That hardly proves that your activities were murderous."

"They were, though. I drove to the Gap, hid in the wood, and waited till she came to swim."

"You were, of course, wearing a man's coat?"

"Yes, though I don't know how you knew. It was cold driving, and I wore one of my brother's that was lying in the car."

"Did you wear the coat to go down to the beach?"

"Yes. It was dithering cold. I don't like bathing in the dawn."

"You went bathing!"

"Of course I did. I couldn't drown her from the shore, could I?"

"And you left the coat on the beach?"

"Oh, no," she said with elaborate sarcasm. "I went swimming in it!"

And Grant breathed again. For a moment he had had a fright.

"So you changed into swimming things, walked down to the beach with your brother's coat over you, and—then what?"

"She was a fair way out. I went in, swam up to her and drowned her."

"How?"

"She said, 'Hello, Judy.' I said, 'Hello.' I gave her a

light tap on the chin. My brother taught me where to hit a person's chin, so as to addle them. Then I dived under her and pulled her through the water by the heels until she was drowned."

"Very neat," Grant said. "You've thought it all out, haven't you? Have you invented a motive for yourself, too?"

"Oh, I just didn't like her. I hated her, if you want to know. Her success and her looks and her self-sufficiency. She got in my hair until I couldn't bear it another day."

"I see. And will you explain why, having achieved the practically perfect murder, you should calmly come here and put a noose around your neck?"

"Because you've got someone for it."

"You mean because we've got Robert Tisdall. And that explains everything. And now having wasted some precious minutes of my time, you might recompense me and rehabilitate yourself at the same time, by telling me what you know of Tisdall."

"I don't know anything. Except that he would be the very last person in the world to commit a murder. For any reason."

"You knew him fairly well, then?"

"No. I hardly knew him at all."

"You weren't—friends?"

"No, nor lovers, if that's what you're trying to say. Bobby Tisdall didn't know I was alive, except to hand me a cocktail."

Grant's tone changed. "And yet you'd go even to this length to get him out of a jam?" he said, quite kindly.

She braced into resentment at the kindness. "If you'd committed a murder wouldn't you confess to save an innocent person?"

"Depends on how innocent I thought the police were. You underrate us, Miss Sellers."

"I think you're a lot of idiots. You've got a man who is innocent. You're busy hounding him to death. And you won't listen to a perfectly good confession when you get one."

"Well, you see, Miss Sellers, there are always things about a case that are known only to the police and are not to be learned from newspapers. The mistake you made was to get up your story from the newspaper accounts. There was one thing you didn't know. And one thing you forgot."

"What did I forget?"

"That no one knew where Christine Clay was staying."

"The murderer did."

"Yes. That is my point. And now—I'm very busy."

"So you don't believe a word I say."

"Oh, yes. Quite a lot of it. You were out all night on Wednesday, you probably went swimming, and you arrived back at lunch-time on Thursday. But none of that makes you guilty of murder."

She got up, in her reluctant, indolent way, and produced her lipstick. "Well," she drawled between applications, "having failed in my little bid for publicity, I suppose I must go on playing blonde nit-wits for the rest of my life. It's good I bought a day-return."

"You don't fool me," Grant said, with a not too grim smile as he opened the door for her.

"All right, then, maybe you're right about that, and blast you anyhow," she burst out. "But you're wrong about his doing it. So wrong that your name will stink before this case is over."

And she brushed past an astonished Williams and two clerks, and disappeared.

"Well," said Williams, "that's the first. Humans are queer, aren't they, sir? You know, if we announced the fact that the coat we want has a button missing, there'd be people who would pull the button off their coats and bring it in. Just for fun. As if things weren't difficult enough without that. Not just the usual type, though, was she, sir?"

"No. What did you make of her, Williams?"

"Musical comedy. Looking for publicity to help her career. Hard as nails."

"All wrong. Legitimate stage. Hates her career. Soft-hearted to the point of self-sacrifice."

Williams looked a little crestfallen. "Of course, I didn't have a chance to talk to her," he reminded.

"No. On looks it was quite a good reading, Williams. I wish I could read this case as well." He sat down and ran his fingers through his hair. "What would you do, Williams, once you had got clear of the Marine?"

Williams understood that he was supposed to be Tisdall.

"I'd take a fairly crowded bus somewhere. First that came to hand. Get off with a crowd of others, and walk off as if I knew where I was going. In fact, wherever I went I'd look as if I knew where I was going."

"And then, what?"

"I'd probably have to take another bus to get out of townified parts."

"You'd get out of built-up areas, would you?"

"Sure!" said Williams, surprised.

"A man's much more conspicuous in open country."

"There are woods. In fact, some of the woods in this part of the world would hide a man indefinitely. And if a man got as far west as Ashdown Forest, well, it'd take about a hundred men to comb Ashdown properly."

Grant shook his head. "There's food. And lodging."

"Sleep out. It's warm weather."

"He's been out two nights now. If he has taken to the country he must be looking shop-worn by this time. But has he? Have you noticed that no one has reported him as buying a razor? There's just the chance that he's with friends. I wonder—" his eyes strayed to the chair where Judy had been sitting. "But no! She'd never risk as big a bluff as that. No need for it."

Williams wished to himself that Grant would go to the hotel and have some sleep. He was taking far too much to heart his failure to arrest Tisdall. Mistakes happened to the best of people, and everyone knew that Grant was all right. He had the Yard solid behind him. Why need he worry himself sick over something that might have happened to anyone? There were one or two crabbers, of course—people who wanted his job—but no one paid any attention to the like of them. Everyone knew what they were getting at. Grant was all right, and everyone knew it. It was silly of him to get so worked up over a little slip.

If a policeman's heart can be said to ache, then Williams's stout heart ached for his superior.

"You can get rid of this disgusting object," Grant said, indicating the coat. "It's twenty years old, at least, and hasn't had a button on it for the last ten. That's one thing that puzzles me, you know, Williams. He had it at the beach, and it was missing when he came back. He had to get rid of that coat somewhere along his route. It isn't a very extensive route, when all is said. And there wasn't time for him to go far off it. He'd be too anxious to get back and cover up his mistake in going away. And yet we haven't turned the coat up. Two duck ponds, both shallow, both well dragged. Three streams that wouldn't hide a penny and wouldn't float a paper boat. Ditches beaten, garden walls inspected on the wrong side, two copses scoured. Nothing! What did he do with it? What would you do with it?"

"Burn it."

"No time. It's damp too. Soaking wet, probably."

"Roll it small and stick it in the fork of a tree. Everyone looks on the ground for things."

"Williams, you're a born criminal. Tell Sanger your theory and ask him to make use of it this afternoon. I'd rather have that coat than have Tisdall. In fact, I've got to have that coat!"

"Talking of razors, you don't think maybe, he took his razor with him, sir?"

"I didn't think of it. Shouldn't think he had the

presence of mind. But then I didn't think he'd have the nerve to bolt. I concentrated on suicide. Where are his things?"

"Sanger took them over here in the case. Everything he had."

"Just see if his razor is there? It's just as well to know whether he's shaved or not."

There was no razor.

"Well!" said Grant. "Who'd have thought it! 'You disappoint me, Inspector,' says he, quietly pocketing the razor, and arranging his get-away with the world's prize chump of a detective watching him. I'm all wrong about that lad, Sergeant. All wrong. I thought first, when I took him from the inquest that he was one of these hysterical, do-it-on-the-spur-of-the-moment creatures. Then, after I knew about the will, I changed my mind. Still thought him a 'poor thing,' though. And now I find he was planning a get-away under my very nose—and he brought it off! It isn't Tisdall who's a washout, it's me!"

"Cheer up, sir. Our luck is out at the moment. But you and I between us, and no one else, so help me, are going to put that coldblooded brute where he belongs," Williams said fervently, not knowing that the person who was to be the means of bringing the murderer of Christine Clay to justice was a rather silly little woman in Kansas City who had never heard of any of them.

11

ERICA STOOD ON THE BRAKE AND BROUGHT HER DISREPU-
table little car to a standstill. She then backed it the
necessary yards, and stopped again. She inspected with
interest the sole of a man's boot, visible in the grass and
gorse, and then considered the wide empty landscape
and the mile-long straight of chalky lane with its
borders of speedwell and thrift, shining in the sun.

"You can come out," she said. "There's no one in
sight for miles."

The boot sole disappeared and a man's astonished
face appeared in the bushes above it.

"That's a great relief to me," Erica observed. "I
thought for a moment that you might be dead."

"How did you know it was me? I suppose you *did*
know it was me?"

"Yes. There's a funny squiggle on the instep part of
your sole where the price has been scored off. I noticed
it when you were lying on the floor of Father's office."

"Oh, yes; that's who you are, of course. You're a
very good detective."

"You're a very bad escaper. No one could have missed your foot."

"You didn't give me much time. I didn't hear your car till it was nearly on me."

"You must be deaf. She's one of the County jokes, poor Tinny. Like Lady Middleway's hat and old Mr. Dyne's shell-collection."

"Tinny?"

"Yes. She used to be Christina, but the inevitable happened. You couldn't *not* have heard her."

"I think perhaps I was asleep for a minute or two. I—I'm a bit short of sleep."

"Yes, I expect so. Are you hungry?"

"Is that just an academic question, or—or are you offering me food?"

Erica reached into the back of the car and produced half a dozen rolls, a glass of tongue, half a pound of butter, and four tomatoes.

"I've forgotten a tin-opener," she said, passing him the tongue, "but if you hit the tin lid hard with a flint it will make a hole." She split a roll with a pen knife produced from her pocket and began to butter it.

"Do you always carry food about with you?" he asked, doubtfully.

"Oh, always. I'm a very hungry person. Besides I'm often not home from morning till night. Here's the knife. Cut a hunk of the tongue and lay it on that." She gave him the buttered roll. "I want the knife back for the other roll."

He did as he was bidden, and she busied herself with the knife again, politely ignoring him so that he should not have to pretend to an indifference that would be difficult of achievement.

Presently he said, "I suppose you know that all this is very wrong?"

"Why is it wrong?"

"For one thing, you're aiding an escaped criminal, which is wrong in itself, and doubly wrong in your father's daughter. And for another—and this is much worse—if I were what they think me you'd be in the gravest danger at this minute. You shouldn't *do* things like that, you know."

"If you were a murderer it wouldn't help you much to commit another one just to keep me from saying I saw you."

"If you've committed one, I suspect you don't easily stop at another. You can only be hanged once. And so you don't think I did it?"

"I'm quite sure you didn't."

"What makes you so sure?"

"You're not capable of it."

"Thank you," he said gratefully.

"I didn't mean it that way."

"Oh! Oh, I see." A smile actually broke through. "Disconcerting but invigorating. George an ancestor of yours?"

"George? Oh. No. No, I can tell lies with the best."

"You'll have to tonight. Unless you are going to give me up."

"I don't suppose anyone will question me at all," she said, ignoring the latter half of his remark. "I don't think a beard becomes you, by the way."

"I don't like it myself. I took a razor with me but couldn't manage to do anything without soap and water. I suppose you haven't soap in the car?"

"I'm afraid not. I don't wash as often as I eat. But there's a frothy stuff in a bottle—Snowdrop, they call it—that I use to clean my hands when I change a wheel. Perhaps that would work." She got out the bottle from the car pocket. "You must be much cleverer than I thought you were, you know."

"Yes? How clever does that make me actually?"

"To get away from Inspector Grant. He's very good at his job, Father says."

"Yes, I think he probably is. If I didn't happen to have a horror of being shut up, I wouldn't have had the nerve to run. As it was, that half-hour was the most exciting thing that ever happened to me. I know now what living at top speed means. I used to think having money and doing what you liked—twenty different things a day—was living at speed. But I just didn't know anything about it."

"Was she nice, Christine Clay?"

He looked disconcerted. "You do jump about, don't you? Yes, she was a grand person." He forgot his food for a moment. "Do you know what she did? She left me her ranch in California because she knew I had no money and hated an office."

"Yes, I know."

"You know?"

"Yes, I've heard Father and the others discussing it."

"Oh. Oh, yes. . . . And you still believe I didn't do it? I must be very bargain counter in your eyes!"

"Was she very beautiful?"

"Haven't you ever seen her, then? On the screen, I mean?"

"No. I don't think so."

"Neither have I. Funny, isn't it. I suppose, roaming from place to place it's easy to miss pictures."

"I'm afraid I don't go to the cinema often. It's a long way to a good one from our place. Have some more tongue."

"She meant to do me such a good turn—Chris. Irony, isn't it? That her gift should be practically my death warrant."

"I suppose you have no idea who could have done it?"

"No. I didn't know any of her friends, you know. She just picked me up one night." He considered the schoolgirlish figure before him. "I suppose that sounds dreadful to you?"

"Oh, no. Not if you liked the look of each other. I judge a lot on looks."

"I can't help feeling that the police may be making a mistake—I mean, that it was just accident. If you'd seen the country that morning. Utterly deserted. No one going to be awake for at least another hour. It's almost incredible that someone should have been out for murder at that time and in that place. That button *might* be an accident, after all."

"If your coat turned up with the buttons on it, would that prove you had nothing to do with it?"

"Yes, I think so. That seemed to be all the evidence the police had." He smiled a little. "But you know more about it than I do."

"Where were you when you lost it—the coat, I mean?"

"We'd gone over to Dymchurch one day: Tuesday, it was. And we left the car to walk along the sea-wall for about half an hour. Our coats were always left lying in the back. I didn't miss mine till we stopped for petrol about half-way home, and I turned around to get the bag Chris had flung there when she got in." His face suddenly flamed scarlet, and Erica watched him in surprise and then in embarrassment. It was moments later before it occurred to her that the tacit admission that the woman was paying was more humiliating to him than any murder accusation. "The coat wasn't there then," he went on hurriedly, "so it could only have gone while we were walking."

"Gypsies?"

"I don't think so. I didn't see any. A casual passer-by, more likely."

"Is there anything to tell that the coat is yours? You'd have to prove it to the police, you know."

"My name is on the lining—one of those tailor's tags, you know."

"But if it was stolen that would be the first thing they'd take off."

"Yes. Yes I suppose so. There's another thing, though. There's a small burn on the right-hand side below the pocket, where someone held a cigarette against it."

"That's better, isn't it! That would settle it very nicely."

"If the coat were found!"

"Well, no one who stole a coat is likely to bring it to the police station just because the police want it. And the police are not looking for coats *on* people. They're looking for discarded ones. So far no one has done anything about getting *your* coat. On your behalf, I mean. To be evidence for you."

"Well, what can I do?"

"Give yourself up."

"What!"

"Give yourself up. Then they'll give you a lawyer and things. And it will be his business to look for the coat."

"I couldn't do that. I just couldn't, What's-Your-Name."

"Erica."

"Erica. The thought of having a key turned on me gives me the jitters."

"Claustrophobia?"

"Yes. I don't really mind closed spaces as long as I know that I can get out. Caves and things. But to have a key turned on me, and then to have nothing to do but sit and think of—I just couldn't do it."

"No, I suppose you couldn't, if you feel like that about it. It's a pity. It's much the most sensible way. What are you going to do now?"

"Sleep out again, I suppose. There's no rain coming."

"Haven't you any friends who'd look after you?"

"With a murder charge against me? No! You overrate human friendship." He paused a moment, and added, in a surprised voice: "No. No, perhaps you don't, at that. I've just not met the right kind before."

"Then we had better decide on a place where I can meet you tomorrow and bring you some more food. Here, if you like."

"No!"

"Where then?"

"I didn't mean that. I mean that you're not meeting me anywhere."

"Why not?"

"Because you'd be committing a felony, or whatever it is. I don't know what the penalty is, but you'd be a criminal. It can't be done."

"Well, you can't stop me dropping food out of the car, can you? There is no law against that, that I know of. It will just happen that a cheese and a loaf and some chocolates will fall out of the car into these bushes tomorrow morning. I must go now. The landscape looks deserted, but if you leave a car standing long enough someone always pops up to make inquiries."

She swept the refuse of the food into the car, and got in herself.

He made a movement to get to his feet.

"Don't be foolish," she said sharply. "Keep down."

He swivelled around on his knees. "All right. You can't object to this position. And it expresses my feelings much better."

She shut the car door, and leaned over it.

"Nut or plain?"

"What?"

"The chocolate."

"Oh! The kind with raisins in it, please. Some day, Erica Burgoyne, I shall crown you with rubies and make you to walk on carpets rich as—"

But the sentence was lost in the roar of Tinny's departure.

12

"KINDNESS," SAID ERICA, TO HER FATHER'S HEAD GROOM, "have you anything laid by?"

Kindness paused in his checking the corn account, shot her a pale glance from a wrinkled old eye, and went on with his adding.

"Tuppence!" he said at length, in the tone one uses instead of a spit.

This referred to the account, and Erica waited. Kindness hated accounts.

"Enough to bury me decent," he said, having reached the top of the column again.

"You don't want to be buried yet a while. Could you lend me ten pounds, do you think?"

The old man paused in licking his stub of pencil, so that the lead made a purple stain on the exposed tip of his tongue.

"So that's the way it is!" he said. "What have you been doing now?"

"I haven't *been* doing anything. But there are some

things I might want to do. And petrol is a dreadful price."

The mention of petrol was a bad break.

"Oh, the car is it?" he said jealously. Kindness hated Tinny. "If it's the car you want it for, why don't you ask Hart?"

"Oh, I *couldn't.*" Erica was almost shocked. "Hart is quite new." Hart being a newcomer with only eleven years' service.

Kindness looked mollified.

"It isn't anything shady," she assured him. "I would have got it from Father at dinner tonight; the money, I mean; but he has gone to Uncle William's for the night. And women are so inquisitive," she added after a pause.

This, which could only refer to Nannie, made up the ground she had lost over the petrol. Kindness hated Nannie.

"Ten pounds is a big bit out of my coffin," he said with a sideways jerk of the head.

"You won't need it before Saturday. I have eight pounds in the bank, but I don't want to waste time tomorrow morning going into Westover for it. Time is awfully precious just now. If anything happens to me, you're sure of eight pounds anyhow. And Father is good for the other two."

"And what made you come to Kindness?"

There was complacence in the tone, and anyone but Erica would have said: Because you are my oldest friend, because you have always helped me out of difficulties since I was three years old and first put my legs astride a pony, because you can keep my counsel and ̇s, because in spite of your cantankerousness you are an old darling.

But Erica said, "I just thought how much handier tea-caddies were than banks."

"What's that!"

"Oh, perhaps I shouldn't have said that. Your wife

told me about that, one day I was having tea with her. It wasn't her fault, really. I saw the notes peering through the tea. A bit germy, I thought. For the tea, I mean. But an awfully good idea." As Kindness was still speechless. "Boiling water kills most things, anyhow. Besides," she said, bringing up as support what she should have used for attack, "who else could I go to?"

She reached over and took the stub of pencil from him, turned over a handbill of the local gymkhana which was lying on the saddleroom table, and wrote in school-girl characters on the back:

I owe Bartholomew Kindness ten pounds. Erica Meir Burgoyne.

"That will do until Saturday," she said. "My check book is finished, anyhow."

"I don't like you frittering away my brass handles all over Kent," Kindness grumbled.

"I think brass handles are very showy," Erica said. "You'd do much better to have wrought iron."

As they went through the gardens together towards his cottage and the tea-caddy, Erica said:

"About how many pawnbrokers are there in Kent?"

"'Bout two thousand."

"Oh, dear!" said Erica. And let the conversation lapse.

But the two thousand pawnbrokers slept with her that night, and leaped awake before her waking eyes.

Two thousand! My hat!

But of course Kindness was just guessing. He probably had never pawned anything in his life. How could he know in the very least how many pawnbrokers there were in a county? Still, there was bound to be quite a number. Even in a well-to-do county like Kent. She had never noticed even one. But she supposed you wouldn't notice one unless you happened to be looking for it. Like mushrooms.

It was half-past six of a hot, still morning as she backed Tinny out of the garage, and no one was awake in the bland white house that smiled at her as she went.

Tinny made a noise at any time, but the noise she made in the before-breakfast silence of a summer morning was obscene. And for the first time Erica was guilty of disloyalty in her feeling for Tinny. Exasperated she had been often; yes, furious; but it had always been the fury of possession, the anger one feels for someone so loved as to be part of oneself. Never in her indignation, never in the moments of her friends' laughter, had she ever been tempted to disown Tinny. Still less to give her up.

But now she thought quite calmly, I shall really have to get a new car.

Erica was growing up.

Tinny expostulated her way through the quiet shining lanes, chuffing, snorting, and shaking, while Erica sat upright in the old-fashioned seat and ceased to think about her. Beside her was a box containing half a spring chicken, bread and butter, tomatoes, shortbread, and a bottle of milk. This—"Miss Erica's lunch"—was the Steynes housekeeper's unwitting contribution to the confounding of the Law. Beyond it, in a brown-paper parcel, was Erica's own subscription—a less delicate but more filling one than the housekeeper's—purchased at Mr.-Deeds-in-the-village. ("Eastindiaman and provision Merchant. All the Best in Season.") Mr. Deeds had provided pink and shining slices of jellied veal ("Do you really want it as thick as that, Miss Erica?") but he had not been able to supply a brand of chocolates with raisins in it. No demand for that, there wasn't.

It had not even crossed Erica's mind that she was tired, that there remained less than an hour before closing-time, and that a starving man might just as well have good solid lumps of plain chocolate as be indulged in his light preference for raisins. No; Erica—although she could not have told you about it—knew all about the importance of little things. Especially the importance of little things when one was unhappy. In the hot and dusty evening she had toured the neighboring villages with a determination that grew with her lack of success. So that now, in the torn and gaping pocket of Tinny's near door, lay four half-pound slabs of chocolate with raisins in it, the whole stock of Mrs.-Higgs-at-Leytham, who at a quarter past seven had been persuaded to leave her high tea ("only for you I'd do it, Miss Burgoyne, not for another soul") and turn the enormous key in her small blistered door.

It was after seven before she had clamored her way through sleeping Mallingford and entered the hot, shadeless country beyond. As she turned into the long straight of the chalky lane where her quick country-trained eyes had noticed that boot yesterday, she wished that Tisdall might have better cover than those gorse bushes. Not cover from the Law, but cover from the sky there was going to be at midday. A blazing day, it was going to be. Tisdall would need all of that bottle of milk and those tomatoes. She debated whether or not it would be a good move to transport the fugitive to other climes. Over to Charing, for instance. There were woods enough there to house an army in safety from sun and law. But Erica had never much liked woods, and had never felt particularly safe in one. It was better to be hot in gorse bushes and be able to see a long way away, than have strangers stumbling over you in the cool of thick trees. Besides, the Tisdall man might refuse the offer of a lift.

There is no doubt as to what the Tisdall man's answer would have been, but the proposition was never put to him. Either he was so dead asleep that not even the uproar of Tinny's advent could rouse him, or he was no longer in that piece of country. Erica went to the end of the mile-long straight, Tinny full out and making a noise like an express train, and came back to the spot where she had stopped yesterday. As she shut off the engine, the silence fell about her, absolute. Not even a lark sang, not a shadow stirred.

She waited there, quietly, not looking about her, her arms propped on the wheel in the attitude of one considering her future movements. There must be no expectancy in her appearance to arouse suspicion in the mind of stray countrymen. For twenty minutes she sat, relaxed and incurious. Then she stretched herself, made sure during the stretch that the lane was still unoccupied, and got out. If Tisdall had wanted to speak to her, he would have reached her before now. She took the two parcels and the chocolate and cached them where Tisdall had been lying yesterday. To these she added a packet of cigarettes produced from her own sagging pocket. Erica did not smoke herself—she had tried it, of course, had not much liked it, and with the logic that was her ruling characteristic had not persisted—and she did not know that Tisdall smoked. These, and the matches, were just "in case." Erica never did a job that was not thorough.

She climbed in again, pressed Tinny into life, and without a pause or backward glance headed down the lane, her face and thoughts turned to the far-off coast and Dymchurch.

It was Erica's very sound theory that no "local" had stolen that coat. She had lived all her life in a country community, and knew very well that a new black overcoat cannot make its appearance even on the meanest back without receiving a truly remarkable amount of attention. She knew, too, that your country-man is not versed in the ways of pawnshops, and that a coat lying in a car would not represent to him a possible cash value, as it would to someone "on the road." If he coveted it at all, it would be for possession; and the difficulty of explaining its appearance would result in his leaving it where it was. The coat, therefore, according to Erica's reasoning, had been taken by a "casual."

This made things at once easier and more difficult. A "casual" is a much more noticeable person than a "local," and so easier to identify. On the other hand, a "casual" is a movable object and difficult to track. In the week that had passed since the theft, that coat might have traversed most of Kent. It might now be—

Hunger gave wings to Erica's imagination. By the time she was in sight of Dymchurch she had, thanks to modern methods of hitch-hiking and old-fashioned methods of stowing away, placed the coat on the back of a clerk in the office of the Mayor of Bordeaux. He was a little pale clerk with a delicate wife and puny baby, and Erica's heart was sore at the thought of having to take the coat from him, even for Tisdall.

At this point Erica decided that she must eat. Fasting was good for the imagination but bad for logic. She stepped on the brake at sight of The Rising Sun, "good pull-up for car men, open all night." It was a tin shed, set down by the roadside with the inconsequence of a matchbox, painted gamboge and violet, and set about with geraniums. The door was hospitably open, and the sound of voices floated out on the warm air.

In the tiny interior were two very large men. The proprietor was cutting very large slices from a very fresh loaf, and the other man was sipping very hot liquid from a very large mug with very great noise. At sight of Erica on the doorstep all these activities ceased abruptly.

"Good morning," said Erica into the silence.

"Morning, miss," said the proprietor. "Cup of tea, perhaps?"

"Well—" Erica looked around. "You haven't any bacon, by any chance?"

"Lovely bacon," said the owner promptly. "Melt in your mouth."

"I'll have a lot," said Erica happily.

"Egg with it, perhaps?"

"Three," said Erica.

The owner craned his neck to see out the door, and found that she really was alone.

"Come," he said. "That's something like. Nice to see a young girl that can appreciate her vittles these days. Have a seat, miss." He dusted an iron chair for her with the corner of his apron. "Bacon be ready in no time. Thick or thin?"

"Thick, please. Good morning." This to the other man, in more particular greeting, as she sat down and so definitely became a partner in this business of eating and drinking. "Is that your lorry out there? I have always wanted to drive one of those."

"Ye'? I've always wanted to be a tightrope walker."

"You're the wrong build," said Erica seriously. "Better stick to lorry driving." And the owner paused in his slicing of the bacon to laugh.

The lorry driver decided that sarcasm was wasted on so literal a mind. He relaxed into amiability.

"Oh, well; nice to have ladies' company for a change, eh, Bill?"

"Don't you have lots of it?" asked Erica. "I thought lorries were very popular." And before the astounded man could make up his mind whether this skinny child was being rude, provocative, or merely matter of fact, she went on, "Do you give lifts to tramps, ever, by the way?"

"Never!" said the driver promptly, glad to feel his feet on firm ground.

"That's a pity. I'm interested in tramps."

"Christian interest?" inquired Bill, turning the sizzling bacon in the pan.

"No. Literary."

"Well, now. You writing a book?"

"Not exactly. I'm gathering material for someone else. You must *see* a lot of tramps, even if you don't give them lifts," she persisted, to the driver.

"No time to see anyone when you're driving that there."

"Tell her about Harrogate Harry," prompted Bill, breaking eggs. "I saw him in your cab last week sometime."

"Never saw anyone in my cab, you didn't."

"Oh, come unstuck, will you. The little lady's all right. She's not the sort to go blabbing even if you did give an odd tramp a lift?"

"Harrogate isn't a tramp."

"Who is he, then?" asked Erica.

"He's a china merchant. Traveling."

"Oh, I know. A blue-and-white bowl in exchange for a rabbit skin."

"No. Nothing like that. Mends teapot handles and such."

"Oh. Does he make much?" This for the sake of keeping the driver on the subject.

"Enough to be going on with. And he cadges an old coat or a pair of boots now and then."

Erica said nothing for a moment, and she wondered if the thumping of her heart was as audible to these two men as it was in her ears. An old coat, now and then. What should she say now? She could not say: Did he have a coat the day you saw him? That would be a complete give-away.

"He sounds interesting," she said, at last. "Mustard, please," to Bill. "I should like to meet him. But I suppose he is at the other end of the country by now. What day did you see him?"

"Lemme see. I picked him up outside Dymchurch and dropped him near Tonbridge. That was a week last Monday."

So it hadn't been Harrogate. What a pity! He had sounded so hopeful a subject, with his desire for coats and boots, his wandering ways, and his friendliness with lorry-drivers who get a man away quickly from possibly unfriendly territory. Oh, well, it was no good imagining that it was going to be as easy as this had promised to be.

Bill set down the mustard by her plate. "Not Monday," he said. "Not that it makes any difference. But Jimmy was here unloading stores when you went by. Tuesday, it was."

Not that it made any difference! Erica took a great mouthful of eggs and bacon to quiet her singing heart.

For a little there was silence in The Rising Sun; partly because Erica had a masculine habit of silence while she ate, partly because she had not yet made up her mind what it would be both politic and productive to say next. She was startled into anxiety when the lorry-driver thrust his mug away from him and rose to go.

"But you haven't told me about Harrogate What's-His-Name!"

"What is there to tell?"

"Well, a traveling china-mender must be chock full of interest. I *would* like to meet him and have a talk."

"He isn't much of a talker."

"I'd make it worth his while."

Bill laughed. "If you was to give Harrogate five bob, he'd talk his head off. And for ten he'll tell you how he found the south pole."

Erica turned to the more sympathetic one of the two.

"You know him? Does he have a home, do you know?"

"In winter he stays put, mostly, I think. But in summer he lives in a tent."

"Living with Queenie Webster somewhere near Pembury," put in the driver, who didn't like the shift of interest to Bill.

He put down some coppers on the scrubbed table and moved to the door.

"And if you're making it worth anyone's while, I'd square Queenie first if I was you."

"Thank you," said Erica. "I'll remember. Thank you for your help."

The genuine warmth of gratitude in her voice made him pause. He stood in the doorway considering her. "Tramps are a queer taste for a girl with a healthy appetite," he said, and went out to his lorry.

13

ERICA'S HEALTHY APPETITE EXTENDED TO BREAD AND
marmalade and several cups of tea, but she absorbed
little information with the nourishment. Bill, for all his
willingness to give her anything she wanted, knew very
little about Harrogate Harry. She had now to decide
whether or not to leave a "warm" Dymchurch and
follow the unknown and elusive Harry into the "cold"
of the Tonbridge country.

"Are most tramps honest, would you say?" she asked
as she was paying her bill.

"We—ll," said Bill, thinking it out, "honest up to the
point of opportunity, if you know what I mean."

Erica knew. Not one tramp in fifty would refuse the
gift of a coat lying unattended. And Harrogate Harry
definitely liked to acquire coats and boots. And Harry
had been in Dymchurch a week last Tuesday. Her job,
therefore, was to follow the china-mender through the
summer landscape until she caught up with him. If
night overtook her in her search she must think of some
really reassuring lie which could be telephoned to her

father at Steynes to account for her absence. The need
for lying caused her the first pang she had suffered so
far in her self-appointed crusade; she had never needed
to shut out her father from any ploy of hers. For the
second time in a few hours her loyalty was divided. She
had not noticed her disloyalty to Tinny; but this time
she noticed and cared.

Oh, well, the day was young, and days just now were
long. And Tinny might be a veteran but she was never
sick or sorry. If luck held as it had begun she might still
be back in her own bed at Steynes tonight. Back at
Steynes—*with the coat!*

Her breath stopped at the very prospect.

She said good-bye to the admiring Bill, promised to
recommend his breakfasts to all her friends, and set
Tinny's nose west and north through the hot flowery
country. The roads were blinding now in the glare of
the sky, the horizons beginning to swim. Tinny swel-
tered stoutly through the green furnace, and was soon
as comfortable as a frying-pan. In spite of her eagerness Erica was forced every few miles to pause and
open both doors while Tinny cooled. Yes, she really
must get another car.

Near Kippings Cross, on the main Tonbridge road,
she repeated as tactics what she had by accident found
serviceable: she pulled up for lunch at a wayside hut.
But this time luck was lacking in the service. The hut
was kept by a jolly woman with a flow of conversation
but no interest in tramps. She had all the normal
woman's intolerance of a waster, and "didn't encour-
age vagrants." Erica ate sparingly and drank her
bottled coffee, glad of the temporary shade; but
presently she rose and went out to find a "better
place." The "better" referring not to food but to
possible information. With a self-control beyond praise
she turned her eyes away from the endless tea-gardens,
green and cool, with gay cloths gleaming like wet stones
in the shadows. Not for her that luxury today. Tea-
gardens knew nothing of tramps.

She turned down a lane to Goudhurst, and sought an inn. Inns had always china to mend, and now that she was in Harrogate's home country, so to speak, she would surely find someone who knew him.

She ate cold underdone beef and green salad in a room as beautiful as any at Steynes, and prayed that one, at least, of the dishes on her table, should be cracked. When the tinned fruit appeared in a broken china rose- bowl she nearly whooped aloud.

Yes, the waitress agreed, it was a pretty bowl. She didn't know if it was valuable or not, she was only there for the season (it being understood that the possible value of household goods could not interest anyone whose playground was the world). Yes, she supposed that someone local mended their china but she didn't know. Yes, she *could* ask, of course.

The landlord, asked who had mended the china bowl so beautifully, said that that particular bowl was bought just as it was, in a job lot of stuff over at Matfield Green. And anyhow it was so old a mend that the man that did it was probably dead by now. But if Erica wanted a man to mend her china, there was a good traveling man who came around now and then. Palmer, by name. He could put fifty pieces together when he was sober without showing a join. But you'd got to be sure he was sober.

Erica listened to the vices and virtues of Palmer, and asked if he was the only one in the district.

The only one the landlord knew. But you couldn't find a better than Harry.

"Harry?"

That was his name. Harrogate Harry they called him. No, the landlord did not know where he was to be found. Lived in a tent Brenchley way, so he understood. Not the kind of household that Erica had better visit alone, he thought he had better say. Harry was no example as a citizen.

Erica went out into the heat encouraged by the news

that for days, sometimes weeks, together, Harry did not stir away from his temporary home. As soon as he made a little extra money, he sat back and drank it.

Well, if one is going to interview a china-mender one's first necessity is broken china. Erica drove into Tunbridge Wells, hoping that the great-aunt who lived somberly in Calverly Park was sleeping off her forbidden pastry and not promenading under the lime trees, and in an antique shop spent some of Kindness's coffin money on a frivolous little porcelain figure of a dancer. She drove back to Pembury and in the afternoon quiet of a deep lane proceeded to drop the dancer with abandon on the running-board of the car. But the dancer was tough. Even when Erica took her firmly by the feet and tapped her on the jamb of the door, she remained whole. In the end, afraid that greater violence might shatter her completely, she snapped off an arm with her finger and thumb, and there was her passport to Harrogate Harry.

You cannot ask questions about a vague tramp who, you think, may have stolen a coat. But to look for a china-mender is quite a legitimate search, involving no surprise or suspicion in the minds of the questioned. It took Erica only ninety minutes to come face to face with Harrogate. It would have taken her less, but the tent was a long way from any made road; first up a cart track through woods, a track impassable even for the versatile Tinny, then across an open piece of gorse land with far views of the Medway valley, and into a second wood to a clearing at its further edge, where a stream ran down to a dark pool.

Erica wished that the tent had not been in a wood. From her earliest childhood she had been fearless by nature (the kind of child of whom older people say out hunting: Not a nerve in her body), but there was no denying that she didn't like woods. She liked to see a long way away. And though the stream ran bright and clear and merry in the sunlight, the pool in the hollow was still and deep and forbidding. One of those sudden, secret cups of black water more common in Sussex than in Kent.

As she came across the clearing carrying the little dancer in her hand, a dog rushed out at her, shattering the quiet with hysterical protest. And at the noise a woman came to the tent door and stood there watching Erica as she came. She was a very tall woman, broadshouldered and straight, and Erica had the mad feeling that this long approach to her over an open floor should end in a curtsey.

"Good afternoon," she called, cheerfully, above the clamor of the dog. But the woman waited without moving. "I have a piece of china—Can't you make that dog be quiet?" She was face to face with her now, only the noise of the dog between them.

The woman lifted a foot to the animal's ribs, and the high yelling died into silence. The murmur of the stream came back.

Erica showed the broken porcelain figure.

"Harry!" called the woman, her black inquisitive eyes not leaving Erica. And Harry came to the tent door: a small weaselish man with bloodshot eyes, and evidently in the worst of tempers. "A job for you."

"I'm not working," said Harry, and spat.

"Oh. I'm sorry. I heard you were very good at mending things."

The woman took the figure and broken piece from Erica's hands. "He's working, all right," she said.

Harry spat again, and took the pieces. "Have you the money to pay?" he asked, angrily.

"How much will it be?"

"Two shillings."

"Two and six," said the woman.

"Oh, yes, I have that much."

He went back into the tent, and the woman stood in the way so that Erica could neither follow nor see. Unconsciously she had, in imagining this moment, always placed herself inside the tent—with the coat folded up in the corner. Now she was not even to be allowed to see inside.

"He won't be long," Queenie said. "By the time you've cut a whistle from the ash tree, it'll be ready."

Erica's small sober face broke into one of its rare smiles. "You thought I couldn't do that, didn't you?" For the woman's phrase had been a flick in the face of a supposed town-dweller.

She cut the wood with her pocket-knife, shaped it, nicked it, and damped it in the stream, hoping that a preoccupation might disarm Queenie and her partner. She even hoped that the last processes of whistle-manufacture might be made in friendly company with the mending of china. But the moment she moved back to the tent, Queenie came from her desultory stick-gathering in the wood to stand guard. And Erica found her whistle finished and the mended figure in her hands, without being one whit wiser or richer than she was when she left the car in the road. She could have cried.

She produced her small purse (Erica hated a bag) and paid her half-crown, and the sight of the folded notes in the little back partition all waiting to do their work of rescue, drove her to desperation. Without any warning and without knowing she was going to say it, she asked the man:

"What did you do with the coat you took at Dymchurch?"

There was a moment of complete stillness, and Erica rushed on:

"I don't want to do anything about it. Prosecuting, or anything like that, I mean. But I do want that coat awfully bad. I'll buy it back from you if you still have it. Or if you've pawned it—"

"You're a nice one!" the man burst out. "Coming here to have a job of work done and then accusing a man of battle and blue murder. You be out of here before I lose my temper good and proper and crack you one on the side of the jaw. Impudent little—with your loose tongue. I've a good mind to twist it out of your bloody head, and what's more I—"

The woman pushed him aside and stood over Erica, tall and intimidating.

What makes you think my man took a coat?"

"The coat he had when Jake, the lorry-driver, gave him a lift a week last Tuesday was taken from a car at Dymchurch. We know that." She hoped the "we" sounded well. And she hoped she didn't sound as doubtful as she felt. They were both very innocent and indignant-looking. "But it isn't a matter of making a case. We only want the coat back. I'll give you a pound for it," she added, as they were about to break in on her again.

She saw their eyes change. And in spite of her predicament a great relief flooded her. The man was *the* man. They knew what coat she was talking about.

"And if you've pawned it, I'll give you ten shillings to tell me where."

"What do you get out of this?" the woman said. "What do *you* want with a man's coat?"

"I didn't say anything about it being a man's." Triumph ran through her like an electric shock.

"Oh, never mind!" Queenie dismissed with rough impatience any further pretense. "What is it to you?"

If she mentioned murder they would both panic, and deny with their last breath any knowledge of the coat. She knew well, thanks to her father's monologues, the petty offender's horror of major crime. They would go to almost any lengths to avoid being mixed up, even remotely, in a capital charge.

"It's to get Hart out of trouble," she said. "He shouldn't have left the car unattended. The owner is coming back tomorrow, and if the coat isn't found by then Hart will lose his job."

"Who's Art?" asked the woman. "Your brother?"

"No. Our chauffeur."

"Chauffeur!" Harry gave a high skirl of laughter that

had little amusement in it. "That's a good one. I suppose you have two Rolls Royces and five Bentleys." His little red eyes ran over her worn and outgrown clothes.

"No. Just a Lanchester and my old Morris." As their disbelief penetrated: "My name is Erica Burgoyne. My father is Chief Constable."

"Ye'? My name is John D. Rockfeller, and my father was the Duke of Wellington."

Erica whipped up her short tweed skirt, gripped the elastic waistband of the gym knickers she wore summer and winter, and pushed the inner side of it towards him on an extended thumb.

"Can you read?" she said.

"Erica M. Burgoyne," read the astonished man, in red on a Cash's label.

"It's a great mistake to be too skeptical," she said, letting the elastic snap back into place.

"So you're doing it for a chauffeur, eh?" Harry leered at her, trying to get back his lost ground. "You're very concerned about a chauffeur, aren't you?"

"I'm desperately in love with him," Erica said, in the tone in which one says: "And a box of matches, please." At school theatricals Erica had always had charge of the curtains.

But it passed. Their minds were too full of speculation to be concerned with emotion.

"How much?" said the woman.

"For the coat?"

"No. For telling you where to find it."

"I told you, I'll give you ten shillings."

"Not enough."

"But how do I know you'll tell me the truth?"

"How do we know you're telling the truth?"

"All right, I'll give you a pound. I shall still have to buy it from the pawnshop, you know."

"It isn't in a pawnshop," the man said. "I sold it to a stone-breaker."

"W-h-a-t!" cried Erica in a despairing wail. "Do I have to begin looking for someone else?"

"Oh, no need to look, no need at all. You hand over the cash, and I'll tell you where to find the bloke."

Erica took out a pound note and showed it to him. "Well?"

"He's working at the Five Wents cross-road, Paddock Wood way. And if he ain't there, he lives in a cottage in Capel. Near the church."

Erica held out the note. But the woman had seen the contents of the purse.

"Wait, Harry! She'll pay more." She moved between Erica and the path through the wood.

"I won't give you a penny more," Erica said incisively. Indignation overcame her awareness of the black pool, the silence, and her dislike of woods. "That's cheating."

The woman grabbed at her purse; but Erica had played lacrosse for her school only last winter. Queenie's eager hand, to her great astonishment, met not the purse but Erica's other arm, and came up and hit her own face with surprising violence. And Erica was around her stately bulk and running across the clearing, as she had swerved and run, half-bored, half-pleased, through many winter afternoons.

She heard them come after her, and wondered what they would do to her if they caught up with her. She wasn't afraid of the woman, but the man was small and light, and for all his drinking might be speedy. And he knew the path. In the shade of the trees, after the bright sunlight, she could hardly see a path at all. She wished she had said that someone was waiting for her in the car. It would have been—

Her foot caught in a root, and she rolled over and over.

She heard him coming thudding down the soft path, and as she sat up his face appeared, as it were swimming toward her, above the undergrowth. In a few seconds he would be on her. She had fallen heavily because she was still clutching something in either hand. She looked to see what she was holding. In one hand was the china figure; in the other her purse and—the whistle.

The whistle! She put it to her mouth and blew a sort of tattoo. Long and short, like a code. A signal.

At the sound the man stopped, only a few yards from her, doubtfully.

"Hart!" she called with all the force of her very good lungs. "Hart!" And whistled again.

"All right," said the man, "all right! you can have your—Hart. Some day I'll tell your pa what's going on around his house. And I'll bet you pay me more than a few quid then, me lady!"

"Good-bye," said Erica. "Thank your wife from me for the whistle."

14

"AND OF COURSE, WHAT *YOU* WANT, INSPECTOR, IS A rest. A little relaxation." The Chief Constable heaved himself into his raincoat. "Overworking yourself disgracefully. That never got a man anywhere. Except into his grave. Here it is Friday, and I dare swear you haven't had a night's sleep or a proper meal this week. Ridiculous! Mustn't take the thing to heart like that. Criminals have escaped before and will escape again."

"Not from me."

"Overdue, then. That's all I can say. Very overdue. Everyone makes mistakes. Who was to think a door in a bedroom was a fire-escape, anyhow?"

"I should have looked in the cupboards."

"Oh, my dear good sir—!"

"The first one opened towards me, so that I could see inside. And by the time he came to the second he had lulled me into—"

"I told you you were losing your sense of proportion! If you don't get away for a little, you'll be seeing cupboards everywhere. You'll be what your Sergeant

Williams calls 'falling down on the job.' You are coming
back to dinner with me. You needn't 'but' me! It's only
twenty miles."

"But meanwhile something may—"

"We have a telephone. Erica said I was to bring you.
Said something about ordering ices specially. You fond
of ices? Anyhow, she said she had something to show
you."

"Puppies?" Grant smiled.

"Don't know. Probably. Never a moment in the
year, it seems to me, when there isn't a litter of sort at
Steynes. Here is your excellent substitute. Good evening, Sergeant."

"Good evening, sir," said Williams, rosily pink from
his high tea.

"I'm taking Inspector Grant home to dinner with
me."

"Very glad, sir. It'll do the Inspector good to eat a
proper meal."

"That's my telephone number, in case you want
him."

Grant's smile broadened as he watched the spirit that
won the empire in full blast. He was very tired. The
week had been a long purgatory. The thought of sitting
down to a meal in a quiet room among leisured people
was like regaining some happier sphere of existence
that he had known a long time ago and half-forgotten
about. Automatically he put together the papers on the
desk.

"To quote one of Sergeant Williams's favorite say-
ings: 'As a detective I'm a grand farmer.' Thank you,
I'd like to come to dinner. Kind of Miss Erica to think
of me." He reached for his hat.

"Thinks a lot of you, Erica. Not impressionable as a
rule. But you are the big chief, it seems."

"I have a picturesque rival, I'm afraid."

"Oh, yes. Olympia. I remember. I don't know much
about bringing up children, you know, Grant," he said
as they went out to the car. "Erica's my only one. Her

mother died when she was born, and I made her a sort of companion instead of letting her grow up in the nursery. Her old nurse and I were always having words about it. Great stickler for the *comme il faut* and all that, Nannie. Then she went to school. Must find your own level, that's all education is: learning to deal with people. She didn't like it, but she stuck it. A good plucked 'un, she is."

"I think she is a charming child," Grant said heartily, answering the "justifying" tone and the Colonel's worried look.

"That's just it, Grant, that's just it! She isn't a child any longer. She should be coming out. Going to dances. Staying with her aunts in town and meeting people. But she doesn't want to. Just stays at home and runs wild. Doesn't care for clothes or pretties or any of the things she should care about at her age. She's seventeen, you know. It worries me. She's taken to gadding about all over the place in that little car of hers. I don't know where she has been half the time. Not that she doesn't tell me if I ask. Always a truthful child. But it worries me."

"I don't think it need, sir. She'll make her own happiness. You'll see. It's rare to meet anyone of that age who has so sure a knowledge of what she wants."

"Hrrmp!" said the Colonel. "And gets it! George will be there for dinner," he added. "George Meir. Cousin of my wife's. Perhaps you know him? Nerve specialist."

"I know him well by reputation, but I've never met him."

"That's Erica's doing. Nice fellow, George, but a bit of a bore. Don't understand what he's talking about half the time. Reactions, and things. But Erica seems to understand the lingo. Good shot, though: George. Nice fellow!"

Sir George was a nice fellow. Grant liked him at sight, and noticing his narrow cheekbones, felt that some other attribute in him must weigh very strongly with Erica to overcome his physical characteristics. He was certainly a pleasant person, with neither the slight flamboyance nor the condescension so common in Wimpole Street. That he could commiserate with Grant on his non-success without making Grant want to hit him, was a test of his worth. Grant, in fact, turned to him in his sore state, as to someone who would understand. This was a man to whom human failure must be a very ordinary affair.

Colonel Burgoyne had forbidden mention of the Clay affair during dinner, but he might as well have bidden the tides cease. They were all talking Tisdall, Colonel included, before the fish had disappeared. All but Erica, who sat at the end of the table in her demure school-supper white dress, listening quietly. She had powdered her nose, but looked no more grown up than she did by day.

"We never picked up his trail at all," Grant said in answer to a question of Meir. "He just disappeared from the moment he left the hotel. Oh, there were dozens of accounts of men like him, of course. But they all led to nothing. We don't know a thing more than we did last Monday. He might have been sleeping out, the first three nights. But you know what last night was like. Torrents. Not even an animal could have stayed out in it. He must have found shelter somewhere, if he's still alive. It wasn't local, the storm. There are floods from here to the Tyne. And yet another whole day has gone past and not a hint of him."

"No chance of his escaping by sea?"

"Not likely. Curiously enough, not one criminal in a thousand escapes that way."

"So much for our island race!" laughed Meir. "The sea's the last thing they think of. You know, Inspector, I don't know if you know it, but you have made the man very vivid in the half-hour we've been talking. And there's something else you've made clear, I think; something you probably are not aware of yourself."

"What is that?"

"You were surprised in your heart of hearts that he had done it. Perhaps even sorry. You hadn't believed it."

"Yes, I think that's true. You'd have been sorry yourself, Sir George," Grant grinned. "He's very plausible. And he stuck to truth as far as it served him. As I told you, we've checked his statement from beginning to end. It's true as far as it can be checked. But that thin story about stealing the car! And losing his coat—the all-important coat!"

"Curiously enough, I don't think the stealing episode is as incredible as it sounds. His main thought for the past few weeks had been escape. Escape from the disgrace of his spent fortune, from the crowd (whom he seems to have begun to value at their proper worth), from the necessity of earning his living again (tramping was just as mad a notion, in the case of a boy with influential connections, as stealing a car: the escape motif again), and latterly escape from the equivocal situation at the cottage. He must have looked forward, you know, with subconscious dread to the leavetaking that was due in a day or two. He was in a highly emotional condition due to his self-disgust and self-questioning (at bottom what he wanted to escape from was himself). At a moment of low vitality (six in the morning) he is presented with the means of physical escape. A deserted country-side and abandoned car. He is possessed for the time being. When he recovers he is horrified, just as he says. He turns the car without having to think twice, and comes back at the best speed he can make. To his dying day he'll never understand what made him steal the car."

"Stealing will pretty soon not be a crime at all, what with all you specialists," the Colonel remarked with a sort of tart resignation.

"Not a bad theory, sir," Grant said to Meir. "Can you make the thin tale about the coat thicker too?"

"Truth is often terribly thin, don't you think?"

"Are you taking the view that the man may be innocent?"

"I had thought of it."

"Why?"

"I have an excellent opinion of your judgment."

"*My* judgment?"

"Yes. You were surprised the man had done it. That means that your first impression was clouded by circumstantial evidence."

"In fact, I'm logical as well as imaginative. Mercifully, since I'm a police officer. The evidence may be circumstantial but it is very satisfying and neat."

"Much too neat, don't you feel?"

"Lord Edward said that. But no policeman feels that evidence is too neat, Sir George."

"Poor Champneis!" the Colonel said. "Dreadful for him. Very devoted they were, I'm told. A nice fellow. Didn't know him, but knew the family in my young days. Nice people. Dreadful for them!"

"I traveled up from Dover with him on Thursday," Meir said. "I had come over from Calais—I've just come back from a medical conference in Vienna—and he joined the boat train with the usual Champneis lordliness at Dover. He seemed very happy to be back. Showed me some topazes he had brought from Galeria for his wife. They corresponded every day by telegram, it seemed. I found that more impressive than the topazes, if I must be frank. European telegrams being what they are."

"Just a moment, Sir George. Do you mean that Champneis hadn't come over on the boat from Calais?"

"No, oh, no. He came home by yacht. The *Petronel*. It belongs to his elder brother, but he lent it to Edward for the voyage back from Galeria. A charming little ship. She was lying in the harbor."

"Then when had Lord Edward arrived in Dover?"

"The night before, I believe. Too late to go up to town." He paused and looked quizzically at Grant.

"Neither logic nor imagination will make Edward Champneis suspect."

"I realize that." Grant went on calmly to prise the stone from a peach, an operation he had suspended abruptly at Meir's phrase about Champneis joining the boat train. "It is of no importance. The police habit of checking up."

But his mind was full of surprise and conjecture. Champneis had distinctly let him understand that he had crossed from Calais on Thursday morning. Not in words but by implication. Grant had made some idle remark, something about the accommodation in the new steamers, and Champneis in his reply had implied that he had been on board that morning. Why? Edward Champneis was in Dover on Wednesday night, and was reluctant to have the fact known. Why? In the name of all that was logical, why?

Because an awkward pause had succeeded the revelation of Champneis's presence in England, Grant said lightly, "Miss Erica hasn't produced the puppies, or whatever it was I was to be shown."

To everyone's surprise Erica grew pink. This was so unheard-of a happening that all three men stared.

"It isn't puppies," she said. "It's something you wanted very much. But I'm terribly afraid you're not going to be happy about it."

"It sounds exciting," admitted Grant, wondering what the child had imagined he wanted. He hoped she hadn't brought him something. Hero-worship was all very well, but it was embarrassing to be given something in full view of the multitude. "Where is it?"

"It's in a parcel up in my room. I thought I'd wait till you had finished your port."

"Is it something you can bring into a dining-room?" her father asked.

"Oh, yes."

"Then Burt will fetch it."

"Oh, no!" she cried, arresting her father's hand on the bell. "I'll get it. I shan't be a minute."

She came back carrying a large brown-paper parcel, which her father said looked like a Salvation Army gift day. She unwrapped it and produced a man's coat, of a grayish black.

"That is the coat you wanted," she said. "But it has all its buttons."

Grant took the coat automatically, and examined it.

"Where in Heaven's name did you get that, Erica?" her father asked, astonished.

"I bought it for ten shillings from a stone-breaker at Paddock Wood. He gave a tramp five shillings for it, and thought it such a bargain that he didn't want to part with it. I had to have cold tea with him, and listen to what the Border Regiment did on the first of July, and see the bullet scar on his shin, before he would give up the coat. I was afraid to go away and leave him with it in case he sold it to someone else, or I couldn't find him again."

"What makes you think this is Tisdall's coat?" Grant asked.

"This," she said, and showed the cigarette burn. "He told me to look for that."

"Who did?"

"Mr. Tisdall!"

"Who?" said all three men at once.

"I met him by accident on Wednesday. And since then I've been searching for the coat. But it was great luck coming across it."

"You met him! Where?"

"In a lane near Mallingford."

"And you didn't report it?" Grant's voice was stern.

"No." Hers quavered just a little, and then went on equably. "You see, I didn't believe he had done it. And I really do like you a lot. I thought it would be better for you if he could be proved innocent before he was really arrested. Then you wouldn't have to set him free again. The papers would be awful about that."

There was a stunned silence for a moment.

Then Grant said, "And on Wednesday Tisdall told

you to look for this." He held forward the burned piece, while the others crowded from their places to inspect.

"No sign of a replaced button," Meir observed. "Do you think it's the coat?"

"It may be. We can't try it on Tisdall, but perhaps Mrs. Pitts may be able to identify it."

"But—but," stammered the Colonel—"if it is the coat do you realize what it means?"

"Completely. It means beginning all over again."

His tired eyes, cold with disappointment, met Erica's kind gray ones, but he refused their sympathy. It was too early to think of Erica as his possible savior. At the moment she was just someone who had thrown a wrench into the machinery.

"I shall have to get back," he said. "May I use your telephone?"

15

MRS. PITTS IDENTIFIED THE COAT. SHE HAD DRIED IT AT the kitchen fire one day when a thermos bottle of hot water had leaked on it. She had noticed the cigarette burn then.

Sergeant Williams, interviewing the farmer who had identified Tisdall's car, found that he was color blind.

The truth stuck out with painful clarity. Tisdall had really lost his coat from the car on Tuesday. He had really driven away from the beach. He had not murdered Christine Clay.

By eleven that Friday evening Grant was faced with the fact that they were just where they were a week previously, when he had cancelled a theater seat and come down to Westover. Worse still, they had hounded a man into flight and hiding, and they had wasted seven days on a dud investigation while the man they wanted made his escape.

Grant's mind was a welter of broken ends and unrelated facts.

Harmer. He came into the picture now, didn't he? They had checked his story as far as it went. He really had made inquiries from the owner of the cherry orchard, and from the post office at Liddlestone at the times he said. But after that, what? After that no one knew anything about his movements until he walked into the cottage at Medley, some time after eight the next morning.

There was—incredibly!—Edward Champneis, who had brought back topazes for his wife, but who, for some reason, was unwilling that his movements on that Wednesday night should be investigated. There could be no other reason for his desire to make Grant believe that he had arrived in England on Thursday morning. He had not come to England secretly. If you want to arrive secretly in a country, arriving in a populous harbor by yacht is not the way to do it. Harbor-master and customs' officials are a constitutionally inquisitive race. Therefore it was not the fact of his arrival that he wanted to hide, but the way in which he had occupied his time since. The more Grant thought about it, the queerer it became. Champneis was at Dover on Wednesday night. At six on Thursday morning his well-loved wife had met her death. And Champneis did not want his movements investigated. Very queer!

There was, too, the "shilling for candles." That, which had first caught his interest and had been put aside in favor of more obvious lines of inquiry, that would have to be looked into.

On Saturday morning the newspapers, beginning to be bored with a four-day-old man hunt, carried the glad news that the hunted man was innocent. "New information having come to police." It was confidently expected that Tisdall would present himself before nightfall, and in that hope reporters and photographers lingered around the County police station in Westover; with more optimism than logic, it would seem, since Tisdall was just as likely to present himself at a station miles away.

But Tisdall presented himself nowhere.

This caused a slight stirring of surprise in Grant's busy mind when he had a moment to remember Tisdall; but that was not often. He wondered why Tisdall hadn't enough sense to come in out of the wet. It had rained again on Friday night and it had been blowing a north-easter and raining all Saturday. One would have thought he would have been glad to see a police station. He was not being sheltered by any of his old friends, that was certain. They had all been shadowed very efficiently during the four days that he was "wanted." Grant concluded that Tisdall had not yet seen a newspaper, and dismissed the thing from his mind.

He had set the official machinery moving to discover the whereabouts of Christine Clay's brother; he had started a train of inquiries which had the object of proving that Jason Harmer had once had a dark coat which he had lately discarded and which had a missing button. And he himself took on the investigation of Lord Edward Champneis. He noticed with his usual self-awareness that he had no intention of going to Champneis and asking for an account of his movements on Wednesday night. It would be highly embarrassing, for one thing, if Champneis proved that he had slept peacefully in his bunk all night. Or at the Lord Warden. Or otherwise had a perfect alibi. For another—oh, well, there was not getting away from the fact; one didn't demand information from the son of a ducal house as one demanded it from a coster. A rotten world, no doubt, but one must conform.

Grant learned that the *Petronel* had gone around to Cowes, where her owner, Giles Champneis, would live in her for Cowes' week. On Sunday morning, therefore, Grant flew down to Gosport, and got a boat across the glittering Spithead to the island. What had been a white flurry of rain-whipped water yesterday was now a Mediterranean sea of the most beguiling blue. The English summer was being true to form.

Grant flung the Sunday papers on the seat beside him

and prepared to enjoy the crossing. And then his eye
caught the *Sunday Newsreel's* heading: The Truth
About Clay's Early Life. And once more the case drew
him into it. On the previous Sabbath, the *Sunday Wire*
had had as its chief "middle" a tear-compelling article
by that prince of newspaper men, Jammy Hopkins. The
article had consisted of an interview with a Nottingham
lace-hand, Miss Helen Cozens, who had, it appeared,
been a contemporary of Christine Clay's in the factory.
It had dealt touchingly with Chris's devotion to her
family, her sunny disposition, her excellent work, the
number of times Miss Helen Cozens had helped her in
one way or another, and it had finished with a real
Hopkins touch of get-togetherness. It had been the fate
of one of these two friends, he pointed out, to climb to
the stars, to give pleasure to millions, to irradiate the
world. But there were other fates as glowing if less
spectacular; and Helen Cozens, in her little two-room
home, looking after a delicate mother, had had a
destiny no less wonderful, no less worthy of the world's
homage. It was a good article, and Jammy had been
pleased with it.

Now the *Sunday Newsreel* appeared with an interview of its own. And it caused Grant the only smile he
had enjoyed that week. Meg Hindler was the lady
interviewed. Once a factory hand but now the mother
of eight. And she wanted to know what the hell that
God-damned old maid Nell Cozens thought she was
talking about, and she hoped she might be struck down
for her lies, and if her mother drank the lord knew it
was no wonder with a nagging dyspeptic piece of acid
like her daughter around, and everyone knew that
Christina Gotobed was out of the factory and away
from the town long before Nell Cozens put her crooked
nose into the place at all.

It was not put just like that, but to anyone reading
between the lines it was perfectly clear.

Meg really had known Christine. She was a quiet girl,
she said, always trying to better herself. Not very

popular with her contemporaries. Her father was dead and she lived with her mother and brother in a three-room tenement house. The brother was older, and was the mother's favorite. When Chris was seventeen the mother had died, and the family had disappeared from Nottingham. They did not belong to the town and had had no roots there, and no one had regretted them when they went. Least of all people who hadn't come into the town until years afterward.

Grant wondered how Jammy would enjoy being taken for a ride by the imaginative Nell. So the elder brother had been the mother's favorite, had he? Grant wondered how much that meant. A shilling for candles. What family row had left such a mark that she should immortalize it in her will? Oh, well! Reporters thought they were clever, but the Yard had ways and means that were not open to the Press, however powerful. By the time he got back tonight, Christine Clay's early life would be on his desk in full detail. He discarded the *Wire* and turned to the other papers in the bundle. The *Sunday Telegraph* had a symposium—a very dignified and conveniently cheap method of filling a page. Everyone from the Archbishop of Canterbury to Jason Harmer had given their personal view of Christine Clay and her influence on her art. (The *Sunday Telegraph* liked influence and art. Even boxers never described punches to it: they explained their art.) The silly little paragraphs were all conventional, except Jason's, which had a violent sincerity beneath its sickly phrases. Marta Hallard was graceful about Clay's genius, and for once omitted to condone her lowly origin. The heir to a European throne extolled her beauty. A flying ace her courage. An ambassador her wit. It must have cost the *Telegraph* something in telephones.

Grant turned to the *Courier,* and found Miss Lydia Keats being informative all over the middle pages on the signs of the Zodiac. Lydia's stock had dropped a little in her own circles during the last week. It was felt that if she had foreseen the Clay end so clearly it was a little weak of her to overlook a small detail like murder. But in the public eye she was booming. There was no fraud about Lydia. She had stated in public, many months ago, what the stars foretold for Christine Clay, and the stars were right. And if there is anything the public loves it is a prophecy come true. They pushed their shuddering spines more firmly into the cushions and asked for more. And Lydia was giving it to them. In small type at the end of the article appeared the information that, thanks to the *Courier's* generosity, its readers might obtain horoscopes from the infallible Miss Keats at the cost of one shilling, coupon on the back page.

Grant tucked the smaller illustrateds under his arm, and prepared to get off the boat. He watched a sailor twisting a hawser around a bollard and wished that he had chosen a profession that dealt with things and not with people.

The *Petronel* was moored in the roads. Grant engaged a boatman and was rowed out to her. An elderly deckhand pushed a pipe into a pocket and prepared to receive them. Grant asked if Lord Giles were on board, happily aware that he was in Buckinghamshire. On hearing that he was not expected for a week, Grant looked suitably disappointed and asked if he might come on board: he had hoped that Giles would show him the craft. The man was pleased and garulous. He was alone on board and had been very bored. It would be a pleasant diversion to show the good-looking friend of Lord Giles around the ship, and no doubt there would be a tip forthcoming. He did the honors with a detail that wearied Grant a little, but he was very informative. When Grant remarked on the splendid sleeping accommodation, the man said that Lord Giles wasn't one for ever sleeping ashore if he could help it. Never so happy as on salt water, Lord Giles wasn't.

"Lord Edward isn't so fond of it," Grant remarked, and the man chuckled.

"No, not Lord Edward, he wasn't. He was ashore the

minute the dinghy could be swung out or a hawser slapped on a quay."

"I suppose he stayed with the Beechers the night you made Dover?"

The deckhand didn't rightly know where he slept. All he knew was that he didn't sleep on board. In fact, they hadn't seen him again. His hand luggage had been sent to the boat train and the rest had been sent to town after him. Because of the sad thing that happened to his lady, that was. Had Grant ever seen her? A film actress, she was. Very good, too. It was dreadful wasn't it, the things that happened in good families nowadays. Even murders. Changed days indeed.

"Oh, I don't know," Grant said. "The older families of England made a pastime of murder if my history books told the truth."

The man was so pleased with his tip that he offered to make cocoa for the visitor, but Grant wanted to get ashore so that he could talk to the Yard. On the way back he wondered just how Champneis had spent that night ashore. The most likely explanation was that he had stayed with friends. But if he had stayed with friends, why the desire to avoid attention? The more Grant thought of it the more out-of-character it was in the man to want to hide anything. Edward Champneis was a person who did what he wanted to in broad daylight and cared not a straw for opinions or consequences. Grant found it difficult to associate him in his mind with any furtive activity whatever. And that very thought led to a logical and rather staggering sequel. It was no petty thing that Champneis had to hide. Nothing but some matter of vast importance would have driven Champneis to prevarication. Grant could dismiss, therefore, any thought of a light love affair. Champneis had, in any case, a reputation that bordered on the austere. And if one dismissed a love affair what was left? What possible activity could a man of Champneis's stamp want to keep secret? Except murder!

Murder was just possible. If that calm security were once shattered, who knew what might flame out? He was a man who would both give and demand fidelity—and be unforgiving to the faithless. Supposing—! There was Harmer. Christine Clay's colleagues may have doubted that she and Harmer were lovers, but the *beau monde,* unused to the partnership of work, had no doubt. Had Champneis come to believe that? His and Christine's love for each other was an equable affair, but his pride would be a very real thing, fragile and passionate. Had he—? That was an idea! Had he driven over to the cottage that night? He was, after all, the only person who knew where she was: nearly all her telegrams had been to him. He was in Dover, and she was only an hour away. What more natural than that he should have motored over to surprise her? And if so—

A picture swam into Grant's mind. The cottage in the summer dark, the lit windows open to the night, so that every word, every movement almost, is audible outside. And in the rose-tangled mass of the garden a man standing, arrested by the voices. He stands there, quite silent, quite still, watching. Presently the lights go out. And in a little while the figure in the garden moves away. Where? To brood on his home-coming; on his cuckold state? To tramp the downs till morning? To see her come to the beach, unexpected, alone? To—

Grant shook himself and picked up the telephone receiver.

"Edward Champneis didn't spend the night of Wednesday on board," he said, when he had been connected. "I want to know where he did spend it. And don't forget, discretion is the better part. You may find that he spent it with the Warden of the Cinque Ports, or something equally orthodox, but I'll be surprised if he did. It would be a good idea if someone got friendly with his valet and went through his wardrobe for a dark coat. You know the strongest card we have is that no one outside the force knows about that button. The fact that we asked for any discarded coat that was found to be brought in doesn't convey much to anyone. The chances are ten to one, I think, that the coat is still with its owner. Keeping a coat, even with a missing button, is less conspicuous than getting rid of one. And that S.O.S. for the coat was only a police circular, anyhow, not a public appeal. So inspect the Champneis wardrobe. . . . No, I haven't got anything on him. . . . Yes, I know it is mad. But I'm not taking any more chances in this case. Only be discreet, for Heaven's sake. I'm in bad enough odor as it is. What is the news? Has Tisdall turned up? . . . Oh, well, I expect he will by night. He might give the Press a break. They're waiting breathless for him. How is the Clay dossier coming? . . . Oh. Has Vine come back from interviewing the dresser—what's-her-name? Bundle—yet? No? All right, I'm coming straight back to town."

As Grant hung up he shut his mind quickly on the thought that tried to jump in. Of *course* Tisdall was all right. What could happen to an adult in the English countryside in summer? Of course he was all right.

16

THE DOSSIER WAS FILLING UP NICELY. HENRY GOTOBED had been an estate carpenter near Long Eaton, and had married a laundry maid at the "big house." He had been killed in a threshing-mill accident, and—partly because his father and grandfather had been estate servants, partly because she was not strong enough to work—the widow had been given a small pension. The cottage at Long Eaton having to be vacated, she had brought her two children to Nottingham, where there was better hope of ultimate employment for them. The girl was then twelve and the boy fourteen. It had been curiously difficult to obtain information about them after that. Information other than the bare official record, that is to say. In the country, changes were slow, interests circumscribed, and memories long. But in the fluctuating life of the town, where a family stayed perhaps six months in a house and moved elsewhere, interest was superficial where it existed at all.

Meg Hindler, the *Newsreel's* protégée, had proved

the only real help. She was an enormous, hearty, loud-voiced, good-natured woman, who cuffed her numerous brood with one hand and caressed with the other. She was still suffering a little from a Nell-Cozens phobia, but when she could be kept off the Cozens tack she was genuinely informative. She remembered the family not because there was anything memorable about them, but because she had lived with her own family across the landing from them, and had worked in the same factory as Chris, so that they sometimes came home together. She had liked Chris Gotobed in a mild way; didn't approve of her stuck-up ideas, of course; if you had to earn your living by working in a factory, then you had to earn your living by working in a factory, and why make a fuss about it? Not that Chris made a fuss, but she had a way of shaking the dust of the factory off her as if it was dirt. And she wore a hat always; a quite unnecessary piece of affectation. She had adored her mother, but her mother couldn't see anything in life but Herbert. A nasty piece of work, if ever there was one, Herbert. As slimy, sneaking, cadging, self-satisfied a piece of human trash as you'd meet in a month of Sundays. But Mrs. Gotobed thought he was the cat's whiskers. He was always making it difficult for Chris. Chris had once talked her mother into letting her have dancing lessons—though what you wanted dancing lessons for, Meg couldn't think: you'd only to watch the others hopping around for a little and you'd got the general idea: after that it was only practice—but when Herbert had heard about it he had quickly put a stop to anything like that. They couldn't afford it, he said—they never could afford anything unless Herbert wanted it—and besides, dancing was a light thing, and the Lord wouldn't approve. Herbert always knew what the Lord would like. He not only stopped the dancing-lesson idea but he found some way of getting the money Chris had saved and that she had hoped her mother would make up to the required amount. He had pointed out how selfish it was of Chris to save money for her own ends when their mother was so poorly. He talked such a lot about their mother's bad health that Mrs. Gotobed began to feel very poorly indeed, and took to her bed. And Herbert helped eat the delicacies that Chris bought. And Herbert went with his mother for four days to Skegness because Chris couldn't leave the factory and it just happened that this was one of the numerous occasions when Herbert was without a job.

Yes, Meg had been helpful. She did not know what had become of the family, of course. Chris had left Nottingham the day after her mother's funeral, and because the rent was paid up to the end of the week Herbert had stayed on alone in the house for several days after. Meg remembered that because he had had one of his "meetings" in the house—he was always having meetings where he could hear the sound of his own voice—and the neighbors had to complain about the noise of the singing. As if there wasn't enough row always going on in a tenement without adding meetings to the din! What kind of meetings? Well, as far as she could remember he had begun with political harangues, but very soon took to religion; because it doesn't matter how you rave at your audience, when it's religion they don't throw things. She personally didn't think it mattered to him what he was talking about as long as he was the person who was talking. She never knew anyone who had a better opinion of himself with less cause than Herbert Gotobed.

No, she didn't know where Chris had gone, or whether Herbert knew her whereabouts. Knowing Herbert, she thought that Chris had probably gone without saying goodbye. She hadn't said goodbye to anyone, if it came to that. Meg's younger brother, Sydney—the one that was now in Australia—had had a fancy for her, but she didn't give him any encouragement. Didn't have any beau, Chris didn't. Funny, wasn't it, that she should have seen Christine Clay on the screen often and often, and never recognized Chris Gotobed. She had changed a lot, that she had. She'd heard that they made you over in Hollywood. Perhaps that was it. And of course it was a long time between seventeen and thirty. Look what a few years had done to her, come to think of it.

And Meg had laughed her ample laugh and revolved her ample figure for the detective's inspection, and had given him a cup of stewed tea and Rich Mixed Biscuits.

But the detective—who was the Sanger who had assisted at the non-arrest of Tisdall, and who was also a Clay fan—remembered that even in a city there are communities who have interests as narrow and memories as long as any village dwellers, and so he had come eventually to the little house in a suburb beyond the Trent where Miss Stammers lived with a toy Yorkshire terrier and the wireless. Both terrier and wireless had been given her on her retirement. She would never have had the initiative after thirty years of teaching at Beasley Road Elementary School to acquire either on her own behalf. School had been her life, and school still surrounded her. She remembered Christina Gotobed very clearly indeed. What did Mr. Sanger want to know about her? Not Mr.? A detective? Oh, dear! She did hope that there was nothing serious the matter. It was all a very long time ago, and of course she had not kept in touch with Christina. It was impossible to keep in touch with all one's pupils when one had as many as sixty in a class. But she had been an exceptionally promising child, exceptionally promising.

Sanger had asked if she was unaware that her exceptionally promising pupil was Christine Clay?

"Christine Clay? The film actress you mean? Dear me. Dear me!"

Sanger had thought the expression a little inadequate until he noticed her small eyes grow suddenly large with tears. She took off her pince-nez and wiped them away with a neatly folded square of handkerchief.

"So famous?" she murmured. "Poor child. Poor child."

Sanger reminded her of the reason for Christine's prominence in the news. But she seemed less occupied with the woman's cruel end than with the achievement of the child she had known.

"She was very ambitious, you know," she said. "That is how I remember her so well. She was not like the others: anxious to get away from school and become wage earners. That is what appeals to most elementary children, you know, Mr. Sanger: a weekly wage in their pockets and the means of getting out of their crowded homes. But Christina wanted to go to the secondary school. She actually won a scholarship—a 'free place,' they call it. But her people could not afford to let her take it. She came to me and cried about it. It was the only time I had known her to cry: she was not an emotional child. I asked her mother to come to see me. A pleasant enough woman, but without force of character. I couldn't persuade her. Weak people can be very stubborn. It was a regret in my mind for years, that I had failed. I had great feeling for the child's ambition. I had been very ambitious once myself, and had—had to put my desire aside. I understood what Christina was going through. I lost sight of her when she left school. She went to work in the factory, I remember. They needed the money. There was a brother who was not earning. An unsympathetic character. And the mother's pension was small. But she made her career, after all. Poor child. Poor child!"

Sanger had asked, as he was taking his departure, how it was that she had missed the articles in the newspapers about Christine Clay's childhood.

She never saw Sunday newspapers, she said, and the daily paper was handed on to her a day late by her very kind neighbors, the Timpsons, and at present they were at the seaside, so that she was without news, except for the posters. Not that she missed the papers much. A matter of habit, didn't Mr. Sanger think? After three days without one, the desire to read a newspaper vanished. And really, one was happier without. Very depressing reading they made these days. In her little home she found it difficult to believe in so much violence and hatred.

Sanger had made further inquiries from many people about that unsympathetic character Herbert Gotobed. But hardly anyone remembered him. He had never stayed in a job for more than five months (the five months was his record: in an ironmonger's) and no one had been sorry to see him go. No one knew what had become of him.

But Vine, coming back from interviewing the one-time dresser, Bundle, in South Street, had brought news of him. Yes, Bundle had known there was a brother. The snapping brown eyes in the wizened face had snapped ferociously at the very mention of him. She had only seen him once, and she hoped she never saw him again. He had sent in a note to her lady one night in New York, to her dressing-room. It was the first dressing-room she had ever had to herself, the first show she had been billed in. *Let's Go!* it was. And she was a success. Bundle had dressed her as a chorus girl, along with nine others, but when her lady had gone up in the world she had taken Bundle with her. That's the sort her lady was: never forgot a friend. She had been talking and laughing till the note was brought in. But when she read that she was just like someone who was about to take a spoonful of ice cream and noticed a beetle in it. When he came in she had said, "So *you*'ve turned up!" He said he'd come to warn her that she was bound for perdition, or something. She said, "Come to see what pickings there are, you mean." Bundle had never seen her so angry. She had just taken off her day make-up to put on her stage one, and there wasn't a spark of color anywhere in her face. She had sent Bundle out of the room then, but there had been a grand row. Bundle, standing guard before the door—

there were lots, even then, who thought they would like
to meet her lady—couldn't help hearing some of it. In
the end she had to go in because her lady was going to
be late for her entrance if she didn't. The man had
turned on her for interrupting, but her lady had said
that she would give him in charge if he didn't go. He
had gone then, and had never to her knowledge turned
up again. But he had written. Letters came from him
occasionally—Bundle recognized the writing—and he
always seemed to know where they were, because the
address was the correct one, not a forwarded affair.
Her lady always had acute depression after a letter
had come. Sometimes for two days or more. She
had said once, "Hate is very *lowering,* isn't it, Bundle?" Bundle had never hated anyone except a cop
who was habitually rude to her, but she had hated
him plenty, and she agreed that hate was very weak-
ening. Burned you up inside till there was nothing
left.

And to Bundle's account of Christine's brother was
added the report of the American police. Herbert
Gotobed had entered the States about five years after
his sister. He had worked for a short while as a sort of
house man for a famous Boston divine who had been
taken (in) by his manners and his piety. He had left the
divine under some sort of cloud—the exact nature of
the cloud was doubtful since the divine, either from
Christian charity or more likely from a reluctance to
have his bad judgment made public, had preferred no
charges—and had disappeared from the ken of the
police. It was supposed, however, that he was the man
who, under the name of the Brother of God, had
toured the States in the rôle of prophet, and had been,
it was reported, both an emotional and financial
success. He had been jailed in Kentucky for blasphe-
my, in Texas for fraud, in Missouri for creating a riot, in
Arkansas for his own safety, and in Wyoming for
seduction. In all detentions he had denied any connec-

tion with Herbert Gotobed. He had no name, he said, other than the Brother of God. When the police had pointed out that relation to the deity would not be considered by them an insuperable obstacle to deportation, he had taken the hint and had disappeared. The last that had been heard of him was that he had run a mission in the islands somewhere—Fiji, they thought—and had decamped with the funds to Australia.

"A charming person," Grant said, looking up from the dossier.

"That's our man, sir, never a doubt of it," Williams said.

"He certainly has all the stigmata: greed, enormous conceit, and lack of conscience. I rather hope he is our man. It would be doing the world a good turn to squash that slug. But why did he do it?"

"Hoped for money, perhaps."

"Hardly likely. He must have known only too well how she felt about him."

"I wouldn't put it past him to forge a will, sir."

"No, neither would I. But if he has a forged will, why hasn't he come forward? It will soon be a fortnight since her death. We haven't a thing to go on. We don't even know that he's in England."

"He's in England all right, sir. 'Member what her housekeeper said: that he always knew where she was? Clay had been more than three months in England. You bet he was here too."

"Yes. Yes, that's true. Australia? Let me see." He looked up the New York report again. "That's about two years ago. He'd be difficult to trace there, but if he came to England after Clay he shouldn't be difficult to trace. He can't keep his mouth shut. Anything quite so vocal must be noticeable."

"No letters from him among her things?"

"No, Lord Edward has been through everything. Tell me, Williams, on what provocation, for what imaginable reason, would a Champneis, in your opinion, tell a lie?"

"Noblesse oblige," said Williams promptly.

Grant stared. "Quite right," he said at length. "I hadn't thought of that. Can't imagine what he could have been shielding, though."

17

So the candles weren't the kind you go to bed with, Grant thought, as the car sped along the embankment that Monday afternoon en route for the Temple; they were the kind you put on altars. The Brother of God's tabernacle had been none of your bare mission tents. It had been hung with purple and fine linen and furnished with a shrine of great magnificence. And what had been merely an expression of Herbert's own love of the theatrical had in most cases (Kentucky was an exception) proved good business. A beauty-starved and theatrically-minded people had fallen hard—in hard cash.

Christine's shilling was the measure of her contempt. Her return, perhaps, for all those occasions when Herbert's Lord had seen fit to deny her the small things her soul needed.

In the green subaqueous light of Mr. Erskine's small room beside the plane-tree, Grant put his proposition to the lawyer. They wanted to bring Herbert Gotobed to the surface, and this was the way to do it. It was quite orthodox, so the lawyer needn't mind doing it. Lord Edward had approved.

The lawyer hummed and hawed, not because he had any real objections but because it is a lawyer's business to consider remote contingencies, and a straightforward agreement to anything would be wildly unprofessional. In the end he agreed that it might be done.

Grant said: "Very well, I leave it to you. In tomorrow's papers, please," and went out wondering why the legal mind delighted in manufacturing trouble when there was so much ready-made in the world. There was plenty in poor Grant's mind at the moment. "Surrounded by trouble," as the spaewives said when they told your cards: that's what he was. Monday would soon be over and there was no sign that Robert Tisdall was in the world of men. The first low howl had come from the *Clarion* that morning, and by tomorrow the whole wolf pack would be on him. Where was Robert Tisdall? What were the police doing to find him? To do Grant justice the discomfort in his mind was less for the outcry that was imminent than for the welfare of Tisdall. He had genuinely believed for the last two days that Tisdall's non-appearance was due to lack of knowledge on Tisdall's part. It is not easy to see newspapers when one is on the run. But now doubt like a chill wind played through his thoughts. There was something wrong. Every newspaper poster in every village in England had read: TISDALL INNOCENT. HUNTED MAN INNOCENT. How could he have missed it? In every pub, railway carriage, bus, and house in the country the news had been the favorite subject of conversation. And yet Tisdall was silent. No one had seen him since Erica drove away from him last Wednesday. On Thursday night the whole of England had been swamped by the worst storm for years, and it had rained and blown for two days afterwards. Tisdall had picked up the food left by Erica on Thursday, but not afterwards. The food she left on Friday was still there, a sodden pulp, on Saturday. Grant knew that

Erica had spent all that Saturday scouring the country-
side; she had quartered the country with the efficiency
and persistence of a game dog, every barn, every
shelter of any description, being subjected to search.
Her very sound theory was that shelter he *must* have
had on Thursday night—no human being could have
survived such a storm—and since he had been in that
chalky lane on Thursday morning to pick up the food
she left, then he could not have gone far afield.

But her efforts had come to nothing. Today an
organized gang of amateur searchers had undertaken
the work—the police had no men to spare—but so far
no news had come. And in Grant's mind was growing a
slow fear that he tried with all his self-awareness to beat
down. But it was like a moor fire. You whipped it to
cinder only to see it run under the surface and break
out ahead of you.

News from Dover was slow, too. The investigation
was hampered beyond any but police patience by the
necessity of *(a)* not offending the peerage, and *(b)* not
frightening the bird: the first applying to a possibly
innocent, the second to a possibly guilty. It was all very
complicated. Watching Edward Champneis's calm
face—he had eyebrows which gave a peculiar expression of repose—while he discussed with him the
trapping of Herbert, Grant had several times forcibly
to restrain himself from saying: "Where were you on
Wednesday night?" What would Champneis do? Look
a little puzzled, think a moment, and then say: "The
night I arrived in Dover? I spent it with the So-and-sos
at Such-and-Such." And then realization of what the
question entailed would dawn, and he would look
incredulously at Grant, and Grant would feel the
world's prize fool. More! In Edward Champneis's
presence he felt that it was sheer insult to suggest that
he might have been responsible for his wife's death.
Away from him, that picture of the man in the garden,
watching the lighted house with the open windows,
might swim up in his mind more often than he cared to

admit. But in his presence, any such thought was fantastic. Until his men had accounted—or failed to account—for Champneis's movements that night, any direct inquiry must be shelved.

All he knew so far was that Champneis had stayed in none of the obvious places. The hotels and the family friends had both been drawn blank. The radius was now being extended. At any moment news might come that my lord had slept in a blameless four-poster and the county's best linen sheets, and Grant would be forced to admit that he had been mistaken when he imagined that Lord Edward was deliberately misleading him.

18

ON TUESDAY MORNING WORD CAME FROM COLLINS, THE
man who was investigating Champneis's wardrobe.
Bywood, the valet, had proved "very sticky going," he
reported. He didn't drink and he didn't smoke and
there seemed to be no plane on which Collins could
establish a mutual regard. But every man has his price,
and Bywood's proved to be snuff. A very secret vice, it
was. Lord Edward would dismiss him on the spot if he
suspected such indulgence. (Lord Edward would probably have been highly pleased by anything so eigh-
teenth century.) Collins had procured him "very special
snuff," and had at last got within inspecting distance of
the wardrobe. On his arrival in England—or rather, in
London—Champneis had weeded out his wardrobe.
The weeding out had included two coats, one dark and
one camel-hair. Bywood had given the camel-hair one
to his brother-in-law, a chorus-boy; the other he had
sold to a dealer in London. Collins gave the name and
address of the dealer.

Grant sent an officer down to the dealer, and as the

officer went through the stock the dealer said: "That coat came from Lord Edward Champneis, the Duke of Bude's son. Nice bit of stuff."

It was a nice bit of stuff. And it had all its buttons; with no sign of replacements.

Grant sighed when the news came, not sure whether he was glad or sorry. But he still wanted to know where Champneis had spent the night.

And what the Press wanted to know was where Tisdall was. Every newspaper in Britain wanted to know. The C.I.D. were in worse trouble than they had been for many years. The *Clarion* openly called them murderers, and Grant, trying to get a line on a baffling case, was harassed by the fury of colleagues, the condolences of his friends, a worried Commissioner, and his own growing anxiety. In the middle of the morning Jammy Hopkins rang up to explain away his "middle" in the *Clarion*. It was "all in the way of business," and he knew his good friends at the Yard would understand. Grant was out, and it was Williams at the other end of the telephone. Williams was not in the mood for butter. He relieved his overburdened soul with a gusto which left Hopkins hoping that he had not irretrievably put himself in the wrong with the Yard. "As for hounding people to death," Williams finished, "you know very well that the Press do more hounding in a week than the Yard has since it was founded. And *all* your victims are innocent!"

"Oh, have a heart, Sergeant! You know we've got to deliver the goods. If we don't make it hot and strong, we'll be out on our ear. St. Martin's Crypt, or the Embankment. And you pushing people off the seats. We've got our jobs to keep just as much as—"

The sound of Williams's hang-up was eloquent. It was action and comment compressed into one little monosyllable. Jammy felt hardly used. He had enjoyed writing that article. He had in fact been full of righteous indignation as the scarifying phrases poured forth. When Jammy was writing his tongue came out of its habitual position in his cheek, and emotion flooded him. That the tongue went back when he had finished did not matter; the popular appeal of his article was secure; it was "from the heart"; and his salary went up by leaps and bounds.

But he was a little hurt that all his enemies-on-paper couldn't see just what a jape it was. He flung his hat with a disgusted gesture on to his right eyebrow and went out to lunch.

And less than five minutes away Grant was sitting in a dark corner, a huge cup of black coffee before him, his head propped in his hands. He was "telling it to himself in words of one syllable."

Christine Clay was living in secret. But the murderer knew where she was. That eliminated a lot of people.

Champneis knew.

Jason Harmer knew.

Herbert Gotobed almost certainly knew.

The murderer had worn a coat dark enough to be furnished with a black button and black sewing thread.

Champneis had such a coat, but there was no missing button.

Jason Harmer had no such coat; and had not lately worn any such coat.

No one knew what Herbert Gotobed wore.

The murderer had a motive so strong and of such duration that he could wait for his victim at six of a morning and deliberately drown her.

Champneis had a possible motive.

Jason Harmer had a possible motive if they had been lovers, but there was no proof of that.

Herbert Gotobed had no known motive but had almost certainly hated her.

On points Gotobed won. He knew where his sister was; he had the kind of record that was "headed for murder"; and he had been on bad terms with the victim.

Oh, well! By tomorrow Gotobed might have declared himself. Meanwhile he would drug himself with black coffee and try to keep his mind off the Press.

As he raised the cup to his lips, his eyes lighted on a man in the opposite corner. The man's cup was half empty, and he was watching Grant with amused and friendly eyes.

Grant smiled, and hit first. "Hiding that famous profile from the public gaze? Why don't you give your fans a break?"

"It's all break for them. A fan can't be wrong. You're being given a hell of a time, aren't you? What do they think the police are? Clairvoyants?"

Grant rolled the honey on his tongue and swallowed it.

"Some day," Owen Hughes said, "someone is going to screw Jammy Hopkins's head off his blasted shoulders. If my face wasn't insured for the sum total of the world's gold, I'd do it myself. He once said I was 'every girl's dream'!"

"And aren't you?"

"Have you seen my cottage lately?"

"No. I saw the photograph of the wreck in the paper one day."

"I don't mind telling you I wept when I got out of the car and saw it. I'd like to broadcast that photograph to the ends of the earth as a sample of what publicity can do. Fifty years ago a few people might have come a few miles to look at the place, and then gone home satisfied. They came in charabanc loads to see Briars. My lawyer tried to stop the running of the 'trips,' but there was nothing he could do. The County Police refused to keep a man there after the first few days. About ten thousand people have come in the last fortnight, and every one of the ten thousand has peered through the windows, stood on the plants and taken away a souvenir. There is hardly a scrap of hedge left—it used to be twelve feet high, a mass of roses— and the garden is a wilderness of trampled mud. I was rather attached to that garden. I didn't croon to the pansies, exactly, but I got a lot of kick out of planting things people gave me, and seeing them come up. Not a vestige left."

"Rotten luck! And no redress. Maddening for you. Perhaps by next year the plants will have taken heart again."

"Oh, I'm selling the place. It's haunted. Had you ever met Clay? No? She was grand. They don't make that kind in pairs."

"Do you know of anyone who would be likely to want to murder her, by any chance?"

Hughes smiled one of the smiles which made his fans grip the arms of their cinema seats. "I know lots who would gladly have murdered her on the spot. But only on the spot. The minute you cooled off, you'd cheerfully die for her. It's most unlikely death for Chris—the one that happened to her. Did you know that Lydia Keats prophesied it from her horoscope? She's a marvel, Lydia. She should have been drowned when she was a pup, but she really is a marvel. I sent her Marie Dacre's year, day, and minute of birth from Hollywood. Marie made me swear an oath before she divulged the awful truth of the year. Lydia hadn't the faintest notion whose horoscope she was doing, and it was marvelously accurate. She'd be a wow in Hollywood."

"She seems to be heading that way," Grant said dryly. "Do you like the place?"

"Oh, yes. It's restful." As Grant raised his eyebrows: "There are so many pebbles on the beach that you're practically anonymous."

"I thought they ran rubbernecking tours for Midwest fans."

"Oh, yes, they run motor-coaches down your street, but they don't tramp your flowers into the ground."

"If you were murdered they might."

"Not they. Murders are ten cents the dozen. Well, I must get along. Good luck. And God bless you. You've done me a power of good, so help me you have."

"I?"

"You've brought to my notice one profession that is worse than my own." He dropped some money on the table and picked up his hat. "They pray for judges on Sundays, but never a word for the police!"

He adjusted the hat at the angle which after much testing had been found by camera-men to be the most becoming, and strolled out, leaving Grant vaguely comforted.

19

THE PERSON WHO WASN'T COMFORTED WAS JAMMY. THE
buoyant, the resilient, the hard-boiled but bouncing
Jammy. He had eaten at his favorite pub (black coffee
might be all very well for worried police officials and
actors who had to think of their figure, but Jammy dealt
only in other people's worries and remembered his
figure only when his tailor measured him) and nothing
during lunch had been right. The beef had been a shade
too "done," the beer had been a shade too warm, the
waiter had had hiccoughs, the potatoes were soapy, the
cabinet pudding had tasted of baking soda, and they
were out of his usual cigarettes. And so his feeling of
being ill-used and misunderstood, instead of being
charmed away by food and drink, had grown into an
exasperation with the world in general. He looked
sourly over his glass at his colleagues and contemporaries, laughing and talking over the coarse white cloths,
and they, unused to a glower on his brow, paused in
their traffic to tease him.

"What is it, Jammy? Pyorrhœa?"

"No. He's practicing to be a dictator. You begin with the expression."

"No you don't," said a third. "You begin with the hair."

"And an arm movement. Arms are very important. Look at Napoleon. Never been more than a corporal if he hadn't thought up that arm-on-chest business. Pregnant, you know."

"If it's pregnant Jammy is, he'd better have the idea in the office, not here. I don't think the child's going to be a pleasant sight."

Jammy consigned them all to perdition, and went out to find a tobacconist who kept his brand of cigarettes. What did the Yard want to take it like that for? Everyone knew that what you wrote in a paper was just eye-wash. When it wasn't bilgewater. If you stopped being dramatic over little tuppenny no-account things, people might begin to suspect that they were no-account, and then they'd stop buying papers. And where would the Press barons, and Jammy, and a lot of innocent shareholders be then? You'd got to provide emotions for all those moribund wage-earners who were too tired or too dumb to feel anything on their own behalf. If you couldn't freeze their blood, then you could sell them a good sob or two. That story about Clay's early days in the factory had been pure jam— even if that horse-faced dame *had* led him up the garden about knowing Chris, blast her. But you couldn't always rise to thrills or sobs, and if there was one emotion that the British public loved to wallow in it was being righteously indignant. So he, Jammy, had provided a wallow for them. The Yard knew quite well that tomorrow all these indignant people wouldn't remember a thing about it, so what the hell! What was there to get sore about? That "hounding innocents to death" was just a phrase. Practically a cliché it was. Nothing in that to make a sensible person touchy. The Yard were feeling a bit thin in the skin, that was what. They knew quite well that this shouldn't have been allowed to happen. Far be it from him to crab another fellow's work, but some of that article had been practically true, now he came to think of it. Not the "hounding to death," of course. But some of the other bits. It really *was* something amounting to a disgrace—oh, well, disgrace was a bit strong; but regrettable, anyhow, that such a thing should occur in a force that thought it was efficient. They were so very superior and keep-off-the-grass when times were good; they couldn't expect sympathy when they made a bloomer. Now if they were to let the Press in on the inside, the way they did in America, things like that simply wouldn't happen. He, Jammy Hopkins, might be only a crime reporter, but he knew just as much about crime and its detection as any police force. If the "old man" were to give him leave, and the police the use of their files, he would have the man who killed Clay inside prison walls—and on the front page, of course—inside a week. Imagination, that's what the Yard needed. And he had plenty of it. All he needed was a chance.

He bought his cigarettes, emptied them gloomily into the gold case his provincial colleagues had given him when he left for London (it was whispered that the munificence was more the expression of thankfulness than of devotion), and went gloomily back to the office. In the front entrance of that up-to-the-minute cathedral which is the headquarters of the *Clarion,* he encountered young Musker, one of the junior reporters, on his way out. He nodded briefly, and without stopping made the conventional greeting.

"Where you off to?"

"Lecture on stars," said Musker, with no great enthusiasm.

"Very interesting, astronomy," reproved Jammy.

"Not astronomy. Astrology." The boy was turning from the shade of the entrance into the sunlit street. "Woman called Pope or something."

"Pope!" Jammy stood arrested halfway to the lift door. "You don't mean Keats, do you?"

"Is it Keats?" Musker looked at a card again. "Yes, so it is. I knew it was a poet. Hey, what's the matter?" as Jammy caught him by the arm and dragged him back into the hall.

"Matter is you're not going to any astrology lecture," said Jammy, propelling him into the lift.

"Well!" said the astonished Musker. "For this relief much thanks, but why? You got a 'thing' about astrology?"

Jammy dragged him into an office and assaulted with his rapid speech the placid pink man behind the desk.

"But, Jammy," said the placid one when he could get a word in edgeways, "it was Blake's assignment. He was the obvious person for it: Doesn't he tell the world every week on Page 6 what is going to happen to it for the next seven days? It's his subject: astrology. What he didn't foresee was that his wife would have a baby this week instead of next. So I let him off and sent Musker instead."

"Musker!" said Jammy. "Say, don't you know that this is the woman who foretold Clay's death? The woman the *Courier* is running to give horoscopes at a shilling a time?"

"What of it?"

"What of it! Man, she's news!"

"She's the *Courier's* news. And about dead at that. I killed a story about her yesterday."

"All right, then, she's dead. But a lot of 'interesting' people must be interested in her at this moment. And the most interested of the lot is going to be the man who made her prophecy come true! For all we know she may have been responsible for giving him the idea; her and her prophecies. Keats may be dead, but her vicinity isn't. Not by a long chalk." He leaned forward and took the card that the Musker boy was still holding. "Find something for this nice boy to do this afternoon. He doesn't like astrology. See you later."

"But what about that story for—"

"All right, you'll have your story. And perhaps another one into the bargain!"

As Jammy was shot downwards in the lift he flicked the card in his hand with a reflective thumb. The Elwes Hall! Lydia was coming on!

"Know the best way to success, Pete?" he said to the liftman.

"All right, I'll buy," said Pete.

"Choose a good brand of hooey."

"You should know!" grinned Pete, and Jammy made a pass at him as he stepped through the doors. Pete had known him since—well, if not since his short-pant days, at least since his wrong-kind-of-collar days.

The Elwes Hall was in Wigmore Street: a nice neighborhood; which had been responsible in no small measure for its success. Chamber music was much more attractive when one could combine it with tea at one's club and seeing about that frock at Debenham's. And the plump sopranos who were flattered at the hush that attended their *Lieder* never guessed at the crepe-versus-satin that filled their listeners' minds. It was a pleasant little place: small enough to be intimate, large enough not to be huddled. As Jammy made his way to a seat, he observed that it was filled with the most fashionable audience that he had seen at any gathering since the Beaushire-Curzon wedding. Not only was "smart" society present in bulk, but there was a blue-blooded leaven of what Jammy usually called "duchesses-up-for-the-day": of those long-shoed, long-nosed, long-pedigreed people who lived on their places and not on their wits. And sprinkled over the gathering, of course, were the cranks.

The cranks came not for the thrill, nor because Lydia's mother had been the third daughter of an impoverished marquis, but because the Lion, the Bull, and the Crab were household pets of theirs, the houses of the Zodiac their spiritual home. There was no mistaking them: their pale eyes rested on the middle distance, their clothes looked like a bargain basement after a stay-in strike, and it seemed that they all wore the same string of sixpenny beads around their thin necks.

Jammy refused the seat which had been reserved for the *Clarion* representative, and insisted on having one among the palms on the far side of the hall below the platform. This had been refused, with varying degrees of indignation, by both those who had come to see Lydia and those who had come to be seen. But Jammy belonged to neither of these. What Jammy had come to see was the audience. And the seat half buried in Messrs. Willoughby's decorations provided as good a view of the audience as anything but the platform itself could afford.

Next to him was a shabby little man of thirty-five or so, who eyed Jammy as he sat down and presently leaned over until his rabbit-mouth was an inch from Jammy's ear, and breathed:

"Wonderful woman!"

This Jammy took to refer to Lydia.

"Wonderful," he agreed. "You know her?"

The shabby man ("Crank," said Jammy's mind, placing him) hesitated, and then said: "No. But I knew Christine Clay." And further converse was prevented by the arrival of Lydia and her chairman on the platform.

Lydia was at the best of times a poor speaker. She had a high thin voice, and when she became enthusiastic or excited her delivery was painfully like a very old gramophone record played on a very cheap gramophone. Jammy's attention soon wandered. He had heard Lydia on her favorite subject too often. His eyes began to quarter the crowded little hall. If *he* had bumped off Clay, and was still, thanks to the inadequacy of the police, both unsuspected and at large, would he or would he not come to see the woman who had prophesied for Clay the end he had brought about?

Jammy decided that, on the whole, he would. The

Clay murderer was clever. That was admitted. And he must now be hugging himself over his cleverness. Thinking how superior a man of his caliber was to the ordinary rules that hedged common mortals. That was a common frame of mind in persons who achieved a planned murder. They had planned something forbidden, and had brought it off. It went to their heads like wine. They looked around for more "dares" to bring off, as children play "last across the road." This, this orthodox gathering of orthodox people in one of the most orthodox districts in London, was a perfect "dare." In every mind in that hall the thought of Christine's death was uppermost. It was not mentioned from the platform, of course; the dignities must be observed. The lecture was a simple lecture on astrology; its history and its meaning. But all these people—or nearly all—had come to the gathering because nearly a year ago Lydia had had that lucky brain wave about the manner of Christine Clay's death. Christine was almost as much part of the gathering as Lydia herself; the hall was full of her. Yes, it would give Jammy, hypothetical murderer, a great kick to be one of that audience.

He looked at the audience now, pluming himself on the imagination that had got him where he was; the imagination that Grant, poor dear idiot, could never aspire to. He wished he had brought Bartholomew along. Bart was much better informed where the society racket was concerned than he was. It was Bart's business to be descriptive: and at whatever was "descriptive"—weddings, motor racing, launches, or what not—the same faces from the racket turned up. Bart would have been useful.

But Jammy knew enough of those faces to keep him interested.

"On the other hand," said Lydia, "Capricorn people are often melancholic, doubtful of themselves, and perverse. On a lower plane still, they are gloomy, miserly and deceptive." But Jammy was not listening. In any case he did not know which of the signs had had

the honor of assisting at his birth, and did not care.
Lydia had several times told him that he was "typically,
oh, but typically, Aries" but he never remembered. All
hooey.

There was the Duchess of Trent in the third row.
She, poor, silly, unhappy wretch, had the perfect alibi.
She had been going to have a luncheon for Christine: a
luncheon that would make her the most envied hostess
in London instead of a rather tiresome back-number,
and Christine had gone and died on her.

Jammy's eye wandered, and paused at a good-
looking dark face in the fourth row. Very familiar that
face; as familiar as the head on a coin. Why? He didn't
know the man; would swear he had never seen him in
the flesh.

And then it came to him. It was Gene Lejeune; the
actor who had been engaged to play opposite Clay in
her third and last picture in England: the picture she
had never made. It was rumored that Lejeune was glad
that he would never have to make that picture; Clay's
brilliance habitually made her men look like penny
candles; but that was hardly a good reason for getting
up at dawn to hold her head under water until she died.
Jammy wasn't greatly interested in Lejeune. Next to
him was a fashion plate in black and white. Marta
Hallard. Of course. Marta had been given the part that
Clay had been scheduled to play. Marta was not in the
Clay class, but holding up production was likely to
prove expensive, and Marta had poise, sophistication,
sufficient acting ability, sufficient personality, and what
Coyne called "class." She was now Lejeune's leading
woman. Or was he her leading man? It would be
difficult to say which of these two was the "supporting"
one. Neither of them was in the first flight. Considered
simply as a partnership, it was likely to prove much
more successful than the Clay-Lejeune one would have
been. A step up—a big step up for Marta—and more
chance to shine for Lejeune. Yes, Christine's death had
been a lucky break for both of them.

He heard in his mind a girl's voice saying, "You, of course, murdered her yourself." Who had said that? Yes, that Judy girl who played dumb blondes. And she had said it about Marta. That Saturday night when he and Grant had met on the doorstep of Marta's flat and had been entertained by her. The Judy person had said it with that sulky air of defiance that she used to life's most trivial activities. And they had taken it as a joke. Someone else had laughed and agreed, supplying the motive: "Of course! You wanted that part for yourself!" And the conversation had flowed on in unbroken superficiality.

Well, ambition was one of the better known incentives to murder. It came, well up the list, just below passion and greed. But Marta Hallard was Marta Hallard. Murder and that brittle, insincere sophisticate were poles apart. She didn't even play murder well on the stage, now he came to think of it. She had always the air of saying at the back of her mind, "Too tiresome, all this earnestness." If she didn't find murder humorless, she would undoubtedly find it plebian. No, he could imagine Marta being a murderee, but not a murderer.

He became aware that Marta was paying no attention whatever to Lydia. All her interest—and it was a fixed and whole-hearted interest—was centered on someone to her right in the row in front. Jammy's eyes followed the imaginary dotted line of her glance and came to rest, a little surprised, on a nondescript little man. Incredulous, he traveled the dotted line again. But the answer was still the small round-faced man with the sleepy expression. Now what could interest Marta Hallard in that very commercial exterior and that far from exciting—

And then Jammy remembered who that little man was. He was Jason Harmer, the song writer. One of Christine's best friends. Marta's "merry kettle." And, if women's judgment was to be accepted, anything but unexciting. In fact, that was the chap who was popularly supposed to have been Christine Clay's lover. Jammy's mind did the equivalent of a long, low whistle. Well, well, so that was Jay Harmer. He had never seen him off a song-cover until now. Queer taste women had, and no mistake.

Harmer was listening to Lydia with a rapt and childlike interest. Jammy wondered how anyone could remain unaware of so concentrated a battery of attention as Marta Hallard was directing on him. There he sat, short-necked and placid, while Marta's brilliant eyes bored into the side of his head. A lot of hooey, that about making people turn by just looking at them. And what, in any case, was the reason for Marta's secret interest? For secret it was. The brim of her hat hid her eyes from her escort, and she had taken it for granted that the eyes of everyone else were on the lecturer. Unconscious of being watched, she was letting her eyes have their fill of Harmer. Why?

Was it a "heart" interest—and if so, just how much of a heart interest? Or was it that, in spite of her companionship of him that night at her flat, she was seeing Jason Harmer as a possible murderer?

For nearly fifteen minutes Jammy watched them both, his mind full of speculation. Again and again his glance went over the crowded little hall and came back to them. Interest there was plenty elsewhere, but not interest like this.

He remembered Marta's instant refutal of the suggestion that there was more than friendship between Harmer and Christine Clay. What did that mean? Was she interested in him herself? And how much? How much *would* Marta Hallard be interested? Enough to get rid of a rival?

He found himself wondering if Marta was a good swimmer, and pulled himself up. Fifteen minutes ago he had laughed at the very thought of Marta as a person passionate to the point of murder. The very idea had been ludicrous.

But that was before he had observed her interest—
her strange consuming interest—in Jason. Supposing—just supposing; to pass the time while that woman made her boring way through the planets and
back again—that Marta *was* in love with this Harmer
fellow. That made Christine a double rival of hers,
didn't it? Christine had been where Marta, for all her
fashionable crust of superficiality and indifference,
would have given her right hand to be: at the top of her
professional tree. So often Marta had been within sight
of that top, only to have the branch she relied on break
and let her down. Certainly, and beyond any doubt,
Marta wanted professional success. And certainly, for
all her fair words, she had bitterly grudged the little
factory hand from the Midlands her staggering, and as
it seemed too easy, achievement. Five years ago Marta
had been very nearly where she was now: famous,
successful, financially sound, and with the top of the
tree—that elusive, giddy top—somewhere in sight. It
had been somewhere in sight for five years. And
meanwhile an unknown dancer from a Broadway
musical had sung, danced, and acted her way to
canonization.

It was no wonder if Marta's fair words where
Christine was concerned were the merest lip-service.
And supposing that Christine had not only the position
she had thirsted after, but the man she desired? What
then? Was that enough to make Marta Hallard hate to
the point of murder?

Where was Marta when Christine was drowned? In
Grosvenor Square, presumably. After all, she was
playing in that thing at the St. James's. No, wait! At
that Saturday night party something was said about her
being away? What was it? What was it? She had said
something about hard-working actresses, and Clement
Clements had mocked, saying: "Hard-working, for-
sooth. And you've just had a week off to go dashing
around the Continent!" She had said: "Not a week,

Clement! Only four days. And an actress can presumably play with a broken spine but never with a gumboil."

Clement had said that the gumboil didn't prevent her having a grand time at Deauville. And she had said: "Not Deauville. Le Touquet."

Le Touquet. That was where she had been. And she had come back in time for the Saturday matinée. They had talked about the reception she had had, and the size of the "house," and the rage of her understudy. She had come back after four days at Le Touquet! She was in Le Touquet, just across the channel, when Christine died.

"If parents would only study their children's horoscopes with the same diligence that they use to study their diets," Lydia was saying, shrill as a sparrow and about as impressive, "the world would be a much happier place."

"Le Touquet! Le Touquet!" exulted Jammy's mind. Now he was getting somewhere! Marta Hallard was not only within reach of Christine on that fatal morning, but *she had the means to cover the distance easily*. Le Touquet had opened the doors of his memory. Clements and she and Jammy in that far corner by the cocktail cupboard, and she answering Clements's idle questions. She had flown over, it appeared, with someone in a private plane, and had come back by the same method. And the plane had been an amphibian!

On that misty morning a plane had landed either on the downs or on the sea, had stayed a little, and had gone again without having entered into the consciousness of any but one lonely swimmer. Jammy was so sure of it that he could see the thing come out of the fog like a great bird and drop on to the water.

Who had piloted that plane? Not Harmer. Harmer hadn't been out of England. That was why the police were taking such an interest in him. Harmer had been only too much on the spot. He had an alibi of sorts, but Jammy didn't know whether it was a good one or not.

The police were so damned secretive. Well, he was on the track of something that the police, for all their vaunted efficiency, had missed. Marta was a friend of Grant's: it was natural that he should overlook her: he had never seen her look at Harmer, as Jammy was seeing her now; and he didn't know about that plane, Jammy would take his oath. And the plane made all the difference.

And if it was a case of a plane, then there were two in the business. The pilot, if not an accomplice, was certainly an accessory before the fact.

At this point Jammy mentally stopped to draw breath. He looked surprisedly along the well-dressed silent rows to the smart black-and-white figure in the middle distance. What connection had that familiar presence with the person his mind had drawn? There was the real Marta Hallard, her *soigné*, gracious, serene self. How had he let his mind make her into something so tortured, so desperate?

But she was still looking every now and then at Jason, her eyes resting longer on him than they did on Lydia. And there was something in that unguarded face that joined the real Marta to that shadowy one that his imagination had created. Whatever she might be, Marta Hallard was after all capable of strong feeling.

A patter like rain fell into Jammy's thoughts; the polite percussion of gloved hand on gloved hand. Lydia had apparently reached her peroration. Jammy sighed happily and felt for his hat. He wanted to get out into the air and think what his next move was to be. He hadn't been so excited since Old Man Willingdon had given him the exclusive story of how and why he had beaten his wife into pulp.

But there was going to be a question time, it would seem. Miss Keats, sipping water and smiling benevolently between sips, was waiting for the audience to collect its wits. Then some bold spirit began, and presently questions were raining around her. Some were amusing; and the audience, a little tired by the warm air, Lydia's voice, and the dullish lecture, laughed easily in relief. Presently the questions grew more intimate, and then—so inevitably that half the audience could see it coming—the query came:

Was it true that Miss Keats accurately foretold the manner of Christine Clay's death?

There was a shocked and eager silence. Lydia said, simply and with more dignity than she usually possessed, that it was true; that she had often foretold the future truly from a horoscope. She gave some instances.

Emboldened by the growing intimacy of the atmosphere, someone asked if she was helped in her reading of horoscopes by second-sight. She waited so long before answering that stillness fell back on the moving heads and hands; their eyes watched her expectantly.

"Yes," she said, at length. "Yes. It is not a matter that I like to discuss. But there are times when I have known, beyond reason, that a thing is so." She paused a moment, as if in doubt, and then took three steps forward to the edge of the platform with such impetuosity that it seemed that she meant to walk forward on to thin air. "And one thing I have known ever since I stepped on the platform. The murderer of Christine Clay is here in this hall."

It is said that ninety-nine people out of a hundred, receiving a telegram reading: *All is discovered: fly,* will snatch a toothbrush and make for the garage. Lydia's words were so unexpected, and their meaning when understood so horrifying, that there was a moment of blank silence. And then the rush began, like the first breath of a hurricane through palm trees. Above the rising babel, chairs shrieked like human beings as they were thrust out of the way. And the more they were thrust aside, the greater the chaos and the more frantic the anxiety of the escapers to reach the door. Not one in the crowd knew what they were escaping from. With most of them it began as a desire to escape from a tense situation; they belonged, as a class, to people who hate "awkwardness." But the difficulty of reaching the door through the scattered chairs and the densely packed crowd increased their natural desire to escape, into something like panic.

The chairman was saying something that was meant to be reassuring, to tide over the situation; but he was quite inaudible. Someone had gone to Lydia, and Jammy heard her say:

"What made me say that? Oh, what made me say that?"

He had moved forward to mount the platform, all the journalist in him tingling with anticipation. But as he laid his hand on the platform edge to vault, he recognized Lydia's escort. It was the fellow from the *Courier*. She was practically the *Courier's* property, he remembered. It was a million to one against his getting a word with her, and, at these odds, it wasn't worth the effort. There was better game, after all. When Lydia had made that incredible statement, Jammy, having abruptly pulled his own jaw into place, had turned to see how two people took the shock.

Marta had gone quite white, and a look of something like fury had come into her face. She had been one of the first to get to her feet, moving so abruptly that Lejeune was taken by surprise and had to fish his hat from under her heels. She had made for the door without a second glance at the platform or Lydia, but since she had had a seat in the front rows had become firmly wedged halfway down the hall, where confusion became worse confounded by someone having violent hysteria.

Jason Harmer, on the other hand, had not moved a muscle. He had gone on looking at Lydia with the same pleased interest during and after her staggering announcement as he had shown before. He had made no move to get up until people began to walk over him. Then he rose leisurely, helped a woman to climb over a chair that was blocking her path, patted his pocket to assure himself that something or other was there (his gloves probably), and turned to the door.

It took Jammy several minutes of scientific shoving to reach Marta, wedged in an alcove between two radiators.

"The silly fools!" she said viciously, when Jammy had reminded her who he was. And she glared, with most un-Hallard-like lack of poise, at her fellow beings.

"Nicer with an orchestra pit between, aren't they?"

Marta remembered that these were her public, and he could see her automatically pull herself together. But she was still what Jammy called "het up."

"Amazing business," he said, prompting. And in explanation: "Miss Keats."

"An utterly disgusting exhibition!"

"Disgusting?" said Jammy, at a loss.

"Why doesn't she turn cartwheels in the Strand?"

"You think this was just a publicity stunt?"

"What do you call it? A sign from Heaven?"

"But you said yourself, Miss Hallard, that night you were so kind as to put up with me, that she isn't a quack. That she really—"

"Of course she isn't a quack! She has done some amazing horoscopes. But that is a very different matter from this finding of murderers at a penny a time. If Lydia doesn't take care," she said after a pause and with venom, "she will end by being an Aimeé McPherson!"

It occurred to Jammy that this was hardly the line he had expected Marta to hand out. He didn't know what he had expected. But somehow it wasn't this. Into the pause that his doubt made, she said in a new crisp tone:

"This isn't by any chance, an interview, is it, Mr. Hopkins? Because if so, please understand quite clearly that I have said none of these things."

"All right, Miss Hallard, you haven't said a word. Unless the police ask me, of course," he added smiling.

"I don't think the police are on speaking terms with you," she said. "And now, if you will be so kind as to stand a little to your left, I think I can get past you into that space over there."

She nodded to him, smiled a little, pushed her scented person past him into the place of vantage, and was swallowed up in the crowd.

"Not a ha'penny change!" said Jammy to himself. And ruefully began to push his way back to where he had last seen Jason Harmer. Dowagers cursed him and debutantes glared, but half Jammy's life had been spent in getting through crowds. He made a good job of it.

"And what do *you* think of this, Mr. Harmer?"

Jason eyed him in a good-humored silence. "How much?" he said at last.

"How much what?"

"How much for my golden words?"

"A free copy of the paper."

Jason laughed, then his face grew sober. "Well, I think it has been a most instructive afternoon. You believe in this star stuff?"

"Can't say I do."

"Me, I'm not so sure. There's a lot in that crack about more things in heaven and earth whatever-it-is. I've seen some funny things happen in the village where I was born. Witchcraft and that. No accounting for any of it by any natural means. Makes you wonder."

"Where was that?"

Jason looked suddenly startled for the first time that afternoon. "East of Europe," he said abruptly. And went on: "That Miss Keats, she's a wonder. Not a canny thing to have around the house, though. No, sir! Must spoil your chances of matrimony quite a bit to be able to see what's going to happen. To say nothing of what has been happening. Every man has a right to his alibis."

Was no one, thought Jammy in exasperation, going to take the expected line of country this afternoon!

Perhaps if he pushed his way into Lydia's presence, she at least would behave according to the pattern he had marked out for her.

"You believe that Miss Keats was genuinely feeling the presence of evil when she made that statement?" he pursued hopefully.

"Sure, sure!" Jason looked a little surprised. "You don't make a fool of yourself that way unless you're pretty worked up."

"I noticed you weren't very surprised by the statement."

"I been in the States fifteen years. Nothing surprises me any more. Ever seen Holy Rollers? Ever seen Coney Island? Ever seen a tramp trying to sell a gold mine? Go west, young man, go west!"

"I'm going home to bed," said Jammy, and took his pushing way through the crowd.

But by the time he had reached the vestibule, he had recovered a little. He adjusted his collar and waited to see the crowd move past. Once outside the inner door, and breathing the secure air of Wigmore Street, they recovered from their fright and broke with one accord into excited speech.

But Jammy gleaned little from their unguarded chatter.

And then over their heads he saw a face that made him pause. A fair face with light lashes and the look of a rather kind terrier. He knew that man. His name was Sanger. And the last time he had seen him was sitting at a desk in Scotland Yard.

So Grant had had a little imagination after all!

Jammy flung his hat disgustedly on and went out to think things over.

20

GRANT HAD IMAGINATION, YES. BUT IT WAS NOT JAMMY'S kind. It would never have occurred to him to waste the time of a perfectly good detective by sending him to look at an audience for two hours. Sanger was at the Elwes Hall because his job for the moment was to tail Jason Harmer.

He brought back an account of the afternoon's drama, and reported that Harmer had been, as far as he could see, quite unmoved. He, Jason, had been accosted by Hopkins from the *Clairon* directly afterwards; but Hopkins didn't seem to get very far with him.

"Yes?" said Grant, lifting an eyebrow. "If he's a match for Hopkins, we must begin to consider him again. Cleverer than I thought!" And Sanger grinned.

On Wednesday afternoon Mr. Erskine telephoned to say that the fish had bitten. What he said, of course, was that "the line of investigation suggested by Inspector Grant had, it would appear, proved unexpectedly successful," but what he meant was that the fish had risen. Would Grant come along as soon as he could to inspect a document which Mr. Erskine was anxious to show him?

Grant would! In twelve minutes he was in the little green-lighted room.

Erskine, his hand trembling a little more than usual, gave him a letter to read.

SIR,

Having seen your advertisement saying that if Herbert Gotobed will call at your office he will hear of something to his advantage, I beg to state that I am unable to come personally but if you will communicate your news to me by letter to 5, Threadle Street, Canterbury, I will get the letter.

Yours faithfully,
HERBERT GOTOBED

"Canterbury!" Grant's eyes lighted. He handled the letter lovingly. The paper was cheap, and the ink poor. The style and the writing vaguely illiterate. Grant remembered Christine's letter with its easy sentences and its individual hand, and marveled for the thousandth time at the mystery of breeding.

"Canterbury! It's almost too good to be true. An accommodation address. I wonder why? Is our Herbert 'wanted,' by any chance? The Yard certainly don't know him. Not by that name. Pity we haven't got a photograph of him."

"And what is our next move, Inspector?"

"You write saying that if he doesn't put in a personal appearance you have no guarantee that he is Herbert Gotobed, and that it is therefore necessary for him to come to your offices!"

"Yes. Yes, certainly. That would be quite in order."

As if it mattered a hoot whether it was in order, Grant thought. How did these fellows imagine criminals were caught? Not by wondering what would be in order, that was certain!

"If you post it straight away, it will be in Canterbury tonight. I'll go down tomorrow morning and be waiting for the bird when he arrives. May I use your telephone?"

He called the Yard and asked, "Are you sure that none of the list of 'wanted' men has a passion for preaching or otherwise indulging in theatricality?"

The Yard said no, only Holy Mike, and everyone in the force had known him for years. He was reported from Plymouth, by the way.

"How appropriate!" Grant said, and hung up. "Strange!" he said to Erskine. "If he isn't wanted, why lie low? If he has nothing on his conscience—no, he hasn't a conscience. I mean, if we have nothing on him, I should have thought the same lad would have been in your office by return of post. He'd do almost anything for money. Clay knew where to hurt him when she left him that shilling."

"Lady Edward was a shrewd judge of character. She had, I think, been brought up in a hard school, and the fact helped her to discriminate."

Grant asked if he had known her well.

"No, I regret to say, no. A very charming woman. A little impatient of orthodox form, but otherwise—"

Yes. Grant could almost hear her saying, "And in plain English what does that mean?" She, too, must have suffered from Mr. Erskine.

Grant took his leave, warned Williams to be ready to accompany him next morning to Canterbury, arranged for a substitute in the absence of them both, and went home and slept for ten hours. In the morning, very early, he and Williams left a London not yet awake and arrived in a Canterbury shrouded in the smoke of breakfast.

The accommodation address proved to be, as Grant had expected, a small newsagent in a side street. Grant considered it, and said: "I don't suppose our friend will show up this end of the day, but one never knows. You go across to the pub over the way, engage that room above the saloon door, and have breakfast sent up to you. Don't leave the window, and keep an eye on everyone who comes. I'm going inside. When I want you I'll sign from the shop window."

"Aren't you going to have breakfast, sir?"

"I've had it. You can order lunch for one o'clock, though. It doesn't look the kind of place that would have a chop in the house."

Grant lingered until he saw Williams come to the upper window. Then he turned into the small shop. A round bald man with a heavy black moustache was transferring cartons of cigarettes from a cardboard box to a glass case.

"Good morning. Are you Mr. Rickett?"

"That's me," Mr. Rickett said, with caution.

"I understand that you sometimes use these premises as an accommodation address?"

Mr. Rickett looked him over. His experienced eye asked, Customer or police? and decided correctly.

"And what if I do? Nothing wrong in that, is there?"

"Not a thing!" Grant answered cheerfully. "I wanted to know whether you knew a Mr. Herbert Gotobed?"

"This a joke?"

"Certainly not. He gave your shop as an address for letters, and I wondered if you knew him."

"Not me. I don't take no interest in the people who has letters. They pay their fee when they come for them, and that finishes it as far as I am concerned."

"I see. Well, I want you to help me. I want you to let me stay in your shop until Mr. Gotobed comes to claim his letter. You have a letter for him?"

"Yes, I have a letter. It came last night. But— You police?"

"Scotland Yard." Grant showed his credentials.

"Yes. Well, I don't want no arrests on my premises. This is a respectable business, this is, even if I do a little on the side. I don't want no bad name hanging around my business."

Grant assured him that no arrest was contemplated. All he wanted was to meet Mr. Gotobed. He wanted information from him.

Oh, well, if that was all.

So Grant was established behind the little tower of cheap editions at the end of the counter, and found the morning passing not so slowly as he had feared. Humanity, even after all his years in the force, still had a lively interest in Grant's eyes—except in moments of depression—and interest proved plentiful. It was Williams, watching a very ordinary small-town street, who was bored. He welcomed the half-hour of conversation behind the books when Grant went to lunch, and went back reluctantly to the frowsy room above the saloon. The long summer afternoon, clouded and warm, wore away into a misty evening, and a too early dusk. The first lights appeared, very pale in the daylight.

"What time do you close?" Grant asked anxiously.

"Oh, tennish."

There was still plenty of time.

And then, about half-past nine, Grant became aware of a presence in the shop. There had been no warning of footsteps, no announcement at all except a swish of drapery. Grant looked up to see a man in monk's garb.

A high-pitched peevish voice said, "You have a letter addressed to Mr. Herbert—"

A light movement on Grant's part called attention to his presence.

Without a moment's pause the man turned and disappeared, leaving his sentence unfinished.

The apparition had been so unexpected, the disappearance so abrupt, that it was a second or two before mortal wits could cope with the situation. But Grant was out of the shop before the stranger was more than a few yards down the street. He saw the figure turn into an alley, and he ran. It was a little back-court of two-story houses, all the doors open to the warm evening, and two transverse alleys leading out of it. The man had disappeared. He turned to find Williams, a little breathless, at his back.

"Good man!" he said. "But it isn't much use. You take that alley and I'll take this one. A monk of sorts!"

"I saw him!" Williams said, making off.

But it was no good. In ten minutes they met at the newsagent's, blank.

"Who was that?" Grant demanded of Mr. Rickett.

"Don't know. Never saw him before as far as I know."

"Is there a monastery here?"

"In Canterbury? No!"

"Well, in the district?"

"Not as I knows."

A woman behind them put down sixpence on the counter. "Goldflake," she said. "You looking for a monastery? There's that brotherhood place in Bligh Vennel. They're by way of being monks. Ropes around their middles and bare heads."

"Where is—what is it? Bligh Vennel?" Grant asked. "Far from here?"

"No. 'Bout two streets. Less as the crow flies, but that won't be much good to you in Canterbury. It's in the lanes behind the Cock and Pheasant. I'd show you myself, if Jim wasn't waiting for his smoke. A sixpenny packet, Mr. Rickett, please."

"After hours," said Mr. Rickett, gruffly, avoiding the detective's eye. The woman's confidence was a conviction in itself.

She looked surprised, and before she should commit herself further Grant pulled his own cigarette-case from his pocket. "Madame, they say a nation gets the laws it deserves. It is not in my weak power to obtain the sixpenny packet for you, but please let me repay your help by providing Jim's smoke." He poured his cigarettes into her astonished hands, and dismissed her, protesting.

"And now," he said to Rickett, "about this brother-hood or whatever it is. Do you know it?"

"No. There is such a thing, now I remember. But I don't know where they hang out. You heard what she said. Behind the Cock and Pheasant. Half the cranks in the world has branches here, if it comes to that. I'm shutting up now."

"I should," Grant said. "People wanting cigarettes are a nuisance."

Mr. Rickett growled.

"Come on, Williams. And remember, Rickett, not a word of this to anyone. You'll probably see us tomorrow."

Rickett was understood to say that if he never saw them again it would be too soon.

"This is a rum go, sir," Williams said, as they set off down the street. "What's the program now?"

"I'm going to call on the brotherhood. I don't think you had better come along, Williams. Your good healthy Worcestershire face doesn't suggest any yearning after the life ascetic."

"You mean I look like a cop. I know, sir. It's worried me often. Bad for business. You don't know how I envy you your looks, sir. People think 'Army' the minute they see you. It's a great help always to be taken for Army."

"Considering all the dud checks on Cox's, I find that surprising! No, I wasn't considering your looks, Williams, not that way. I was just talking 'thoughtless.' It's a one-man party, this. You'd better go back to the aspidistra and wait for me. Have a meal."

They found the place after some search. A row of first story windows looked down upon the alley, but the only opening on the ground floor was a narrow door, heavy and studded. The building apparently faced into a court or garden. There was neither plate nor inscription at the door to give information to the curious. But there was a bell.

Grant rang, and after a long pause there was the

sound, faint through the heavy door, of footsteps on a stone floor. A small grill in the door shot back, and a man asked Grant's business.

Grant asked to see the principal.

"*Whom* do you wish to see?"

"The principal," said Grant firmly. He didn't know whether they called their Number One abbot or prior; principal seemed to him good enough.

"The Reverend Father does not give audience at this hour."

"Will you give the Reverend Father my card," Grant said, handing the little square through the grill, "and tell him that I shall be grateful if he would see me on a matter of importance."

"No worldly matter is of importance."

"The Reverend Father may decide differently when you have given him my card."

The grill shot back with an effect which might in a community less saintly have been described as snappish, and Grant was left in the darkening street. Williams saluted silently from some paces distance and turned away. The distant voices of children playing came clearly from adjoining streets, but there was no traffic in the alley. Williams's footsteps had faded out of hearing long before there was the sound of returning ones in the passage beyond the door. Then there was the creak of bolts being drawn and a key turned (What did they shut out? Grant wondered. Life? Or were the bars to keep straying wills indoors?). The door was opened sufficiently to admit him, and the man bade him enter.

"Peace be with you and with all Christian souls and the blessing of the Lord God go with you now and for ever, amen," gabbled the man as he shot the bolts again and turned the key. If he had hummed a line of "Sing to me sometimes" the effect would have been exactly similar, Grant thought.

"The Reverend Father in his graciousness will see you," the man said, and led the way up the stone passage, his sandals slapping with a slovenly effect on the flags. He ushered Grant into a small white-washed room, bare except for a table, chairs, and a Crucifix, said "Peace be with you," and shut the door, leaving Grant alone. It was very chilly there, and Grant hoped that the Reverend Father would not discipline him by leaving him there too long.

But in less than five minutes the doorkeeper returned and with great impressiveness bowed in his principal. He uttered another of his gabbled benedictions and left the two men together. Grant had expected the fanatic type; he was confronted instead with the successful preacher; bland, entrenched, worldly.

"Can I help you, my son?"

"I think you have in your brotherhood a man of the name of Herbert Gotobed—"

"There is no one of that name here."

"I had not expected that that was the name he is known by in your community, but you are no doubt aware of the real names of the men who enter your order."

"The worldly name of a man is forgotten on the day he enters the door to become one of us."

"You asked if you could help me."

"I still wish to help you."

"I want to see Herbert Gotobed. I have news for him."

"I know of no one of that name. And there can be no 'news' for a man who has joined the Brotherhood of the Tree of Lebanon."

"Very well. You may not know the man as Gotobed. But the man I want to interview is one of your number. I have to ask that you will let me find him."

"Do you suggest that I should parade my community for your inspection?"

"No. You have some kind of service to which all the brothers come, haven't you?"

"Certainly."

"Let me be present at the service."

"It is a most unusual request."

"When is the next service?"

"In half an hour the midnight service begins."

"Then all I ask is a seat where I can see the faces of your community."

The Reverend Father was reluctant, and mentioned the inviolability of the holy house, but Grant's casually dropped phrases on the attractive but obsolete custom of sanctuary and the still-surviving magic of King's Writ, made him change his mind.

"By the way, will you tell me—I'm afraid I'm very ignorant of your rules and ways of life—do the members of your community have business in the town?"

"No. Only when charity demands it."

"Have the brothers no traffic with the world at all then?" Herbert was going to have a perfect alibi, if that were so!

"For twenty-four hours once every moon, a brother goes into the world. That is contrived lest the unspottedness of communal life should breed self-righteousness. For the twelve hours of the day he must help his fellow beings in such ways as are open to him. For the twelve hours of the night he must meditate in a place alone: in summer in some open place, in winter in some church."

"I see. And the twenty-four hours begin—when?"

"From a midnight to a midnight."

"Thank you."

21

THE SERVICE WAS HELD IN A BARE CHAPEL, CANDLE-LIT
and white-washed, very simple except for the magnificence of the altar at the East gable. Grant was surprised
by the appearance of the altar. Poor the brothers might
be, but there was wealth somewhere. The vessels on
the white velvet cloth, and the Crucifix, might have
been a pirate's loot from a Spanish American cathedral. He had found it difficult to associate the Herbert
Gotobed he knew by reputation with this cloistered and
poverty-struck existence. Being theatrical to no audience but oneself must soon pall. But the sight of that
altar gave him pause. Herbert was perhaps running
true to form after all.

Grant heard no word of the service. From his seat in
the dim recess of a side window he could see all the
faces of the participants; more than a score of them;
and he found it a fascinating study. Some were cranks
(one saw the same faces at "anti" meetings and folk-
dance revivals), some fanatics (masochists looking for a
modern hair shirt), some simple, some at odds with

themselves and looking for peace, some at odds with the world and looking for sanctuary. Grant, looking them over with a lively interest, found his glance stayed as it came to one face. Now what had brought the owner of that face to a life of seclusion and self-denial? A round sallow face on a round ill-shaped head, the eyes small, the nose fleshy, the lower lip loose, so that it hung away from his teeth as he repeated the words of the service. All the others in that little chapel had been types that fitted easily into recognized niches in the everyday world: the principal to a bishopric, this one to a neurologist's waiting-room, this to a depot for unemployed. But where did that last one fit?

There was only one answer. In the dock.

"So that," said Grant's other self to him, "is Herbert Gotobed." He could not be sure, of course, until he had seen the man walk. That was all he had ever seen of him: his walk. But he was ready to stake much on his judgment. The best of judges were at fault sometimes—Gotobed might turn out to be that lean and harmless-looking individual in the front row—but he would be surprised if Gotobed were any but that unctuous creature with the loose lower lip.

As the men filed out after midnight, he had no more doubt. Gotobed had a peculiar walk, a gangling, shoulder-rotating progression which was quite his own.

Grant followed them out and then sought the Reverend Father. What was the name of the last man to leave the chapel?

That was Brother Aloysius.

And after a little persuasion Brother Aloysius was sent for.

As they waited Grant talked conventionally of the Order and its rules and learned that no member could own any worldly property or have communication for worldly purposes with human beings. Such trivial worldlinesses as newspapers were, of course, not even thought of. He also learned that the principal intended in about a month's time to take over a new Mission in

Mexico, which they had built out of their funds, and that the privilege of electing his successor lay entirely with him.

A thought occurred to Grant.

"I don't want to be impertinent—please don't think this idle curiosity—but would you tell me whether you have decided in your mind on any particular person?"

"I have practically decided."

"May I know who it is?"

"I really do not know why I should tell to a stranger what I am not prepared to tell to the brothers of my own Order, but there is no reason to conceal it if I may trust your secrecy." Grant gave his word. "My successor is likely to be the man you have asked to see."

"But he is a newcomer!" Grant said before he thought.

"I am at a loss to know how you knew that," the Reverend Father said sharply. "It is true Brother Aloysius has been with us only a few months, but the qualities necessary for the priorship" (so he was a prior!) "are not developed with length of service."

Grant murmured agreement, and then asked which of their community had been on an errand in the streets this evening.

None of them, the prior said firmly; and the conversation was brought to an end by the entrance of the man Grant wanted.

He stood there passively, his hands folded within the wide sleeves of his dark-brown gown. Grant noticed that his feet were not sandaled but bare, and remembered that there had been no warning of his approach when he had presented himself in the newsagent's. The looker-on in Grant wondered whether it was an appearance of humility or the convenience of a noiseless tread which appealed so greatly to Herbert.

"This is Brother Aloysius," the prior said, and left them with a blessing, a much more poetic performance than the doorkeeper's.

"I am from Messrs. Erskine, Smythe, and Erskine, the

lawyers in the Temple," Grant said. "You are Herbert Gotobed."

"I am Brother Aloysius."

"You were Herbert Gotobed."

"I never heard of him."

Grant considered him for a moment. "I'm sorry," he said. "We're looking for Gotobed about a legacy that has been left him."

"Yes? If he is a brother of this order, your news will be of little interest to him."

"If the legacy were big enough, he might realize that he could do far more for the cause of charity outside these walls than in them."

"Our oath is for life. Nothing that happens outside these walls is of interest to any member of our order."

"So you deny that you are Herbert Gotobed?"

Grant was conducting the conversation automatically. What his mind was occupied with, he found, was that the expression in the man's small pale eyes was hate. He had rarely seen such hate. But why hate? That was what his mind asked. It should be fear, surely?

Grant felt that to this man he was not a pursuer but someone who had butted in. The feeling stayed with him while he took his leave and all the way back to the hotel opposite the tobacconist's.

Williams was brooding over a cold meal he had caused to be set for his superior.

"Any news?" Grant asked.

"No, sir."

"No word of Tisdall? Have you telephoned?"

"Yes, I telephoned about twenty minutes ago. Not a word, sir."

Grant slapped some slices of ham between two pieces of bread. "Pity," he said. "I'd work much better if Tisdall were out of my mind. Come on. There isn't going to be much bed for us tonight."

"What is it, sir? Did you find him?"

"Yes, he's there all right. Denied he was Gotobed. They're not allowed to have any worldly transactions.

That is why he was so shy in the shop. Didn't even wait to see who the second person behind the counter was: just fled at the very prospect of a watcher. That's what's worrying me, Williams. He seems much more occupied with not being chucked out of the order than with being run in for murder."

"But his running out of the shop might have been because he wanted to keep on in hiding. That monastery place is as good a hide-out as a murderer could wish for."

"Ye-s. Yes, but he's not frightened. He's angry. We're spoiling something for him."

They had been going quietly downstairs, Grant eating large mouthfuls of his improvised sandwich. As they approached the ground floor they were confronted by an enormous female who blocked their exit from the stairway. She had no poker in her hand, but the effect was the same.

"So that's what you are!" she said, with concentrated venom. "A couple of sneaking fly-by-nights. Come in here, as large as life, you do, and make me and my poor husband buy the best of everything for your meals—chops at tenpence each, and tongue at two-and-eightpence the pound, to say nothing of English tomatoes to suit your very particular tastes—and all we get for our expense and our trouble is a couple of empty rooms in the morning. I've a good mind to ring up the police and give you in charge—if it weren't for—"

"Oh, for God's sake!" Grant said angrily; and then began to laugh. He hung over the banisters laughing helplessly, while Williams talked to the angry hostess.

"Well, why didn't you say you were bobbies?" she said.

"We're *not* bobbies," Williams said, ferociously, and Grant laughed the more, and dragged him from the scene.

"Gilbertian!" he said, wiping his eyes. "Quite Gilbertian. Did me a lot of good. Now, listen. These monks, or whatever they esteem themselves, retire to their cells at midnight and don't move out of them till six. But Herbert gets in and out of that building more or less when he likes. I don't know how he works it: those first-floor windows are low enough to drop from but much too high to get back into, and he doesn't look like a gymnast. But get out he does. No one knew—or at least, the powers that be didn't know—he was out tonight. Well, I have a hunch that he's going walking again tonight, and I want to see where to."

"What makes you think so, sir?"

"Just instinct. If I were Herbert I'd have a base to conduct operations from. I walked around the block before I came back to the hotel. There are only two points where the monastery property abuts on the street. At the side where the door is; and at the very opposite side where the garden ends in a wall that looks fifteen feet high. There's a small gate there; iron and very solid. It's a long way from the living quarters, and I think our original side is the most helpful. But I want you to keep watch on the garden side, and tail anyone who comes out. I'll do the same on the door side. If nothing happens by six o'clock you can creep home and go to bed."

22

GRANT HAD BEEN WAITING FOR WHAT SEEMED AN ETERNI-
ty. The night was soft, with a damp air, and smelled
pleasantly of green things and flowers. Somewhere
there was a lime tree. There was no sky, only a thick
misty dark above. Bells chimed every now and then,
with aloof sweetness. In spite of himself, Grant found
the peace of the night invading him; his mind grew
blurred and incurious and he had to whip it to
wakefulness.

And then, a few moments after half-past two had
struck, something happened, and his mind leaped
without any goading. He had heard no sound, but in
the lane in front of the monastery there was movement.
It was too dark to see a shape; all that happened was
that the darkness moved, as a curtain might stir in a
current of air. Someone was in the street.

Grant waited. The movement grew less, became
more blurred, and ceased. Whoever was there had
moved away from him. Grant slipped his unlaced boots
from his feet and strung them across his shoulder;

every step on a shod foot would be audible on a night like this. Silently he moved down the lane and past the high wall of the house. Out of its shadows the visibility was slightly better: he could see the movement in front of him again. He followed it with every sense alert; it was not only difficult to gauge his exact distance from it, but almost impossible to tell if it stopped for a moment. In the street beyond it was easier; the movement in the darkness became a form. A form retreating swiftly and effortlessly into the night. Grant set out to keep pace with it. Down the little streets of two-story houses. Past small houses with small gardens. Past an occasional small paddock.

And then Grant felt gravel pavement under his stocking feet and cursed. The man was making for the country; for the outer suburbs at least.

For about twenty minutes Grant followed that half-seen figure through a dark and silent world. He did not know his surrounding; he had to follow the figure blindly. He did not know when a step came, or a declivity, or an obstacle. And a bad stumble might be fatal to the night's work. But as far as he could see, his quarry never hesitated. This was not a flight; it was a journey he had done often before.

Presently Grant could tell that they were in more or less open country. If there were houses they were built behind the original field hedges—a new suburb, probably. The hedges made it difficult to see the man he was following; their dark mass made a gloomy background for a moving figure. And then Grant suddenly found that he had lost him. Nothing moved in front of him any more. He stood still instantly. Was the man waiting for him? Or had he disappeared into an opening? Several times, when pebbles had slid under his own tread, he had wondered if the man suspected his presence. There had been as far as he could see no pause for reconnoitering in the man's progress. But now there was a complete absence of any movement at all.

Grant went forward step by step, and found himself

level with an opening in the hedge. A gate. He wished passionately that he could use his torch. This blindfold moving through an unknown country was getting on his nerves. He decided to risk a guess that this was where the man had gone, and moved into the entrance. Immediately there was soft sand under his feet. He paused doubtfully. Was it only a sand-pit? What was the man planning? An attack?

Then he remembered that fine red sand which decorates the trim approaches to new villas, and breathed again. Reassured he moved forward, finding with one foot the cut edge of turf, and letting it lead him to the building which must be in front of him somewhere. It loomed quite suddenly in the darkness. A white-washed house of perhaps eight rooms. Its paleness made it slightly luminous even on so dark a night; and against its ghostly shimmer he saw the man again. He was standing still, and it seemed to Grant that he was looking back at him. He realized too late that he too was now standing where a wing of the house made a background for him. He dropped to his knees. And after a moment the man moved on and vanished round the corner of the house.

Grant made the best of his way to the corner and waited, pressed up against the wall. But there was no sound, no breathing, not a movement; the man had gone on; he was wasting time. He stepped around the corner. A soft wool substance smothered him, falling over his face and being drawn tightly about his neck. A split second before the folds closed on his throat, Grant got his fingers between the stuff and his flesh. He held on with all his might, and then, using the material as purchase, bent forward abruptly and felt the man's body come sliding over him, head first to the ground. The weight knocked Grant down, and the vile suffocating thing was still over his head, but his hands were free. He reached out for his opponent and felt with passionate gladness the restriction around his throat relax. He was still blind and suffocating, but he was in no immediate danger of being throttled. He was, in fact, doing his best to throttle the other man, if only he could find his throat. But the man was twisting like an eel, and using his knees with malicious art. This was not the first time that Herbert Gotobed had fought foul. Grant wished, hitting blindly and finding only seed-sown grass, that he could see for just thirty seconds. He let go the part of his assailant he happened to be holding—he was not sure whether it was a leg or an arm—and did his best to roll away. It was not success-ful, since the man had just as firm a grip of him. But he had time to reach into his pocket and close his fingers around his torch. His hand was prisoned there as he was rolled on to his back, but with all his might Grant hit with the free hand into the breath that was sobbing into his face. His knuckles hit bone and he heard the snap of teeth meeting. The man's full weight descended on him. He wrenched himself free from it, and dragged the torch from his pocket. Before he had got it out, the man was moving again. He had only rocked him. He flashed the torch on him, and before the light had reached his face the man leaped. Grant stepped aside and swung the weapon at him as he came. It missed him by a hair's breadth and they went down together. Grant lacked stance for the reception of such a weight: all his attention had been on his own blow; he hit the ground with violence. In the dimness of the moment, when all his faculties were trying to summon his stunned body to its duty, he wondered detachedly how the man would kill him?

To his surprise he felt the weight of the man's body lift, something hit him across the side of the head, and he was aware, even while his ears sang, that the man had gone from his side.

He dragged himself to a sitting position; sitting, incidentally, on the stone he had been hit with (by its feel its proper place was a rockery), and was groping for his torch preparatory to following the man, when a woman's voice said out of the dark in a whisper:

"Is that you, Bert? Is anything wrong?"

Grant's hand lighted on the torch, and he got to his feet.

The light shone into eyes big and brown and soft as a deer's. But the rest of the face was not soft.

She drew in her breath as the light flashed, and made a movement backwards.

"Stay still," said Grant in a voice that brooked no disobedience, and the movement ceased.

"Don't talk so loud," she said urgently. "Who are you, anyway? I thought you were—a friend of mine."

"I'm a detective inspector—a policeman."

This statement, Grant had found, produced invariably one of two expressions: fear or wariness. Quite innocent people often showed the first; but the second was a give-away. It gave away the woman now.

Grant's light flashed on the house—a one story building with small attic rooms.

"Don't do that!" she hissed. "You'll waken her."

"Who is 'her'?"

"The old lady. My boss."

"You a maid here?"

"I'm the housekeeper."

"Just the two of you in the house?"

"Yes."

He indicated with his light the open window behind her. "Is that your room?"

"Yes."

"We'll go in there and talk."

"You can't come into the house. You can't do anything to me. I haven't done anything."

"Would you mind!" said Grant, in a tone that belied the meaning of the phrase.

"You can't come into the house without a warrant. I know!" She was standing against the window-sill now, defending her room.

"You don't need a warrant for murder," Grant said.

"Murder!" She stared at him. "What have I to do with murder?"

"Will you get in, please, and put on the light."

She did as she was bidden, climbing over the sill with the ease of practice. As the light clicked, Grant stepped over the sill and drew the curtains.

It was a very pleasant bedroom, with eiderdown on the bed and shaded light on the table.

"Who is your employer?" he asked.

She gave her employer's name, and admitted that she had been there only a few months.

"Where was your last reference from?"

"A place in Australia."

"And what relation are you to Herbert Gotobed?"

"Who's that?"

"Come, don't let's waste time, Miss.—What name do you use, by the way?"

"I use my own name," she glared at him. "Rosa Freeson."

Grant tilted the lamp for a better view of her. He had never seen her before. "Herbert Gotobed came out here to see you tonight and you were waiting for him. You will save yourself a lot of trouble if you tell me all about it, now."

"I was waiting, if you must know, for Bert. He's the milk roundsman. You can't run me in for that. You can't blame me much, either. A girl has to have a little fun in a place like this."

"Yes?" He moved toward the built-in wardrobe. "Stay where you are," he said.

The wardrobe held nothing but women's clothes; rather too good for her position but none of them very new. Grant asked to see the contents of the chest of drawers, and she showed them sullenly. They were all quite normal. He asked where her boxes were.

"In the box room in the attic," she said.

"And what are the suit-cases under the bed?"

She looked ready to strike him.

"Let me see what is in these."

"You have no right! Show me your warrant. I won't open anything for you."

"If you have nothing to hide, you can't possibly object to my seeing what is inside."

"I've lost the key."

"You're making me very suspicious."

She produced the key from a string around her neck and pulled out the first suit-case. Grant, watching her, thought for the first time that she was not all white. Something in her movements, in the texture of her hair, was—what? Negro? Indian? And then he remembered the South Sea Mission which Herbert had run.

"How long since you left the Islands?" he asked conversationally.

"About—" She stopped, and finished immediately, "I don't know what you're talking about."

The first suit-case was empty. The second was full to the brim with men's clothes.

"Male impersonator?" asked Grant, who in spite of his swollen feet and aching head was beginning to feel happier. "Or just old-clothes dealer?"

"These are the clothes of my dead fiancé. I'll thank you not to be funny about them."

"Didn't your fiancé wear a coat?"

"Yes, but it was mussed up when he was killed."

"Oh? How was he killed?" Grant asked amiably, his hands running through the clothes.

"Motor accident."

"You disappoint me."

"Come again?"

"I'd expected a more imaginative end from you. What was your fiancé's name?"

"John Starboard."

"Starboard! That cancels out the motor accident."

"I suppose you know what you're talking about. I don't."

"It wasn't your fiancé's coat you kept in that now empty suit-case, by any chance?"

"It was not."

Grant's searching hand paused. He withdrew it holding a bundle of passports: four in all. One was a

British one issued to Herbert Gotobed; one was an American one in the name of Alexander Byron Black; one a Spanish one, issued to a deaf-mute, one Jose Fernandez; and the fourth an American one for William Cairns Black and his wife. But the photographs were all of the same man: Herbert Gotobed; and the wife's photograph was that of Rosa Freeson.

"A collector, your fiancé. An expensive hobby, I've always understood." He put the passports into his pocket.

"You can't do that. They're not yours. I'll scream the house down. I will say you came in and attacked me. Look!" She pulled her wrap open and began to tear her nightdress.

"Scream as much as you like. Your old lady would be very interested in these passports. And if you have any designs on the old lady, by the way, I should advise you to reconsider them. Now I shall retrieve my boots. They are lying somewhere in the garden. Though God alone knows if my feet will go into them. My advice to you, Mrs. Cairns Black, is to do nothing at all until you hear from me. We have nothing against *you*, so far, so don't begin putting ideas into our heads by doing anything you might regret."

23

GRANT MANAGED TO GET HIS BOOTS ON (BY DINT OF thinking strenuously of something else, his childhood's recipe for painful moments), but after two or three steps hastily took them off again, and hobbled homeward as he had come: stocking-soled. It was not easy to find his way back, but he had an excellent bump of locality (it was said at the Yard that if you blindfolded Grant and turned him until he was dizzy he still knew where north was) and the general direction was clear enough to him. He stood in a doorway on the opposite side of the street and watched the officer on the beat go by, rather than ask a direction and have to explain himself. No member of the C.I.D. likes to appear before a borough policeman with his boots in his hands.

He wrote a note asking Williams to telephone the Yard when he came in at six and ask for any information they might have about a sect or order or whatnot called the Tree of Lebanon, and to waken him when the answer came. He then fell into bed, and slept dreamlessly, the passports under his pillow until Williams called him just before ten o'clock.

"News of Tisdall?" Grant said as his eyes opened.

But there was no news.

The Yard said that the Holy Order of the Tree of Lebanon had been founded by a rich bachelor in 1862, for the furtherance of the monastic life, he having been what was then known as jilted by the object of his affections. He himself had been the first prior, and all his wealth had been used to endow the foundation. The rule of poverty had been very strict, money being used only for charities approved by the prior of the moment, so that by the present day the order had the reputation of having a lot of money laid away. A prior was nominated by his predecessor, but a prior could be superseded at any moment by the unanimous vote of the brethren.

Grant drank the horrible coffee supplied by the establishment, and considered things. "That is what our Herbert wants: the priorship. He has the prior dancing on a stick. It's almost incredible that a man like the prior could be such a fool. But then! Think of the fools we've known, Williams."

"I'm thinking, sir," Williams said, eloquently.

"All those hard-headed self-made pieces of original conglomerate who fall for a few honeyed words from a confidence man in a hotel lobby! And of course Herbert has no ordinary gift of tongues. Perhaps he worked his churches in America as leaven to the prior's interest. Anyhow, he's the prior's fair-haired boy at the moment. With the prospect of having a fortune in his hands if he plays his cards rightly for the next few weeks. Not much wonder he was scared of getting in wrong. He wanted to know just how much his sister had left him, without compromising himself with his brethren. If she had left him enough to make it worth his while, he'd give up the monastic life. I shouldn't think it appeals greatly to him. Even with occasional visits to the villa."

"How long do you think he'd stay in any case, sir?"

"Till he had transferred enough hard cash to his own particular charities. Oh, well, these," he indicated the passports, "will be enough to frame a nice little indictment on, so that we can have him under our hands when we want him. The thing that disappoints me, Williams, is where is the murder in all this? I don't mean that he didn't do it. I've no doubt that he was having his twenty-four hours off at the time. But why did he do it? He came to England when he heard that she was coming. I think, judging by his woman's clothes, that he was possibly broke when he arrived. That was why he took to the Tree of Lebanon. But the possibilities of the Tree must have occurred to him pretty soon. Why kill his sister?"

"Went to see her and had a quarrel. The queer hour that's puzzled us all would be quite normal for him. Six o'clock would be just as usual as lunchtime."

"Yes, that's true. I'm going now to find out from the Reverend Father whether Brother Aloysius was out of the monastery a fort-night yesterday. The Reverend Father would have sat on a very high horse yesterday, but he'll talk when he sees what his favorite looks like on these passports."

But the Reverend Father was not receiving callers. The little *guichet* displayed the sour face of the doorkeeper, who delivered his stolid message in answer to all Grant's questions, whether the phrase was relevant or not. Herbert's golden tongue had been at work. The *guichet* shut, and Grant was left helpless in the little lane. There was nothing for it but a warrant. He went slowly away, his feet still aching; admired the job Herbert had made of oiling the cellar entrance in the pavement, and climbed into his car. Yes, he had better get that warrant.

He went back to the hotel for his pajamas, razor, and toothbrush (he had no intention of spending another night there) and was leaving a message for the sleeping

Williams, when he was called to the telephone by the Yard.

Would he go to Dover? The man there wanted him. Something had turned up, it seemed.

He changed the message for Williams, threw his things into the car, found time to wonder why he over-tipped the frowsy virago for her inattendance, disgusting food, and deplorable cooking, and set out for Dover.

Something had turned up. That could only mean Champneis. Something out of the ordinary. If they had merely found where Champneis had spent the night, it would have been reported by telephone in the ordinary way. But—something had turned up.

Rimell, the detective in charge—a kind, melancholy-looking boy, whose greatest asset was his unlikeness to the popular conception of a detective—was waiting for Grant at the police-station door, and Grant drew him into the car. Rimell said that he had, after endless delving, unearthed an old fellow called Searle, a retired deckhand, who had been coming home from his granddaughter's engagement party about half-past twelve on the Wednesday night—or rather, the Thursday morning. He was alone, because very few people lived down the harbor way nowadays. They'd got ideas and lived up the hill in gimcrack villas you'd be afraid to sneeze in. He had stopped a minute or two when he had got to the sea level, to look at the harbor. It still made him feel fine to look at riding-lights at night. It was beginning to mist over, but it was still clear enough to see the outlines of everything. He knew the *Petronel* was coming in—had seen her through his glasses before he went to the party—and so he looked for her now, and saw her lying, not at the jetty, but out in the water at anchor. As he watched, a small motor-boat came out from her side and made for the shore, going slowly with a quiet *chug-chug* as if not anxious to call attention to itself. As it touched the jetty steps a man moved out of the shadows by the quay. A tall figure whom Searle identified as Lord Edward (he had seen him often and had in fact once served aboard a previous yacht of his brother's) appeared from the boat and said, "Is that you, Harmer?" and the smaller man had said, "It's me," and then, in a low tone, "Customs all right?" Lord Edward had said, "No trouble at all," and they had gone down into the motorboat together and pushed off. The mist had come down quickly after that, blotting out the harbor. After about fifteen minutes Searle had gone on his way. But as he was going up the street, he heard a motor-boat leave the *Petronel.* Whether it came ashore or went out of the harbor he didn't know. He didn't think at the moment any of all this was of any importance.

"Great Heavens!" said Grant. "I can't believe it. There just—there just isn't one single thing in all the world that these two men have in common." (His subconscious added before he could stop it: Except a woman.) "They just don't touch anywhere. And yet they're as thick as thieves." He sat silent a little. "All right, Rimell. Good work. I'm going to have lunch and think this over."

"Yes, sir. May I give you a friendly piece of advice, sir?"

"If you must. It's a bad habit in subordinates."

"No black coffee, sir. I expect you had four cups for breakfast and nothing else."

Grant laughed. "Why should you worry?" he said, pressing the starter. "The more breakdowns, the quicker the promotion."

"I grudge the money for wreaths, sir."

But Grant was not smiling as he drove lunchwards. Christine Clay's husband and her reputed lover had midnight business together. That was strange enough. But that Edward Champneis, fifth son of the seventh Duke of Bude, and a reputable if unorthodox member of his race, should have underhand traffic with Jason Harmer, of Tin Pan Alley was definitely stranger. What was the common bond? Not murder. Grant refused to

consider anything *so outré* as murder in couples. One or
other might have wanted to murder her, but that they
should have forgathered on the subject was unimagina-
ble. The motor-boat had left the *Petronel* again, Searle
said. Supposing only one of them had been in it? It was
only a short distance north along the coast to the Gap
at Westover; and Harmer had turned up at Clay's
cottage two hours after her death. To drown Clay from
a motor-boat was the ideal way. As good as his groyne
theory, with escape both quicker and easier. The more
he thought of the motor-boat, the more enamored of
the method he grew. They had checked the boats in the
vicinity as a matter of routine at the time of the first
investigation; but a motor-boat has a wide cruising
radius. But—oh, well, just "but"! The theory was
fantastic. Could one imagine Jason saying, "You lend
me your boat and I'll drown your wife," or Champneis
suggesting, "I'll lend you the boat if you'll do the
work." These two had met for some other reason
altogether. If murder had resulted, then it had been
unplanned, incidental.

What then had they met for? Harmer had said
something about Customs. It had been his first greeting. He had been anxious about it. Was Harmer a drug
fiend?

There were two things against that. Harmer didn't
look like an addict. And Champneis would never have
supplied the stuff. Risk might be the breath of life to
him, but that kind of risk would be very definitely out.

What, then, was to be kept from the eyes of the
Customs? Tobacco? Jewels? Champneis had shown
George Meir, next morning, the topazes he had
brought back for Christine.

There was one thing against all of it. Smuggling
Edward Champneis might descend to, as a ploy, a mere
bit of excitement; but Grant could not see him smuggling for the benefit of Jay Harmer. One ran one's head
continually against that. What had these two men in
common? They had something. Their association

proved it. But what? They were, as far as anyone knew, the merest acquaintances. Not even that. Champneis had almost certainly left England before Harmer had arrived, and Christine had not known Harmer until they worked together on these English pictures.

No digestive juices flowed in Grant's alimentary tracts during that lunch; his brain was working like an engine. The sweetbreads and green peas might as well have been thrown into the chef's waste bin. By the time coffee had arrived he was no nearer a solution. He wished he was one of these marvelous creatures of super-instinct and infallible judgment who adorned the pages of detective stories, and not just a hard-working well-meaning, ordinarily intelligent Detective Inspector. As far as he could see, the obvious course was to interview one or other of these men. And the obvious one to interview was Harmer. Why? Oh, because he'd talk more easily. Oh, yes, all right, and because there was less chance of running into trouble! What it was to have someone inside you checking up your motives for everything you did or thought!

He refrained from his second cup of coffee, with a smile for the absent Rimell. Nice kid. He'd make a good detective some day.

He rang up Devonshire House, and asked if Mr. Harmer could make it convenient to see Alan Grant (no need to advertise his profession) this evening between tea and dinner.

He was told that Mr. Harmer was not in London. He had gone down to see Leni Primhofer, the continental star, who was staying at Whitecliffe. He was writing a song for her. No, he was not expected back that night. The address was Tall Hatch, Whitecliffe, and the telephone number Whitecliffe 3025.

Grant rang Whitecliffe 3025, and asked when Mr. Harmer could see him. Harmer was in the country motoring with Fräulein Primhofer and would not be back before dinner.

Whitecliffe is a continuation of Westover: a collec-

tion of plutocratic villas set on the cliff beyond the cries
of trippers and the desecration of blown newspaper
pages. Grant still had a room at the Marine, and so to
Westover he went, and there Williams joined him. All
he could do now was to wait for a warrant from the
Yard and a visit from Harmer.

It was cocktail time when Harmer presented himself.

"Are you asking me to dinner, Inspector? If not, say
you are and let the dinner be on me, will you; there's a
good sport. Another hour of that woman and I shall
be daffy. Loco. Nuts. I have known stars in my time,
but holy mackerel! she takes the cake. You'd think
with her English being on the sticky side that she'd
let up now and then to think a bit. But no! Jabbers
right along, with German to fill in, and bits of French
dressing here and there to make it look nice. Waiter!
What's yours, Inspector? Not drinking? Oh, come on!
No? That's too bad. One gin and mixed, waiter. You
don't need to climb on the wagon with a waist like
that, Inspector. Don't say you're Prohibition from conviction!"

Grant disclaimed any crusading interest in the drink
traffic.

"Well, what's the news? You have got news, haven't
you?" He became serious, and looked earnestly, at
Grant. "Something real turned up?'

"I just wanted to know what you were doing in
Dover on that Wednesday night."

"In Dover?"

"A fortnight last Wednesday."

"Someone been pulling your leg?"

"Listen, Mr. Harmer, your lack of frankness is
complicating everything. It's keeping us from running
down the man who killed Christine Clay. The whole
business is cockeyed. You come clean about your
movements on that Wednesday night, and half the
irrelevant bits and pieces that are weighing the case
down can be shorn off and thrown away. We can't see

the outline of it with all the bits that are covering it up and hanging on to it. You want to help us get our man, don't you? Well, prove it!"

"I like you a lot, Inspector. I never thought I'd like a cop so much. But I told you already: I lost my way looking for Chris's cottage, and slept in the car."

"And if I bring witnesses to prove that you were in Dover after midnight?"

"I still slept in the car."

Grant was silent, disappointed. Now he would have to go to Champneis.

Harmer's little brown eyes watched him with something like solicitude.

"You're not getting your sleep these days, Inspector. Heading for a breakdown. Change your mind and have a drink. Wonderful how a drink puts things in their place."

"If you didn't insist on sleeping in the car, I'd have a better chance of sleeping in my bed," Grant said angrily, and took his leave with less than his usual grace.

He wanted to get at Champneis before Jason Harmer had time to tell him that Grant had been making inquiries. The best way to do that was to telephone and ask Champneis to come down to Westover. Offer to send a police car for him at once. And if necessary keep Harmer talking until Champneis would have left town.

But Champneis had already left town. He was in Edinburgh addressing a polite gathering on "The Future of Galeria."

That settled it. Long before anyone could get to him, Harmer would have communicated with him either by telegram or telephone. Grant asked that both means of communication should be tapped, and went back to the lounge to find Jason still sitting over his drink.

"I know you don't like me, Inspector, but honest to God I like you, and honest to God that woman is a holy terror. Do you think you could sort of forget that we are famous-detective and worm-of-a-suspect, and eat together after all?"

Grant smiled, against his will. He had no objections.

Jason smiled too, a little knowingly. "But if you think by the end of dinner I won't have slept in that car, don't kid yourself."

In spite of himself, Grant enjoyed that meal. It was a good game: trying to trap Jason into some kind of admission. The food was good. And Jason was amusing.

Another telephone message came to say that Lord Edward was returning on the first train in the morning, and would be in London by tea-time. Grant could expect the warrant for Gotobed by the first post in the morning.

So Grant went to bed at the Marine, puzzled but not suicidal; at least there was a program for the morrow. Jason too slept at the Marine, having declared his inability to face Leni any more that day.

24

THE KITCHEN OF THE MARINE WAS IN THE ROOF; THE latest discovery of architects being that smells go upward. It had set out to be an all-electric kitchen, that being also in the recent creed of architects. But it was not in the creed of Henri, chef of chefs. Henri was Provençal, and to cook by electricity, my God, it was a horror, but a horror! If God had meant us to cook by lightning, He would not have invented fire. So Henri had his stoves and his braziers. And so now, at three in the morning, a soft glow from the banked-up fires filled the enormous white room. Full of high lights, the room was: copper, silver, and enamel. (Not aluminum. Henri fainted at the mention of aluminum.) The door stood half open, and the fire made a quiet ticking now and then.

Presently the door moved. Was pushed a little further ajar. A man stood in the opening, apparently listening. He came in, silent as a shadow, and moved to the cutlery table. A knife gleamed in the dimness as he took it from the drawer. But he made no sound. From the table he moved to the wall where the keys hung on their little board, each on its appointed hook. Without fumbling he took the key he wanted. He hesitated as he was about to leave the room, and came back to the fire as if it fascinated him. His eyes in the light were bright and excited, his face shadowed.

By the hearth lay kindling wood for some morning fire. It had been spread on a newspaper to dry thoroughly. The man noticed it. He pushed the cut wood to one side and lifted the rest of the paper into the small square of firelight. For a moment he read, so still in that silent room that it might have been empty.

And suddenly all was changed. He leaped to his feet, ran to the electric button, and switched on the lights. Ran back to the paper and snatched it from its bed of sticks. He spread it on the table with shaking hands, patting it and smoothing it as if it were a live thing. Then he began to laugh. Softly and consumedly, drumming with his fists on the scrubbed wood. His laughter grew, beyond his control. He ran to the switch again and snapped on all the lights in the kitchen; one, two, three, four, five, six, seven, eight. A new thought possessed him. He ran out of the kitchen, along the tiled corridors, silent as a shadow. Down the dim stairs he sped, flight after flight, like a bat. And now he began to laugh again, in sobbing gusts. He shot into the darkness of the great lounge and across it to the green light of the reception desk. There was no one there. The night porter was on his rounds. The man turned a page of the registration book, and ran a wavering finger down it. Then he made off up the stairs again, silent except for his sobbing breath. In the service room on the second floor he took a master key from its hook, and ran to the door of Room 73. The door yielded, he put out his hand to the switch, and leaped on the man in the bed.

Grant struggled out of his dream of contraband, to

defend himself against a maniac who was kneeling on his bed shaking him and repeating between sobs: "So you were wrong, and it's all right! You were wrong, and it's all right!"

"Tisdall!" said Grant. "My God, I'm glad to see you. Where have you been?"

"Among the cisterns."

"In the *Marine?* All the time?"

"Since Thursday night. How long is that? I just walked in at the service door late at night. Rain like stair rods. You could have walked the length of the town in your birthday suit, and there wouldn't have been anyone to see. I knew about the little attic place because I saw it when workmen were here one day. No one's ever there but workmen. I come out at night to get food from the larder. I expect someone's in trouble about that food. Or perhaps they never missed it? Do you think?"

His unnaturally bright eyes scanned Grant anxiously. He had begun to shiver. It did not need much guess-work to place his probable temperature.

Grant pushed him gently down to a sitting position on the bed, took a pair of pajamas from the drawer, and handed them over.

"Here. Get into these and into bed at once. I suppose you were soaking when you arrived at the hotel?"

"Yes. My clothes weighed so much I could hardly walk. But it's dry up in the roof. Warm too. Too warm in the day-time. You have a n-n-nice taste in n-n-night wear." His teeth were chattering; reaction was flooding him.

Grant helped him with the pajamas and covered him up. He rang for the porter and ordered hot soup and the presence of a doctor. Then he sat down at the telephone and told the good news to the Yard, Tisdall's over-bright eyes watching him, quizzically. When he had finished he came over to the bed and said: "I can't tell you how sorry I am about all this. I'd give a lot to undo it."

"Blankets!" said Tisdall. "Sheets! Pillows! Eider-down! Gosh!" He grinned as far as his chattering teeth and his week's growth of beard would let him. "Say 'Now I Lay Me' for me," he said. And fell abruptly asleep.

25

IN THE MORNING, BECAUSE THE DOCTOR SAID THAT "THERE was a certain congestion which in the subject's weakened condition might at any moment develop into pneumonia," Grant summoned Tisdall's Aunt Muriel, whom the Yard obligingly found, Tisdall having refused to consider the presence of any aunts. Williams was sent to Canterbury to arrest Brother Aloysius, and Grant planned to go back to town after lunch to interview Champneis. He had telephoned the good news of Tisdall's reappearance to Colonel Burgoyne, and the telephone had been answered by Erica.

"Oh, I'm so glad for you!" she said.

"For *me?*"

"Yes, it must have been awful for you."

And it was only then that Grant realized quite how awful it had been. That continual pushing down of an unnamed fear. What a nice child she was.

The nice child had sent over for the patient in the course of the morning a dozen fresh eggs taken from the Steynes nests that very hour. Grant thought how typical it was of her to send fresh eggs, and not the conventional flowers or fruit.

"I hope she didn't get into trouble for giving me food that time?" Tisdall asked. He always talked as if the occurrences of the last week were many years away; the days in the attic had been a lifetime to him.

"On the contrary. She saved your neck and my reputation. It was she who found your coat. No, I can't tell you about it now. You're supposed not to talk or be talked to."

But he had had to tell all about it. And had left Tisdall saying softly to himself, "Well!" Over and over again: "Well!" in a wondering tone.

The shadow of the Champneis interview had begun to loom over Grant. Supposing he said frankly: "Look here, both you and Jason Harmer went out of your way to lie to me about your movements on a certain night, and now I find that you were together at Dover. What were you doing?" What would the answer be? "My dear sir, I can't answer for Harmer's prevarications, but he was my guest on the *Petronel* and we spent the night fishing in our motor-boat." That would be a good alibi.

And still his mind dwelled on the contraband idea. What contraband was of interest to both Champneis and Harmer? And it didn't take a whole night to hand over even a whole cargo load of contraband. Yet neither of them had an alibi for that night. What had they done with the hours from midnight to breakfast?

He had felt, ever since Rimell's revelation at Dover, that if he could remember what Champneis had been talking about just before his fib about the day of his arrival, all would be clear to him.

He decided to go downstairs and have his hair cut before he left the Marine. He was to remember that haircut.

As he put out his hand to push the swing door open, he heard Champneis's voice in his mind, drawling a sentence.

So *that* was what he had been talking about!

Yes. Yes. Pictures ran together in Grant's mind to make a sequence that made sense. He turned from the saloon door to the telephone and called the Special Branch. He asked them half a dozen questions, and then went to have his hair cut, smiling fatuously. He knew now what he was going to say to Edward Champneis.

It was the busy time of the morning and all the chairs were full.

"Won't be a minute, sir," an anxious supervisor said. "Not a minute if you will wait."

Grant sat down by the wall and reached for a magazine from the pile on a shelf. The pile fell over; a well thumbed collection, most of them far from new. Because it had a frontispiece of Christine Clay, he picked up a copy of the *Silver Sheet,* an American cinema magazine, and idly turned over the pages. It was the usual bouquet. The "real truth" was told about someone for the fifty-second time, being a completely different real truth from all the other fifty-one real truths. A nit-wit blonde explained how she read new meaning into Shakespeare. Another told how she kept her figure. An actress who didn't know one end of a frying-pan from the other was photographed in her kitchen making griddle cakes. A he-man star said how grand he thought all the other he-man stars. Grant turned the pages more impatiently. He was on the point of exchanging the magazine for another when his attention was suddenly caught. He read through an article with growing interest. At the last paragraph he got to his feet, still holding the paper and staring at the page.

"Your turn now, sir," the barber said. "This chair, please."

But Grant took no notice.

"We're quite ready for you now, sir. Sorry you've been kept waiting."

Grant looked up at them, only half conscious of them.

"Can I have this?" he asked, indicating the magazine. "It's six months old. Thank you," and rushed out of the room.

They stared after him, and laughed a little, speculating as to what had taken his fancy.

"Found his affinity," someone suggested.

"Thought they were extinct, affinities," another countered.

"Found something to cure his corns."

"No, gone to consult his best friend."

And they laughed and forgot him.

Grant was in the telephone booth, and the impatient gentleman in the patent-leather shoes was beginning to wonder if he was ever coming out of it. He was talking to Owen Hughes, the cinema star. That was why the patent-leather gentleman didn't go upstairs to the numerous booths on the ground floor. He was hoping to hear some of the conversation. It was about whether someone had mentioned something in a letter to someone.

"You *did!*" Grant said. "Thanks! That's all I wanted to know. Keep it under your hat. That I asked, I mean."

Then he had asked for the Thames police, pulling the door tighter and so exasperating the waiting gentleman.

"Has 276 River Walk a motor-boat, do you know?"

There was a consultation at the other end.

Yes, 276 had a boat. Yes, very fast. Sea-going? Oh, yes, if necessary. Used it for fowling along the Essex flats, they thought. Used to navigation of the lower river, anyhow? Oh, yes.

Grant asked if they would have a boat ready for him in about an hour and a half, by which time he'd be in town, he hoped. He'd take it as a great favor.

Certainly, they would.

Grant telephoned to Barker—at which point the patent-leather gentleman gave it up—and asked that if Williams was back in town within the next ninety minutes he should meet Grant at Westminster Pier. If Williams was not back in time, then Sanger.

Grant took full advantage of the lunch-time lull in traffic, and in unrestricted areas excelled himself in the gentle art of speed with safety. He found Williams waiting for him, a little breathless, since he had that moment arrived from the Yard and sent the disappointed Sanger back. Williams had no intention of being out of anything, if he could help it. And the Superintendent had said that something exciting was due to break.

"Well, was the Reverend Father shocked?" Grant asked.

"Not as shocked as Brother Aloysius. He didn't for a moment imagine we'd got anything on him. By the way he behaved, I should think some other police forces must be anxious to catch up with him."

"I shouldn't wonder."

"Where are we going, sir?"

"Chelsea Reach. Beloved of painters and folk-dancers."

Williams looked benignly at his superior and noticed how much better he was looking now that the Tisdall boy had turned up.

The police boat drew in to the bank at 276 River Walk where a large grayish motor-boat was moored. The police boat edged gingerly nearer until only a foot separated the gunwales.

Grant stepped across. "Come with me, Williams. I want witnesses."

The cabin was locked. Grant glanced up at the house opposite and shook his head. "I'll have to risk it. I'm sure I'm right, anyhow."

While the river police stood by, he forced the lock and went in. It was a tidy, seamanlike cabin; everything was neat and ship-shape. Grant began to go through the lockers. In the one under the starboard bunk he found what he was looking for. An oilskin coat. Black.

Bought in Cannes. With the button missing from the right cuff.

"You take that, Williams, and come up to the house with me."

The maid said that Miss Keats was in, and left them in a dining-room on the ground floor; a very austere and up-to-the-minute apartment.

"Looks more like a place to have your appendix out than to put roast beef into you," Williams observed.

But Grant said nothing.

Lydia came in, smiling, her bracelets jangling and her beads clashing.

"I'm sorry I couldn't take you upstairs, my dear Leo person, but I have some clients who mightn't understand that this is just a friendly visit."

"So you knew who I was, at Marta's?"

"Of course. You don't flatter my powers of divination, my dear Mr. Grant. Won't you present your friend?"

"This is Sergeant Williams."

She looked faintly disconcerted, Grant thought, but managed to be gracious to the sergeant. Then she saw what was under Williams's arm.

"What are you doing with my coat?" she asked sharply.

"Then it is your coat? The one in the locker of the boat?"

"Of course it is my coat! How dare you force my cabin! It is always kept locked."

"The lock will be repaired, Miss Keats. Meanwhile I regret to tell you that I must arrest you for the murder of Christine Clay at the Gap at Westover on Thursday morning, the 15th, and warn you that anything you say may be used in evidence against you."

Her face changed from her habitual expression of satisfaction to the convulsed fury he had seen when Judy Sellers had made light of her powers. "You can't arrest me," she said. "It is not in my stars. Who should know if not I? The stars have no secrets from me. The stars have predicted a glorious destiny for me. It is you, poor mistaken fool, who will go on stumbling and making mistakes. My sign is achievement. Whatever I will I can do. It is set there in the sky that it shall be so. Destiny. 'Some are born great'—that is true and the rest is lies. One is born great or is not great at all. I was born to achieve. To be a leader. To be looked up to by mankind—"

"Miss Keats, I should be grateful if you would prepare to come with us at once. Any clothes you want can be sent after you."

"Clothes? What for?"

"For use in prison."

"I don't understand. You can't put me in prison. It isn't in my stars. They said that what I wanted I could do."

"Everyone can do what they want if they want it enough. But no one with impunity. Will you send for your maid and explain to her? She will fetch your hat if you want it."

"I don't want it. I am not going with you. I am going to a party this afternoon at Marta's. She's got Christine's part, you know. In the new film. That's one good turn I did. It was all written a long time ago what we should do. It falls into place, like the cog things in a musical box, you know. Or perhaps you don't know. Are you musical? And from Marta's I'm going to Owen Hughes. After that we shall see. If you come back in the evening we can talk about it. Do you know Owen? A charming person. He had his appointed place too. If it hadn't been for Owen it would never have come into my head. No, I don't mean that. Great enterprises belong to great minds. They would happen in any case. But the releasing agent is often very small. Like electric light and the switch. I used that simile in a lecture in Scotland the other week. It went very well. Neat, don't you think? Will you have some sherry? I'm afraid I'm very remiss. It's the consciousness of these people upstairs waiting to be told."

"Told what?"

"About me, of course. No, about themsleves. That is what they came for. I'm a little muddled. They want to know what destiny has in store for them. And only I can tell them. Only I, Lydia Keats—"

"May I use your telephone, Miss Keats?"

"Certainly. It is in the cupboard place in the hall. One of the new colored kind. The telephone, not the cupboard. What was I saying?"

Grant said to Williams, "Ask them to send Reynolds around at once."

"Is that the painter? I shall be glad to meet him. He was born to greatness. It is not a matter of application, or mixing pigments, you know. It is having the matter in you. And that the stars arrange. You must let me do a horoscope for you. You are a Leo person. Very attractive people. Kingly born. I have been sorry sometimes that I was not August born. But Aries people are leaders. Talkative, too, I'm afraid." She giggled. "I do talk a lot they tell me. Chatterbox, they called me as a child—"

26

HALF AN HOUR LATER REYNOLDS, THE POLICE SURGEON, gave the screaming, raving thing that had been Lydia Keats a morphine injection so that they might remove her to the station in some sort of decency.

Grant and Williams, standing in the door, watching the disappearing ambulance, found no words.

"Well," Grant said at length, pulling himself together, "I suppose I'd better get along and see Champneis."

"The people that made the laws of this country ought to be shot," Williams said with sudden venom.

Grant looked startled. "Capital punishment, you mean?"

"No! Closed hours."

"Oh, I see. There's a flask in my cupboard. You can help yourself."

"Thank you, sir. Don't take on, miss!" This to the sobbing maid in the background. "Things like that will happen."

"She was a very kind mistress to me," she said. "It hurts me to see her like that."

"Take care of that coat, Williams," Grant said as they went down the path to the car that had been sent for them, glad beyond speech to leave the house behind.

"Tell me, sir, how did you find out it was that woman of all people?"

Grant produced the pages he had torn from the magazine.

"I found that in a magazine in the barbershop at the Marine. You can read it for yourself."

It was an article written by some Midwest sob sister, who had been in New York for a vacation. New York was full of film stars who had either run out on their studies or were on their way back to them, and in New York also was Miss Lydia Keats. And the thing that most impressed the sob sister was not shaking hands with Grace Marvel, but the success of Miss Keats's prophecies. She had made three startling ones. She had prophesied that within three months Lyn Drake would have a serious accident; and everyone knew that Lyn Drake was still on his back. She had said that Millard Robinson would within a month lose a fortune by fire; and everyone knew how the reels of the new million-dollar film had been burned to a cinder. And her third statement prophesied the death by drowning of a woman star of the first magnitude, whose name, of course, she gave, but the sob sister equally of course could not reveal. "If this third prophecy, so circumstantial, so unequivocal, comes true, then Miss Keats is established as the possessor of one of the most uncanny talents in the world. All humanity will be besieging her. But don't go swimming with Miss Keats, little blonde star! The temptation might be too much for her!"

"Well, I'll be damned," said Williams, and was silent until Grant dropped him at the Yard.

"Tell the Superintendent I'll be in as soon as I've seen Lord Edward," Grant said, and was driven on to Regent's Park.

In an atmosphere of marble mantelpieces and sheepskin rugs he waited half an hour before Champneis arrived.

"How are you, Inspector? I hear from Binns that you've been waiting. Sorry to subject you to the furnishings longer than is vitally necessary. I hope you drink tea? But if you don't there are what my uncle called 'cordials.' A much nicer word than 'drinks,' don't you think? Have you news?"

"Yes, sir. I'm sorry to break in with it when you're just after a journey."

"It can't be worse than the drawing-room lecture of my great-aunt's yesterday. I only went for the old lady's sake, but I found that she thought I should have cancelled it. It would have been more 'fitting.' So tell me the bad news."

Grant told him what had happened, and he listened gravely, the unusual defensive flippancy gone.

"Is she insane?" he asked, when Grant had finished.

"Yes. Reynolds thinks so. It may be hysteria, but he thinks it's insanity. Delusions of greatness, you know."

"Poor wretch. But how did she know where my wife was?"

"Owen Hughes told her in a letter from Hollywood. He forgot that it was a secret that she had taken his cottage. He even mentioned the early-morning swimming."

"So simple. I see. . . . Was she very expert with a motor-boat, then?"

"She had been practically brought up on one, it seems. Used the river constantly. No one would have thought of questioning her comings and goings. She may have made that night journey down the river more than once before the opportunity she was looking for turned up. Curious, but one never thinks of the river as a high road to anywhere. We had considered the possibility of a motor-boat, naturally, but not a motor-boat from London. Not that it would have helped us very much if it had. The man's coat she wore was very misleading. Lots of women wear men's oilskins, yachting; but I don't think it would have occurred to me."

There was a short silence.

Each man watched in his mind that boat's journey down the misty river, out to the many-lighted estuary, and along the many-lighted coast. One little town after another, from flaring dockyard lights among the flats to twinkling villa lights among the cliffs, must have lit that progress. But later, there must have been darkness; complete darkness and silence, as the summer fog pressed down on the water. What had her thoughts been, in that time of waiting? Alone, with time to reflect. And with no stars to remind her of her greatness. Or was her madness even then so sure that she had no doubts?

And afterward—Each man watched that too. The surprise. The friendly greeting. Chris's green cap bobbing alongside the gray hull—the cap that had never been found. The woman leaning over to talk to her. And then—

Grant remembered those broken nails on Christine's hands. It had not been so easy, then.

"That finishes the case, sir, but it was really something else that brought me to see you. Another case altogether."

"Yes? Here's tea. You needn't wait, Binns. Sugar, Inspector?"

"I want to know where you took Rimnik."

Champneis paused with the sugar poised. He looked both surprised and amused and—somehow—admiring.

"He is with friends of Harmer's, near Tunbridge Wells."

"May I have the exact address?"

Champneis gave it, and also gave Grant his tea. "Why do you want Rimnik?"

"Because he is in this country without a passport—thanks to you!"

"He was. The Office issued him a landing permit this morning. It took a lot of eloquence—Britain the lover

of justice, the defender of the persecuted, the home of
the righteous homeless: all that stuff—but it worked.
Chests still swell in Whitehall, do you know? They were
like a collection of pouter pigeons when I finished."

He looked at the Inspector's disapproving face. "I
didn't know that that little business had been a worry to
you."

"Worry!" Grant burst out. "It nearly ruined everything. You and Harmer both lying about what you had
done that night—" He found that he was treading on
delicate ground and pulled himself up.

But Champneis had understood. "I really am sorry,
Inspector. Are you going to arrest me? Can one be
arrested retrospectively, so to speak?"

"I don't think so. I shall have to inquire about it. It
would give me great pleasure." Grant had recovered
his temper.

"All right. Let's postpone the arrest. But tell me how
you found out? I thought we'd been so clever."

"I might never have found out if it hadn't been for a
good bit of work by a young officer—Rimell—at
Dover."

"I must meet Rimell."

"He found that you and Harmer had met that night
and had been worried about the Customs."

"Yes. Rimnik was in a cupboard in my cabin. It was
an exciting half-hour. But the Customs and Harbor
Masters are only human."

This Grant took to mean that they knocked off the
Champneis pegs and lacked the nerve to knock on the
bulkheads. "It was then I began to feel that if I could
remember something you had said just before—you
misled me about the time of your arrival in Dover, I
would have the key to everything. And I remembered
it! You said that Galeria's only hope was Rimnik, and
that Rimnik would turn up again when his party was
ready. But the big stumbling block was in seeing the
connection between you and Harmer. It was so simple
and so obvious I couldn't find it. You liked and admired

one another immediately your wife introduced you. I must say he did a beautiful job of throwing dust in my eyes, putting on that resentful—underprivileged-classes act. I should have thought more about my recognition of your—"

"My what?"

"Unorthodoxy." Both men smiled. "Once I groped my way through that difficulty, the rest was easy. The Special Branch knew all about Rimnik's disappearance, his being refused a passport, and Britain's refusal to have him here. They even knew that he was supposed to be in England, but had no confirmation of it. So the motor-boat came ashore a second time?"

"That night, you mean? Yes. Harmer drove us over to his friend's place. He has guts; he was scared stiff, I think, but he went through with it. I see Tisdall has turned up," he said as Grant rose to go. "That must be an enormous relief to you. Is he ill?"

"No. He has a chill, and he's overwrought, of course. But I hope he's going to be all right."

"In the midday edition I bought at York, I read a harrowing description of his sufferings. Knowing the Press, I believed with confidence that not a word of it was true."

"Not a word. That was just Jammy Hopkins."

"Who is Jammy Hopkins?"

"Who is—" Words failed the Inspector. He looked enviously at Champneis. "Now I know," he said, "why men go out into the waste places of the earth!"

27

HERBERT GOTOBED LEFT ENGLAND ABOUT A MONTH LATER on his way to explain to the inquisitive police of Nashville, Tennessee, what he had done with the two thousand dollars old Mrs. Kinsley had given him to build a church with.

And on the day that he sailed—although neither party knew of the other's activities—Erica had a dinner-party at Steynes, "to take the taste of the last one away" as she said bluntly to Grant, when she invited him. The only addition to the original personnel was Robin Tisdall, and Grant found himself ridiculously relieved to find that her small nose was still as casually powdered, and her frock still as childish as on the first occasion. He was afraid that contact with anyone as good-looking and ill-used as Robin Tisdall would have bred a self-awareness that would be the end of her girlhood. But it seemed as if nothing could make Erica self-conscious. She treated Tisdall with the same grave matter-of-factness she had used when she had told him that his shirt collar was too tight. Grant saw

Sir George's eyes going from one to the other in glad amusement. Their glances met, and moved by a common impulse the two men raised their glasses in a small gesture of mutual congratulation.

"Are you drinking a toast?" Erica asked. "I'll give you one. To Robin's success in California!"

They drank it with a will.

"If you don't like the ranch," Erica said, "wait till I am twenty-one and I'll buy it from you."

"Would you like that sort of life?" His tone was eager.

"Of course I should." She turned to Grant, beginning to say something.

"You'll have to come out and see it long before you're twenty-one," Robin persisted.

"Yes, that would be nice." She was sincere but inattentive. "Mr. Grant" (for some reason she never called him Inspector) "if I get those tickets from Mr. Mills myself will you come with me to the Circus at Christmas?"

She was very faintly pink, as if she had asked a forward thing. A phenomenon in Erica, who was forward by nature and never knew it.

"Of course I will," Grant said, "with the greatest pleasure."

"All right," she said. "That's a promise." She lifted her glass. "To Olympia, at Christmas!"

"To Olympia at Christmas!" Grant said.